First published in Great Britain 2011
by Mills & Boon, an imprint of Harlequin (UK) Limited,
Large Print edition 2011
Eton House, 18-24 Paradise Road, Richmond, Surrey TW9 1SR

© Stacey Kayne 2008

ISBN: 978 0 263 22386 6

Harlequin (UK) policy is to use papers that are natural,
renewable and recyclable products and made from wood grown in
sustainable forests. The logging and manufacturing process conform
to the legal environmental regulations of the country of origin.

Printed and bound in Great Britain
by CPI Antony Rowe, Chippenham, Wiltshire

THE GUNSLINGER'S UNTAMED BRIDE

BY

STACEY KAYNE

'Am I in *jail*?'

Warm throaty laughter drew Lily's gaze to a pair of sparkling blue eyes. Flutters erupted low in her belly. A sudden heat flooded her face, and she averted her gaze from the handsome stranger.

'Mind telling me what you're doing up here, Lily?' The corners of his mouth slid upwards again, and Lily was quite certain she'd never known a man with such a charming disposition.

'Sheriff Barns!' The stranger glanced over his shoulder as a man burst in through the door.

'What is it, Davy?'

'*Barns?*' said Lily.

The Sheriff looked back at her, and Lily realized she'd spoken the name aloud.

'That's right,' he said. 'Juniper Barns.'

Lily couldn't draw her next breath. His narrowing blue eyes suggested her expression revealed her shock. *He can't be.*

Sheriff Barns didn't take his eyes off her—eyes that didn't seem quite as warm and gentle as a moment ago. 'Heard of me, have you?'

Her gaze dropped to the holster strapped to his lean hips, the pearl grip of one of his guns visible beneath his vest. *Oh, God.* She glanced up and fear shivered through her.

She'd come to Pine Ridge to kill the sheriff.

Stacey Kayne has always been a day-dreamer. If the comments on her elementary school report cards are any indication, it's a craft she mastered early on. Having a passion for history and a flair for storytelling, she strives to weave fact and fiction into a wild ride that can capture the heart. Stacey lives on a ranch near the Sierra Nevada, with her high-school sweetheart turned husband and their two sons. Visit her website at www.staceykayne.com

Dedicated to…
Robyn, Alyssa & Ali
Inspirations of strength,
intelligence and courage.
Stick to your guns—follow your dreams.

Special Thanks to…
My family for their unending support
and patience.

Sheila Raye, Marlene Urso and Carla James,
my fearless critique partners.

My wonderful agent, Kim Lionetti.

Linda Fildew and Lydia Mason for their
editorial expertise and making my job a joy.

All my readers!

Prologue

Fall 1876
California Foothills

"Juniper Barns!"

Juniper's horse crested the last rise of swaying yellow grasses as his name carried back on the breeze in an angry shout. He reined in, his gaze locking on five riders mounted in front of the ranch house that had been his sanctuary for the past six years.

Sprays of light from the setting sun glinted off their guns, raising the fine hairs on the back of Juniper's neck. Sensation tingled in the tips of his fingers. He forgot about the exhaustion tugging at his muscles and the sweet scent of freshly baked bread that had been calling him home for supper. His free hand flexed, his palm burning for the grip of his gun concealed beneath his range coat.

A kid didn't shoot thirteen men into their dusty graves without making enemies. He'd known there'd be a day when the demons of his past would come to call.

One of the men shouted Juniper's name toward the house as he dismounted.

That day had come.

"He's not here!"

The woman who'd raised him from the age of fourteen stood on the covered porch, baby Isaac in her arms. Rachell's four- and five-year-old daughters huddled against her skirt. May's ebony braids set her apart from her younger sister, April, whose hair was as red as her mother's.

Juniper urged his horse forward. His gaze homed in on the man at the base of the stairs. As Juniper neared the house, the stranger turned toward the sound of his approaching horse.

Flat forehead, square chin, dark beady eyes...features similar to that of Dan Yates.

He hadn't forgotten a single face of the men who'd fallen to his guns. They rose up in his mind at odd times, haunting him.

He tugged on the reins, slowing his mare as she crossed the yard.

"Stop where you are," the man called, raising his rifle.

May's scream pierced the air.

"June!" her little sister shouted.

"It's all right," he called out, wanting to calm his sisters. "Go on inside with your mama." His gaze flickered toward Rachell. She glanced out at the golden hills stretching toward the Sierras. Juniper prayed Jed and the others would take their time getting back. As much as he valued their protection, he didn't want to see any of them get hurt on his account.

Rachell's fearful green eyes met his gaze.

"Go on," he urged.

June, she silently mouthed, hugging her infant son to her chest.

"Wait just a damn minute!" Yates shouted.

"Go," he said, before turning his attention to Yates. "No sense in scaring the girls." June shifted the brim of his hat up over his blond hair to keep a clear view of the other four riders. He felt a rush of relief as the door closed behind Rachell and her children. "Your business is with me."

Narrowed dark eyes moved over him. "I doubt that. I'm looking for a gunfighter from Missouri way. Goes by the name of Juniper Barns."

June leaned forward, crossing his wrists over the saddle horn. "You found him."

Low chuckles rumbled from the men mounted behind their friend. Yates only scowled. "Like hell."

Juniper wished he could deny the fact. No matter how badly he wanted to, he couldn't erase his past, and he refused to hide behind those who would defend his actions. He'd done what he'd had to, and he held himself accountable.

He dismounted slowly, keeping his hands in clear view, though the men before him didn't seem to recognize him as a threat.

"You related to Dan Yates?" Juniper asked, facing the man standing a few yards away from him.

Dark eyes widened in surprise. "I don't know what your game is, kid."

Nearly twenty years old, Juniper was hardly a kid—no more a kid than he'd been at the age of thirteen when his uncle had shoved him into the street, forcing him to draw his guns to stay alive.

"I'm looking for the man who shot my brother down six years ago in Mason, Missouri. I don't care if I have to beat that information out of you or the woman."

Tension coiling through his shoulders, Juniper widened his stance.

"Just tell me where to find Barns and there'll be no need for you to come to harm."

"If you didn't intend harm, you wouldn't be here. If you had any sense, you'd never have come." He brushed back the edges of his range coat, tucking the heavy canvas behind the weight of a double holster he'd worn every day since his father had died at the hands of outlaws.

The man's gaze landed on the matching Colts, his eyes widening with recognition of the twin pearl grips.

"This family doesn't deserve trouble from my past. You want to have it out with me, *fine*. Name the place."

Sheer hatred hardened the man's expression. "I spent five years in prison waiting to get out and avenge my brother's death. It took me a year to find you and I'll damn well shoot you where you stand."

The men mounted behind Yates stepped down from their saddles. Yates raised his hand. "Stay back," he ordered, keeping his gaze trained on Juniper. "He's *mine*."

"Don't make your brother's mistake."

"My brother is dead!" Yates shouted.

"By his own doing," Juniper felt inclined to point out. "I warned him to walk away from my uncle's bet. He didn't listen."

They never listened.

"You think those fancy pistols make you some kind of special, don't you?"

"Mister, I wish to God I'd never strapped on a gun. I'll tell you exactly what I told your brother. I got no will to kill you. You can walk away right now."

Yates tossed his rifle aside. "Your luck just ran out. No one's ever outdrawn me, and I've been hunting you for a long time." The man hunched forward, bending at the knees, his elbows hiked high.

Juniper had to wonder if Yates was giving his impression of a giant crab.

"When I'm done with you," Yates said, his fingers flexing above his holster, "I'll be sure to show your family the same respect you showed mine."

Rebelling against a lash of fear, a numbing calm settled over Juniper as he accepted the challenge. Keeping his gaze on Yates, he noted the position of the four armed men standing behind him. Killing didn't take any great skill. For Juniper, it was merely reflex.

His senses keen, his arms idle yet poised, he waited, in no more a hurry to kill than he was to die.

As if sensing the change in him, Yates narrowed his gaze, a look of caution stealing into his eyes. Sweat trickled down from his temples.

"What are you waiting for?" Juniper taunted. "Shoot me."

Yates tensed. His breathing began to sound labored. All bad signs—for Yates.

"Flinch and I'll kill you," Juniper warned. "Say the word and you can walk away."

Yates went for his gun, the dark metal making it a fraction out of his holster before bullets exploded from Juniper's twin revolvers. He fired four consecutive shots, his aim shifting to the men beyond Yates's falling form. Metal pinged and sparked as two revolvers fell to the ground. The fourth bullet chipped wood from a rifle grip in another pair of hands.

His fingers on the triggers, two men in his sights, Juniper stared at four gaping expressions. All four had just seen proof that it wouldn't take more than a blink for him to drop every one of them.

He didn't have to check Yates to know the man was lying in a pool of blood, a hole through his heart. Juniper had learned, his first time in the street, wounding an adversary only meant he'd also suffer a bullet before having to fire another. The men staring at him hadn't challenged him—yet.

"Anyone else here for vengeance?" His low tone was barely a rustle on the breeze, his heart slugging slow and hard against his chest.

"No," one of them called out, still shaking the sting from his fingers. "I got no quarrel with you."

A second man vigorously shook his head. "We, uh—"

"Ride or die."

They scrambled onto their horses, hooves trampling weapons as they made a hasty retreat.

Juniper stood just beyond the porch, watching all four fade into the distance. The moment they disappeared over the western hillside, the tremors hit, staggering him.

He leaned forward, planting his hands on his knees. His gaze landed on Yates lying in a circle of crimson, his glassy eyes reflecting blue sky and white clouds.

Nausea rose up like a wave of fire.

The sound of his sisters' sobs filtered outside as Juniper sucked air. Hearing the door squeak open, he turned toward the house.

"Rachell, don't let—"

April shoved past her mother before he could tell them to stay inside. "June!" She crossed the porch in a flash of red hair and leaped from the steps into his arms.

Holding her face to his chest, he rushed up to the porch, but he was too late. May stood beside her mother, her wide eyes locked on the man lying in the dirt.

"Is he…dead?"

Rachell turned her oldest daughter toward the door and ushered her back into the house. "We're just glad you're okay," she said as Juniper shut the door behind them.

May glanced at his holster and took a step back, her frightened expression hitting him like a blow to the gut. She stiffened as her gaze shifted toward the sound of horses approaching from the northeast pasture.

"It's your daddy and Uncle Ben and his boys," Juniper said, and realized his whole life was about to be exposed. Ben's sons were just a bit younger than him and had no idea their adopted cousin hid a blood-stained past.

He crouched down to place April on her feet. May rushed forward, crowding into his arms beside her sister. Juniper hugged them both, relief warring with a deep sense of loss. Though he wasn't related to this family by blood, they'd given him the first real home he'd ever known, sealing his place in the family the day their first daughter had been born. "Now I'll have May and June," Rachell had said, June being the nickname Rachell had given him, and he'd never been so honored. April and May were his sisters in every way that mattered.

"You girls stay inside with your mama until your daddy comes for you, okay?"

Both girls nodded, moving toward their mother as he straightened. Juniper was afraid to look at her, ashamed of the terror he'd brought into their home.

The moment he'd taken this man's life, his own had been stolen. Once the others reached town, word would spread about the gunslinger from Missouri.

More would come. He couldn't stay.

"You did what you had to."

Rachell's gentle voice penetrated the anguish welling up inside him, pulling at his emotions as he felt the door close on the people he loved, the home he'd just lost.

Chapter One

Spring 1883
San Francisco

"Admit it, Lily. Your competitiveness has finally gotten the best of you."

"I'll admit nothing of the kind." Quite pleased with her new business venture, Lily Carrington eased back into the burgundy velvet of her office chair and lifted a cup of steaming hot chocolate to her lips.

Reginald spared her a quick glare, his thin lips set in a grim line as he continued to riffle through the box of disorganized company files atop her desk.

"It's no matter," she said. "McFarland is simply being a sore loser by withholding the payroll records and turning over the company files in such disarray. I'll sort through every page if I have to. There's more than one way to obtain payroll records. Surely someone on-site has kept a log of employees, work hours and pay rates."

"Take my advice, sweetness." Reginald tossed another file into the box, then brushed his fingers against his blue silk jacket as though his hands had been soiled. "Sell it."

"I will *not.* You're being rash."

"I'm being realistic." He dropped into the leather chair on the opposite side of her desk. A wedge of sunlight gleamed against the dark hair slicked back against his scalp. Stiff tracks left by his comb added to his look of severity. Even so, with his slight build and delicate facial structure, Regi was no more intimidating than a stern librarian or a cranky banker.

As her second cousin and top financial advisor, it was Regi's job to be circumspect about business matters, but Lily had run the numbers before going after the lumber company. With proper management, the Sierra lumber camp and mill would become a valuable asset to L. P. Carrington Industries.

"Lily, it's no secret that this entire venture is nothing but a folly to put ol' McFarland in his place."

A smile curved her lips before she took another sip of creamy cocoa, the taste nearly as sweet as her victory. She wouldn't deny the fact. The old goat had dared to come to her offices a few months ago seeking financial assistance, only to refuse to sit across the bargaining table from a *woman.* If that hadn't been insult enough, he'd later publicly ridiculed her before hundreds of colleagues at a charitable ball, calling her a disgrace to respectable businessmen.

A disgrace, was she? She hadn't been the one sitting idly by while her stock was discreetly bought out from under her. Her initials had been the prefix of Carrington Industries for five splendidly success-ful years. At twenty-five years old, Lily *was* L. P. Carrington Industries, owning more than eighty-five percent of the company. The supposed board of trust-ees, her old and ailing relatives, only cared that their bank accounts were brimming.

The fact that McFarland wasn't making this particu-lar takeover an easy endeavor didn't take away from her delight at seeing the utter defeat and humiliation in his face as she had personally claimed the title of *her* new lumber company.

"L. P. Carrington Lumber," she said brightly. "I like the sound of it."

Reginald groaned as he reached toward the tray holding her silver chocolate pot. "Face it, strumpet, he let this money pit go because it was failing."

"You didn't see his face when I walked in. He didn't want to part with Pine Ridge."

"So you've taken the man's prized possession. You don't need to prove anything further." He sat back in his chair and pulled a silver flask from the inside of his jacket.

"Regi! It's barely ten o'clock in the morning!"

"And yet my head is throbbing as though I've suf-fered an entire day of your takeover activities."

Lily crossed her arms in disapproval as he poured a clear trail of spirits into his hot chocolate. He capped the flask and tucked it back into his jacket.

"I don't need to see the outstanding payroll records

to surmise that this company is about to implode." Regi sat back, sipping his potent chocolate. "The accounting records reveal plenty. McFarland took out more than he put in and had nothing left to pay his employees, nor was he willing to dip into his personal funds to compensate for the loss."

"Exactly. The company failure was due to *his* poor management. I didn't walk into this completely blind, Reginald. The potential is there."

"Darling, you hardly need another source of income. And we have enough work to juggle without taking on a camp full of filthy oxen men who haven't been paid in weeks. This lumber business will be nothing but a drain on our time and resources."

"I'm keeping my new company. Success is the best revenge."

Regi took a deep drink, his dark eyes shining with mirth. "*This* is why men cower in fear when you enter a boardroom."

She didn't appreciate his catty tone. "They *do*."

"Yes, love, I know. I'm the one standing right beside you as they tremble. No one is questioning your success."

"That's not the point," she said, straightening her posture. She tugged at the bottom of her fitted waistcoat, smoothing wrinkles from the black-and-gray pinstriping.

Reginald rubbed at his temple. "What exactly is the point, love? I keep forgetting. Could it be that you need another excuse to stay cooped up in this pampered palace of an office?" He splayed his hands toward satin-lined walls trimmed with gold moldings. "Look at you. Impeccable style, flawless skin, every straw-berry-blond curl swept up in sheer perfection, *and all of it going to waste.*"

"I don't care for your perspective. Looking my best is hardly wasteful."

"I dare say ten years ago you'd have been the belle of every debutante ball, had you bothered to attend them."

Unlike the rest of the Carrington women, Lily didn't judge her worth by the size of her wedding dowry. She preferred to follow her mother's example and shun tradition. It was, after all, what everyone expected of her, for poor orphaned Lily to adopt her mother's reckless ways. She did hate to disappoint.

"If you'll recall, I was banned from such fest-ivities."

Regi's tittering laugh increased her annoyance. "I assure you, no one has forgotten. You did pull off your own ruin with certain aplomb. And for what? To spend your days intimidating stuffy old men in gray suits and looking over the shoulders of all our accountants? Every day you descend from your living quarters bound and bustled in San Francisco's finest fashions. You need to get out once in a while, Lily. *Strut your fancy wares.*"

"I'm a businesswoman, Reginald, not a peacock."

"You hardly need to be an exotic bird to get some fresh air. Take time for a social tea, a stroll through

Ghirardelli Square for heaven's sake. You need a lover, Lil, not more work."

One brief interlude had been plenty to keep her focused on the finer things in life—business and chocolate. No one had been complaining about her social life while she'd doubled the family fortunes. Regi was the only one who'd made any attempt to understand her, or at least humor her ambitions.

"You socialize enough for both of us," she said. "Someone has to run this place."

"If your aunt Iris knew how I've aided and abetted your spinster ways, she'd turn over in her grave."

Regi also knew how to get under Lily's skin.

"Doubtful," Lily said, her frown deepening at the thought of her late, harping guardian. "The old biddy could hardly be troubled to lift a finger in life, much less 'roll over.' And you are deliberately toying with my temper."

"On the contrary, I'm simply pointing out the obvious. You already work nonstop. This isn't a small undertaking, Lily."

"A successful lumber company will be a perfect addition to L. P. Industries."

"Yes, love, but we're talking about a *bankrupt* lumber camp. According to the latest financial records, McFarland hadn't paid his employees in over a month, which is why he was looking for outside funding. Are we to make good on those back wages? All we have is a list of names, with no hint of their position in the company or pay rate. We don't even know if the camp is abandoned or filled with disgruntled employees."

"We'll gather a team to assess the situation and obtain the payroll files. We'll send a messenger immediately with notices explaining the change of ownership and temporary freeze of financial assets."

Reginald scooted to the edge of his cushion and braced his hands wide on her desk. "Just for a moment let's be reasonable. What do you know of lumberjacks?"

"They chop down trees."

Regi laughed. "Oh, bravo. And when these jolly beasts of labor, who 'chop down trees,' come tromping from the woods demanding to be paid, what then, my darling?"

Lily refilled her cup and smiled brightly. "Refer them to you, of course, my financial counsel."

Regi arched a dark eyebrow. "I'd laugh if I didn't know you have a streak of viciousness in you. I can hardly counsel a woman who does not heed my advice."

"I'm neither naive nor inexperienced. Anything worth the effort is seldom easy."

The glint in Reginald's brown eyes told her he was quite aware of that fact.

"If they want their jobs they'll have to be patient while we work through McFarland's mess. Otherwise they're welcome to take up banners with those obnoxious men of the labor unions and harping ladies of

Women's Suffrage, and march the streets. Goodness knows one can never please the masses."

"You have never tried to please the masses," Regi said. "So why not just please your cousin. Let this one go."

"No."

Regi's gaze narrowed. "When this lumber-camp jaunt goes up in smoke, I will expect a full I-should-have-listened-to-Reginald apology."

"I always listen to you, Regi," she said as she began thumbing through the box of files. "You've been my trusted friend since I arrived in San Francisco."

"Which says little of my sensibilities," he muttered.

"We will split the list of employees and see if we can't match them to job references buried in the rest of this mess."

Reginald stood and snatched the stack of paper she held out to him. "You realize we do employ secretaries?"

"Yes. Tell Emily I'd like another pot of hot chocolate."

"Right after I notify some of the staff that they'll be taking a trip to the mountains."

Lily slid her chair up to the desk and opened the file with rows of names listed in alphabetical order, management mingled with the most common of workers. It was no wonder McFarland's company had gone under. The man clearly had no business sense.

Her gaze scanned down the first page. A name caught her attention, forcing her to reread the line.

Barns, Juniper. *Juniper Barns.*

The name slapped across her senses like a razor strap. A name she'd heard over and over in her mind since she was twelve years old, since the night her father's business partner had stood on the front porch of her childhood home in Missouri, holding a hat and a gun belt.

"I'm sorry, Rose. Red won't be coming back. He was killed in Mason by a gunslinger named Juniper Barns. Gunned him down with those pearl-handled six-shooters."

Her mother had been devastated. Folks had said the influenza had killed her a few weeks later, but Lily knew better. Rose Palmer had stopped living that night on the porch. She'd let the sickness take her.

He'd killed her. The gunfighter had shattered Rose's heart by taking her husband.

Juniper Barns. The man who'd stripped the sun from Lily's sky. He'd stolen her parents, her life, forcing her into the care of strangers, relatives her mother had shunned so she could be with the man she loved. Lily didn't have to wonder why her mother had run off to Missouri, preferring her quiet life in the small cottage on a flower-filled meadow with her and Daddy. Dear Lord, how Lily'd missed her home, the wide-open sky, the scent of spruce and aspen, the sound of her mother's soft voice, her father's strong embraces…

Old rage welled up and coiled across her shoulders. How many nights had she lain awake in her fancy prison, anger burning away tears she had refused to cry as she wished for the opportunity to shoot down the outlaw who'd stolen her family and turned her life into endless torment?

Juniper Barns. Lily's hand trembled as she brushed her finger over the letters. Not exactly a common name.

A man ain't no better than his name.

Her father's voice echoed in her mind. They were some of the last words he'd spoken to her. She remembered the last time she'd stood with him in the sun-sprayed meadow filled with tall grasses and wildflowers, his strong arms closed around her, his big hands helping her to steady the revolver as she took aim at a bottle sitting on a rock in the distance.

He stepped away. She squeezed the trigger, kicking off a shot. Glass exploded into glistening shards.

"That's my girl!"

There was always the threat of raiders in the high country. Daddy had insisted she practice with a revolver as well as a rifle. He said she was to tell her mother about neither.

"Your mama would have my hide for teaching you to handle a six-shooter, but she's a delicate sort of flower. My baby girl is pure Palmer. You don't have to be a man to defend your name and protect what's yours. Out here, we look out for our own. You got that, Lily girl?"

"I got it," she said, thinking of the gun belt tucked safely in her wardrobe upstairs.

You don't have to be a man to defend your name....

A name the Carringtons had forbidden her to speak in their presence. She'd gotten even with the Carringtons, making her true initials, L. P., the prefix of the company name when she'd taken over Carrington Industries.

"Lily Palmer," she said to herself, the name sounding foreign to her ears. Had she been labeled a Carrington for so long, she'd forgotten her true self? Her chest ached at the thought.

"What's that, love?" Regi asked, stepping back into the open doorway of her office.

"I think you're right," she said, shaking off the chill of old memories. "I need a breath of fresh air."

His face lit up with a smile. "Wouldn't hurt."

"Emily?" she called out.

The young woman who worked as her secretary and housekeeper stepped into the room. "Yes, Miss Carrington?"

"Pull out my spring dresses and have Charles retrieve my trunks." She pushed back from her desk and stood. "Some winter dresses, as well," she added, remembering the drastic temperature fluctuations of the higher elevations.

Emily gave a firm nod. "Right away."

"Your trunks?" said Regi. "You intend to take a trip now and dump this lumber mess onto my lap?"

"Of course not. I'll be accompanying our lawyers and accountants. I want to leave within a week."

Reginald stared at her as though she'd suddenly sprouted wings. "You're not serious."

"Weren't you the one just telling me I need to get out more?"

"I meant a trip to the zoo, a stroll through the park, not jaunting off into the *wilderness!*"

"How better to learn about my new company than to pay a visit? I won't have to rely on long-distance reports. It's the perfect solution."

"Lily, I…" His hands clenched into fists. "I *forbid* it."

Realizing he was quite serious, Lily couldn't fight her smile. She was Lily *Palmer* Carrington, and she did as she pleased.

Lily breathed in the strong, nostalgic scent of spruce and pine as their carriage rounded the mountainside. Her gaze moved across a green canopy of giant pines rising up from a canyon below. She had to wonder why she'd waited so long to venture beyond the crowded parlors, tight streets and stifling buildings of San Francisco.

They'd left the valley at daybreak, and the moment they'd gone beyond the rolling green hills and into the forest of pines, she'd felt a sense of homecoming. Every bend in the road and new stretch of scenery had brought heartache and beauty…a longing for the life she'd lost.

A few hours back they'd stopped to rest the horses. She had stepped from the carriage into a grass-filled meadow bursting with wildflowers—clusters of orange, lavender and white. Granite mountains spiked up beyond the perimeter of towering pines. It was like stepping into her childhood, surrounded by the sights and scents of *home,* awakening memories she hadn't realized she'd forgotten. Her eyes had burned at the vision of her mother standing in a similar meadow... the closest she'd come to crying since her mother's death. Perhaps this was why she'd waited so long to leave the city. It had taken this long to let go, to find her place in the confines of the Carrington family.

A tree branch scratched across the window as the road cut inland again, and Lily sat back in her seat. Their armed guard had the best view. In front of the carriage, he rode his own mount, a beautiful black stallion. She'd been tempted to ask to sit atop the carriage with the driver, which would have been utterly inappropriate and would likely have given Reginald heart failure.

"Would you please close that shade?" he snipped. Huddled against his side of the coach, he held one of his scented handkerchiefs over his mouth and nose. He'd been sulking beside her for the past three days. "The carriage is filling with dust."

She pulled down the heavy flap. Regi fanned his kerchief, wafting them with his pungent cologne.

"Honestly, Reginald, a little dust won't kill you."

"No, love, that's your job. You may have been raised in the wild, but *I* was not. You heard the driver, these roads are frequented by bandits."

She glanced at the men seated across from them, all dressed in tailored suits and bowler hats. Her accountants watched her cousin in mild amusement. Brilliant advisors and established family men in their late thirties and early forties, Johnson, Brown and Allen didn't seem to share Reginald's distress.

"We're nearly to Pine Ridge, Regi, and we haven't had a single altercation." Other than his incessant complaints. "I didn't force you to come along," she said, settling back against the velvet seat.

"No, your uncle did. My grandfather clearly hates me."

Lily wasn't sure her uncle Alder liked anyone.

"I want to get in and out, Lily. Just grab your files and perhaps we can make it back to that valley inn by nightfall."

"It's going to take a couple of days, Reginald." She was counting on it. While she had a company agenda, her main interest centered on one employee.

Her chest tightened at the thought of facing her father's killer. She slid her hand into a pocket sewn into the thick folds of her skirt. Her fingers brushed the wooden grip and cold metal of her father's revolver. She'd loaded the gun just as he'd taught her, leaving the first chamber empty.

"Miss Carrington is quite right," said Mr. Allen, removing his spectacles. He tucked the wire frames into the valise on his lap, along with his newspaper. "We have a payroll to disperse. Today will likely be spent simply organizing paperwork, and then we still have the task of tallying wages."

Reginald shook his head. "Utter suicide," he murmured. "All of this could have been done at the office."

"Hush," Lily said, growing annoyed with his constant pessimism. "We've taken the necessary safety precautions and no one knows we have the funds or has reason to suspect we're bringing them. Surely our employees have waited long enough for their pay. Once we have the proper documentation, I'm sure they'll be grateful for their wages and we can move on to establishing some new order."

Reginald glared at her over his silk hankie as he took another strong whiff of perfume.

The carriage slowed before rocking to a stop.

A rush of nerves and anticipation swirled through Lily. The driver's seat creaked as he stepped down. Light spilled into the dim cab as Mr. Dobbs, her armed guard, swung the door wide. He was a rather large and brooding fellow, but the hint of a smile twitched beneath the curve of his black mustache.

"Miss Carrington," he said, holding his hand out to assist her onto the step. "We've reached the lumber mill at Pine Ridge."

She placed her gloved hand over his palm and emerged from the carriage into the cool mountain air. She was glad she'd dressed warmly. Her full skirt belled out, wedges of a heavy tapestry in green, blue and brown paisleys tucked into folds of dark green velvet. As her accountants followed her, Lily brushed heavy wrinkles from her green velvet waistcoat and fluffed the layered bustle crushed by hours of travel. The sound of rushing water drew her gaze to a breath-taking sight.

She walked to the edge of the high cliff overlooking a wide stream. Clear, sparkling water rushed over rocks and giant boulders. On the other side of the river the land had been stripped bare, giving a clear view of miles of green ripples, a weaving of forest valleys and tree-topped mountains.

"Oh, my goodness. It's like standing on the edge of the world. *And knowing I own it.*"

"Be sure they put that on our matching headstones." Reginald stepped beside her, his frown firmly in place.

"How can you look at such beauty with a scowl?"

"Perhaps you should glance behind you, sweets."

Lily turned, glancing past the carriage, and her good spirits plummeted. *What a complete and utter mess.*

Pine Ridge appeared to be no more than a maze of logs, piles of planks, and poles with cables strung in all directions. Splintered wood and shavings littered the rutted ground. For all the piles of planks and logs, the dozen or so small cabins spaced across the yard seemed rather flimsily constructed, pieced together of mismatched boards and spare wood.

Aside from thin trails of smoke rising from stove-pipes on two of the cabins, the cluttered camp appeared to be abandoned.

"Oh, my."

"Hmm. I'll be expecting that apology by the end of the day."

"Did they know we were coming, Miss Carrington?" asked Mr. Dobbs.

"No." She drew a deep breath and went to stand with her men. "I didn't think it wise to announce our arrival while carrying such delicate cargo."

Dobbs nodded in agreement.

A screeching whine echoed from downstream.

"The mill seems to be running," she said, unable to see beyond the bend in the river and a thicket of pines. "Shall we make our way through the camp?"

Brown and Johnson each lifted an end of the lockbox holding the payroll. Mr. Allen gripped the handles of three leather cases containing their ledgers and accounting files.

"What should I do with the luggage?" asked the driver, standing near his team of horses. Their trunks were still strapped to the top of the carriage.

"Leave them for now," she said, setting off across the grounds. "And wait here for us." If no one was around to collect their pay, they may indeed be traveling back to the valley as Regi had hoped.

Lily carefully picked her way across the rutted dirt, stepping over splintered wood and chunks of tree bark. The scent of freshly baked bread grew strong as they passed a few cabins, none of them appearing to be more than common living quarters. The distant sound of a cow echoed across the yard, along with the cluck of chickens—all good signs of inhabitants.

The squeak of hinges drew them to a stop. A man stepped out from one of the ramshackle cabins to their right. His hat hid all but the shaggy brown beard of his face as he fumbled with the closure of his trousers. His other hand gripped an ax. Finished with his pants, he tucked his hands and the ax through red suspenders, then froze at the sight of them.

"Good afternoon," said Dobbs.

The lumberjack quickly shrugged his suspenders into place, his hand taking a rather firm hold on his ax.

Dobbs stepped in front of Lily, blocking her view. "Who's in charge of this camp?" he asked.

"You the new owner who's holdin' our pay?"

"I'm a representative of L. P. Carrington," he answered as Lily moved beside him.

"I wouldn't be shouting that to the treetops," the man advised. "Ever since that 'Frisco bigwig put the stop on our pay, Sheriff's been a mite busy. He'll be wanting to see you when he returns."

"A sheriff?" Lily glanced at Reginald.

Regi shrugged his shoulders as Dobbs continued his inquiry.

"Where do I find the man in charge here?"

The lumberjack scratched at his whiskery jaw. "Depends on where you're standin' and the time of day. Bein' that it's noon, Cook's in charge. Elsewise, Grimshaw runs the mill and assigns the bullheads. The Swede carries some weight, but he mostly brings down the heavy for the sheriff."

Lily wasn't sure the man was speaking English, having understood very little of what he'd said. "Where is the sheriff?" she asked.

"Ma'am," he said, quickly pulling off his battered hat. "Ruckus on the mountain." He motioned his ax toward the rise of trees beyond the river. "I suppose Grimshaw is who you'd want to see," he said to Dobbs. "Follow that path." He pressed his hat over matted brown hair and pointed his ax toward a dirt path leading through the thicket of pines on the far side of camp. "The whine of the saw or Jim's swearing will lead you to the millhouse."

"Lovely." Reginald motioned for Lily to go ahead of him.

"The lady might choose to stay in the carriage," the timberman advised before setting off across the grounds.

"Not likely," Reginald muttered.

"Come along," she said to the others.

Reaching the far side of camp, she ducked beneath chains and stepped over steel tracks as she started up the hillside leading to the millhouse. The wide path cut through a patch of tall timbers. Tracks for rail cars ran along one side. She wondered why this thicket of trees hadn't been cleared. Perhaps to cut down on noise, she thought, hearing the whine of a saw through the tall timbers. Lifting her skirt, she trudged up the hillside.

Up ahead stood a giant open-ended barn. As she reached the top of the hill, the piercing whine of the saw fell silent. The sound of rushing water and the chirping of birds was as loud as steady traffic moving through San Francisco streets. Much like those busy streets, flatbed rail cars piled with cut wood were lined along the tracks leading to smaller open-frame buildings farther down the embankment of the river.

"Watch your footing," she said to Johnson and Brown as they carried the heavy lockbox across a wide grid of steel tracks. Cautiously she stepped into the millhouse, a massive structure filled with machinery and oval tables surrounded by flat hand saws. Other tables supported circular blades in a variety of sizes. The strong scent of sawdust coated her senses. In a place she'd expect to find covered in bark and shavings, the floor was swept surprisingly clean. At the far end, ramps led down to what appeared to be a giant pond filled with logs.

"I think we got it working, Jim."

Two men huddled over one of the tables near the center of the room.

"Good afternoon, gentlemen," she called out.

Both men jumped as though she'd raged at them. Two clean-shaven jaws dropped open as they met her gaze. Both men wore ivory hats tugged low on their brows, blue denims and ivory shirts.

"I'm looking for Mr. Grimshaw."

"That's me," said the taller of the two, wiping a red handkerchief over the black grease on his fingers. "Who are you?"

"We're representatives of L. P. Carrington Industries,"

said Reginald. "I'm Reginald Carrington. This is Miss Carrington and our accountants, Mr. Johnson, Allen and Brown." Each man tipped his hat with the introduction. "Our man, Mr. Dobbs," Regi added, motioning to their menacing guard whose presence was title enough. "Are you the manager here?"

"I run the place," Grimshaw said with a nod. "This is Ted Mathews, one of our tree fellers." He jammed his thumb toward the man beside him.

"Delighted," Reginald said, flashing a rather patronizing smile, which wasn't missed by the two men and annoyed Lily.

"We'd like to have a look at your payroll files," he continued.

"Did the sheriff know you was coming?" asked Grimshaw, slowly strolling toward them.

"I wasn't even aware that we had a sheriff," said Lily. "We've come to retrieve the payroll files. Where is your office?"

The two men stared at her for a moment before looking at each other then glancing at Regi.

"Miss Carrington has asked you a question."

"I, uh…" Again, Grimshaw turned toward the equally vacant expression of his co-worker.

"Surely you have employee files," said Lily.

"Yes, ma'am."

"We would like to see them."

"I'll be truthful with you. Those files aren't as sharp as they ought to be."

"We'll be able to straighten them out," said Reginald.

He pulled a stack of papers from his briefcase and held it out to Grimshaw. "Our estimated payout is listed on top. Beneath you'll find a cross-reference for employees. We'll need you to confirm positions and pay rates."

Grimshaw glanced at the papers. The man beside him leaned in. "You brought the payroll up here?" Grimshaw said, alarm tightening his features.

"This is the Pine Ridge Lumber Camp, is it not?" asked Mr. Dobbs.

"Yeah, but pay's usually passed out in The Grove. Sheriff set that up right off when he took over."

"The grove?" said Lily

"It ain't really a grove, just a spot in the lower hills where some of the family types put down stakes and planted some fruit trees. It's got all the particulars of a township, banking office, church, brothel and general store. A man wants his pay, he goes to The Grove office."

"'Cept for here lately," said Mathews. The mill worker's mouth slanted with a frown.

"What are you suggesting?" asked Reginald. "That we distribute payroll down in The Grove?"

"I reckon. You'd need to run it past the sheriff. He ought to be back later today. He has final say about such things. He put a stop to pay coming up the mountain a couple years back. Too many blind bends in these mountain roads for a man to be riding with cash in his pockets, that's what he told McFarland."

"Then we'll distribute wages in The Grove," said Lily. "In order to do that, we'll need to see your filing system."

Grimshaw poked a finger at the sweat-dampened hair beneath his hat, his tense expression unwavering. "Filing system?"

Good gracious. Did she have to repeat everything? "You do manage this camp, do you not?"

"I manage the workload. We used to have a site manager, but here lately, ain't no one can manage this camp but the sheriff."

"Told you to sell," Regi said beneath his breath.

"I appreciate your situation, Mr. Grimshaw," Lily said, ignoring her cousin's gloating smile. "I assure you we can find all we need if you'll just show us where to look."

"Time cards would do," said Johnson. "Any documentation used to keep track of hours and pay rate."

"Oh, yeah. We got all that up in the office."

Irritation snapped at her nerves. Grimshaw was clearly the sort who only understood English spoken by a *man.* "Would you be so kind as to show us to the office?"

His twisted expression suggested he'd rather not.

"Cook sent your dinners." A young boy darted in from outside. He held a tin plate covered by another in each hand.

"Set 'em over there on a bench and change the blades on table four."

"I'll help you take out the dull blades," said Mathews, rushing off to assist the boy.

Lily watched the boy set the tin plates aside on a workbench and pull on a pair of heavy leather gloves. Cuts and scars covered his slender fingers.

"The boy works here?" she said to Grimshaw.

"A lot of our workers moved on to other lumber camps after the second pay hold. My oldest boy's been helping to pick up the slack. Davy, say hello to Miss Carrington."

His young face glanced up. He touched a gloved hand to the brim of his hat. "Ma'am," he said before turning back to his task.

"Do we have an age limit for employees?"

Grimshaw's eyes narrowed in clear annoyance. "He's thirteen, a smart boy and a hard worker. We've had boys as young as ten work the flumes and other odd jobs."

"I see," she said, deciding to keep her disapproval to herself for now.

Grimshaw turned away, clearly agitated. "Office is this way."

Lily motioned for Reginald and her men to follow him. As they filed up a set of stairs at the north end of the building, she glanced back at the boy lifting a circular saw from a spot on the wall. He seemed awfully young to be handling such dangerous equipment.

"Oh, hey," he said brightly, peering out a wide-open section of the millhouse, "Günter's back."

"Who is Günter?" she asked, stepping toward him as she glanced through the thicket of trees.

"The deputy. That big Swede right there," he said, pointing toward the camp, which now teemed with workers. A giant of a man with pure white hair stood out from the other men. "If he's back in camp, Sheriff must be back, too."

Just the man they needed. With the others already up in the mill office, this was her chance to ask the local lawman about any outlaws infiltrating her camp.

She hurried toward the path.

"Ma'am?" Davy called after her. "You like I should come with you?"

"I can manage," she called back, thinking he ought to be in school where he could learn to speak proper English.

At the bottom of the hill, she discovered this was indeed a functioning camp. Hulking, sweaty men were everywhere, barking out orders, stacking boards, pulling chains, lifting crates—where had they all come from?

She stepped around a pile of logs, seemingly unnoticed by the men milling about like work ants.

Where had the deputy gone off to?

"Lady! Heads up!"

Lily turned toward the sharp call, just as something struck the side of her head. In a flash of pain and bright light, the world went dark.

Chapter Two

Juniper surveyed the growing circle of men as he tethered his horse outside the cabin serving as the Pine Ridge Lumber Camp jailhouse. Only two things drew such a crowd. There wasn't enough rooting and shouting going on for it to be a fight.

Someone had smuggled a woman into camp.

Cursing beneath his breath, he started toward what could well turn into a riot. He didn't get paid enough for this job. Hell, just like the rest of the camp, he hadn't been paid in nearly two months. He needed to get down the mountain and check on John's widow. His friend's death was the most recent of fatalities in a lumber camp sliding downhill at an alarming pace.

"Afternoon, Sheriff," one of the men said as Juniper nudged his way past him and into a strum of murmuring voices.

"What's going on?" he asked, working through the crowd of men. Just as he'd suspected, he spotted pale skin and colorful ruffles through the shifting veil of bodies. Women weren't allowed up at the lumber camp for one obvious reason—they tended to bring out the worst in lonely, rowdy timbermen. To his immediate alarm, she seemed to already be in a horizontal position.

Good God.

He shoved his way through, then drew to a hard stop.

What the hell?

A pretty lady lay unconscious on a spot of open ground. The woman's peaceful expression and fancy prim attire shocked him far more than any display of indecency. The men surrounding her seemed just as stunned, none of them daring to go within a foot of her.

Juniper knelt beside her and pressed his fingers to her slender neck where her pulse beat strong and steady. A sigh of relief broke from his chest.

She sure didn't look like a prostitute or a destitute wife who'd come up here to find out why her husband hadn't brought home his much-needed earnings. Her green velvet waistcoat, matching leather gloves and colorful fancy skirt had a look of wealth about them. What was she doing way up here?

"What happened?" he demanded, glaring up at the others.

"I didn't mean to hit her, Sheriff." Slim, one of the log drivers, stepped forward. He twisted his hat in his hands, his eyes wide with fear as he stared at the woman. "I was moving a load."

"She ain't dead, is she, Sheriff?" someone asked.

"No," he said, sliding his fingers into reddish-blond hair, knocking out hairpins as his fingers moved through the silken mass, searching her scalp for damage. He didn't feel any fractures. A good-size lump protruded from the right side of her head.

"Where'd she come from?" he asked, glancing around the circle.

"I looked 'round and there she was," said Slim. "I shouted a warning, and she turned straight into the log." He clucked his tongue. "Knocked her right out."

Dainty as she was, he was afraid to move her, unsure if the blow had jarred her spine.

"I want to know what she's doing here," he shouted. "Who does she belong to?"

Murmurs went through the crowd, every man looking to another.

"No one was with her?" he said to Slim.

"Not so far as I could see, but I wasn't lookin' beyond the path of that log."

She moaned, and the group fell silent. The circle around Juniper drew tighter as the men leaned in.

"Miss?" Juniper brushed a finger across her petal-soft cheek. Long auburn lashes fluttered. She opened her eyes. The smallest rim of green lined the dilated centers.

She shifted, pushing her elbows up beneath her as she started to sit up. Long shiny hair tumbled to her shoulders in a shimmer of russet and gold. "I…" She winced, her eyes pinching shut. "My…"

Juniper quickly slid his hand beneath her head as she dropped back down.

"Easy, sweetheart."

She blinked up at him. Her lips tipped with a smile.

Juniper's mouth went dry. She sure was pretty.

"Oh my," she said, sounding breathless.

"You've taken a swift hit to the head."

"I must have." Her eyelids drooped.

"Can you tell me your name?"

"Lily."

Lily. What was this sweet, delicate flower doing way up here? Her weight relaxed against his palm.

"Lily? Can you hear me? *Lily?*"

She didn't stir.

Definitely a concussion. She'd moved enough to assure him nothing was broken. Needing to get her out of the sun and away from all the onlookers, he slid his arms beneath her shoulders and the bulk of her skirt. As he straightened, something solid jabbed against his ribs. He shifted her against him, firming his hold on her, and was pretty damn sure he felt the outline of a revolver packed into the green and blue folds of her skirt.

At least she had enough sense to travel armed.

He glanced up at the crowd of woodsmen. "Anyone willing to claim her?"

The eager expressions of the men told him that was about the stupidest question he could have asked.

"I will!" shouted one.

"I'll take her off your hands, Sheriff," called another.

He shook his head and carried her toward his office. Whatever her reasons for coming up here, riling the interest of a bunch of salivating lumberjacks was only going to get her into more trouble than she could handle.

"Find Marty and Günter," he said to no one in particular. "Tell them to hightail it to my office."

"You *arresting* her?" someone shouted after him.

"*I sure am!* She's breaking Pine Ridge law by being here. When I find out who's responsible for bringing her up here, he'll be packing his gear."

"Juniper?" His deputy hurried toward him. "She hurt?" Günter rushed ahead to open the door of the sheriff's office.

"Most likely a concussion," he said, hoping that was the worst of her injuries. He carried her inside and carefully stepped into one of the two jail cells.

"Who is she?"

"Hell if I know. Go see if you can find Marty," he said, placing her on a fairly clean cot. "I'd feel better if he had a look at her head before we send her down the mountain."

As the door shut behind his deputy, Juniper slid his hand into Lily's skirt pocket. Just as he'd suspected, his fingers closed over a gun. Expecting a dainty Derringer or stylish Colt, the .44 Smith & Wesson surprised him. A right decent weapon by his standards and any man's whose life depended on speed and accuracy. The plain wooden grip showed signs of heavy use, some of the varnish having worn through. He opened the cylinder, noting the empty first chamber and clean barrel. To his relief, the use hadn't been recent.

He glanced again at the woman. She seemed far too delicate to be carrying such a thing. Not that he blamed her for packing iron in such rough country, but why in creation would she have come all the way up here with nothing but a hard-used pistol in her pocket?

Leaving her in the cell, he tugged off his hat and tossed the brown Stetson onto his desk. He set the lady's revolver on a stack of reports. Crouching before the cabinet that held a pitcher and washbasin, he took out a clean towel. After pouring some water into the white basin, he dunked in the cloth, wrung it out and went back to Lily.

Such a tiny little thing, he thought as he knelt beside her. Not much over five feet, and he'd bet ten pounds of her slight weight was sheer clothing, her full skirt fluffed up by a stack of petticoats. He laid the cool wet cloth over the bump hidden beneath her hair and stepped back.

She seemed comfortable enough, though her fitted jacket did look rather constrictive. He wondered if he should open the high collar. He reached for the pearl buttons, then decided against it.

"Wake up, pretty lady."

Günter stomped into the cabin. "Marty went up to check a bad-tempered ox. I sent a man after him."

Juniper released a sigh of disappointment. "All right. As soon as he gets back, send him over."

"Da." Günter poked his head inside the jail cell, taking a closer look at Lily. "Pretty, ya?"

"Yeah. A regular sleeping beauty. Go on and get some chow before Cook closes the kitchen."

Günter didn't hesitate. Once Cook locked his doors there'd be no chance of getting a hot meal. "I'll bring you a plate."

Juniper wasn't sure when they expected him to eat—he'd hardly slept in a week. Between gun-toting damsels, renegade lumberjacks, crazed oxen and L. P. Carrington's latest notice starting riots all over this mountain, he had more trouble than he could handle. The sheriff's office had somehow become the headquarters for company complaints. Much more of this and he'd be making a trip to 'Frisco for a little one-on-one with L. P. Carrington. The man clearly had more money than smarts.

Work had been rendered, timber cut and hauled off the mountain. These men needed their wages, not letters asking for patience while some overstuffed suit polished his coins.

He leaned down and stroked a few strands of red-dish-blond hair away from Lily's face. Her long auburn lashes rested peacefully against her fair skin.

He had a hunch he wasn't the only one on the

warpath. This wouldn't be the first time a scorned lover had shown up at the lumber camp with a pistol in her pocket. If that was the case, one of their lumberjacks had been a right lucky man.

Lily woke with a dull headache.

She didn't bother to open her eyes, not wanting to increase the throbbing in her skull. She needed hot chocolate. Reaching out, she blindly searched for the servant bell on her night table, yet the table eluded her.

"Emily?" she called.

"Whoever Emily is," said a low, smooth voice, "it's fair to say she ain't comin'."

Lily sat bolt upright. She barely caught a glimpse of the man moving toward her before her brain seemed to slam forward, pounding stars into her eyes.

She swayed. "Oh, my goodness."

"Easy, now." Warm hands closed over her shoulders and eased her back down. "You took a swift blow to the head."

Eyes of the palest blue gazed down at her. She had a vague recollection of peering up into those cerulean depths once before.

"How's the eyesight?" he asked.

Her gaze moved over his tanned features, sharp jawline and wavy blond hair with startling clarity. He held one hand up, two of his long fingers creating a vee.

"How many fingers do you see?"

"Two," she said, smiling despite her headache. She sat up, slowly this time, and leaned back against the wall.

His swift smile didn't help her wooziness. The handsome stranger eased back. Light glinted off the silver star pinned to his dark leather vest.

The sheriff. She glanced past him and noticed the metal bars.

"Am I in *jail?*"

Warm throaty laugher drew her gaze back to sparkling blue eyes. Flutters erupted low in her belly. She definitely remembered him, and was quite certain she'd found him just as striking the first time she'd looked into those sky-blue eyes.

A sudden heat flooded her face, and Lily averted her gaze.

"You're getting some color back in your cheeks," he said, which only increased the heat flaring into her face.

Good gracious. Lily Carrington did not swoon over men!

Glancing back at the sheriff, she now knew why. Lily Carrington had never been in the presence of a man like the sheriff of the Pine Ridge Lumber Camp.

He took a step back, his broad shoulders seeming to block out the rest of the world as he leaned against the metal door frame. He crossed his law-enforcing arms over his strong chest, creating a formidable barrier between her and the open doorway of the cell.

"Mind telling me what you're doing up here, Lily?"

Her eyes surged wide. How did he know her name?

"Don't remember telling me your name?"

"No," she said, lightly touching the tender spot on the side of her head. "I'm not even sure how I ended up in here."

Golden eyebrows pinched inward, a look of concern narrowing his eyes. "Do you know where you're at?"

"The Pine Ridge Lumber Camp."

He smiled at her answer. The reaction caused an alarming effect on her pulse.

"Yes, ma'am. How many women do you reckon we have here at the lumber camp?"

"I haven't a clue."

"None. Do you know why, Lily?"

"No."

"Same reason this logging camp has to employ its own sheriff. It's not safe. I have enough work cut out for me without our rowdy crews fighting over a woman."

She certainly wasn't a woman willing to be fought over! "This is all a terrible misunderstanding. I've come to Pine Ridge on business."

"I am aware." The corners of his mouth slid upward again, and Lily was quite certain she'd never known a more handsome man with such a charming disposition. "Or was that pistol in your pocket purely for protection?"

Her mouth dropped open. Her hand slid to her empty skirt pocket.

"It's on my desk."

Her gaze darted to the side. Her father's gun sat atop a stack of papers on the sheriff's desk.

Oh, dear.

"If that revolver wasn't so polished, I'd worry about the missing bullet."

Lily groaned and slumped back onto the cot.

"Lily, why don't you tell me what this is all about?"

She stared into his gentle blue eyes and wondered if he used such charm to interrogate all his prisoners.

"I can't cut you loose in this lumber camp, but if you tell me what's going on, maybe I can help."

Yes, perhaps he could. "I'm—"

"Sheriff Barns!"

He glanced over his shoulder as Davy burst in through the door.

"What is it, Davy?"

"Barns?" said Lily.

The sheriff looked back at her, and Lily realized she'd spoken the name aloud. "That's right," he said. "Juniper Barns."

Lily couldn't draw her next breath. His narrowing blue eyes suggested her expression revealed her shock.

He can't be.

"Well, heck. You already found her," Davy said before stepping back outside.

Sheriff Barns didn't take his eyes off her, eyes that didn't seem quite so warm and gentle as a moment ago. "Heard of me, have you?"

He wasn't much older than her, *far too young*. She'd been only twelve years of age when her father had been killed, nearly thirteen years ago.

"Does your father work up here, Sheriff Barns?"

"No, ma'am. I've got no blood kin left to speak of. My father died in *Missouri* nearly fourteen years ago."

His emphasis on Missouri throbbed through her mind as chills raced across her skin. Her gaze dropped to the holster strapped to his lean hips, the pearl grip of one of his guns visible beneath his vest.

Gunned him down with those pearl-handled six-shooters.

Oh, God. She glanced up and fear shivered through her.

She'd come to Pine Ridge to kill the sheriff.

And he knew it.

"Where are you from, Lily?"

He'd killed her father. "San Francisco."

"Born and raised?"

There was no running from the situation. She'd waited twelve years for this day, to meet the man who'd stolen her life.

"No."

"Hell," he muttered, dropping his gaze. "Why can't the past ever stay where it belongs?"

Lily couldn't stop staring at him, the clear blue eyes that had seemed so warm a moment ago, such handsome features… He just didn't fit.

"Guess that explains why you'd be foolish enough to show up alone in a camp full of lumberjacks." He swore beneath his breath.

"You can't be the Juniper Barns from Missouri."

"I am, though I haven't stepped foot in Missouri since I was fourteen."

"But—"

"But nothing. I'm assuming you knew at least one of the men who fell to my guns."

"My father," she said, her mind still refusing to comprehend that this man was the callous killer who'd murdered him. Her heart thundered painfully in her chest as he stared back at her, his gaze so intent she could hardly draw breath.

"My God," he said in a whisper. "You're Red's daughter."

Her eyes surged wide.

"Lily," he said reflectively, as though he'd just recalled her name. *"Lily Palmer."*

"None of this is right," she said, fighting the sudden burn of tears.

"I am sorry," he said.

"You're *sorry?*"

"Damn right. I'm sorry your father felt the need to call me out."

Her father wouldn't have done any such thing!

"I'm sorry as hell for every circumstance that led to this moment, where I'm staring into the pretty green eyes of a woman who's come to shoot me."

"You can't have— My father wouldn't—"

"I am and he did." Juniper Barns pushed away from the cell.

Lily flinched back against the cot.

"I'll be right back," he said, shutting and locking the cell door as he left.

"Wait! Where are you go—" The cabin door slammed shut.

Lily pressed her hands to her chest, her heart beating fit to burst. He wasn't supposed to be so young. All the stories, the images in her mind… This was all wrong.

What kind of a boy shot men for sport? Yet…he'd said her father had been the one to call him out.

He had to be lying. He was covering for his father. Red Palmer had been a gentle giant, Mother always seeming so tiny and frail beside him. He was as kind as he was big. He had to travel for work, but they'd hardly been destitute.

He wouldn't do such a thing!

The cabin door opened and Lily surged to her feet. Sheriff Barns opened the cell and ducked inside. She realized anew just how tall he truly was. He stepped toward her, and she bumped against the cot, her mind a tangle of fear and confusion.

"I'm not going to hurt you, Lily."

His gentle voice prickled her skin. She didn't know how to react to him, a confusion intensified by the sadness vivid in his expression.

She had expected Juniper Barns to be...older and *mean.*

Cold steel closed over her wrists, jarring her from the mental haze. She gasped at the sight of handcuffs circling her wrists. "What are you—?"

"Getting you out of here before I have a chance to find out if your bounty-hunting father passed on his skill with a gun."

"*What!* My father was a sa—" He strapped a bandanna around her mouth. She screamed into the roll of cotton.

He knocked her back. Lily landed on the cot, flat on her back. Her heart lurched as he reached for her skirts.

Lily thrashed against his hold.

A second bandanna went around her booted ankles. He pulled her up into a sitting position and sat back on his heels.

Fear transfixed her as he stared at her.

"Aside from the fact that it's just not safe for you up here, I don't feel like taking a bullet this afternoon. And I'm not about to raise my gun to a woman."

"I 'ily 'ar-eon!" The roll of fabric in her mouth kept her from pronouncing her full name. Why hadn't she said her full name sooner?

He lifted her with startling ease, cradling her in his arms. She tried to twist from his grasp, but it was no use. His sturdy hold imprisoned her against his chest. He eased the door open with the toe of his boot and scouted the area.

"There's no reason to fret, Miss Palmer," he soothed, the warmth of his lips alarmingly close to her ear.

"'Ar-eon,'" she corrected, but the word *Carrington* didn't go beyond the gag in her mouth. "I 'ily 'ar-eon!"

"Chuck will get you safely down the mountain."

"I grabbed all the blankets I could find, Sheriff, just like you said."

Lily turned her face toward the gritty voice and saw a wall of plaid shirt before she was shrouded in gray wool.

"Thanks, Chuck. I don't want her bumping her head."

They were truly trying to sneak her out of camp! She heard the jingle of harnesses and snorting of animals as she was placed on something soft. She wiggled free of the blanket and gazed up at blue sky and the sheriff towering over her. She squirmed as he used a strip of rope to tie the chain linking her handcuffs to the spring of a wagon seat.

He eased back.

Her bound hands prevented her from sitting up.

The rogue! She adamantly shook her head, terrified he was about to leave her. The wagon rocked as the man in the plaid shirt climbed into the seat and propped his boots on the front of the buckboard, directly above her. An older man with a thick gray beard, he squinted down at her.

"Sheriff done you a favor," he said. "Pine Ridge ain't no place for a woman."

A *woman?* She was the owner! "I 'ily 'ar-eon!"

Juniper Barns leaned close. "Chuck's a little rough around the edges," he whispered, "but trustworthy as they come. He'll get you to the valley. This is enough fare to take the stage back to 'Frisco." His hand pushed into her skirt pocket.

He reached up and stroked her hair, sending a shiver of fear down her spine.

"Swelling's gone down," he said. "Do yourself a favor, Lily. Don't come back."

You stupid clod! I own this camp! Useless muffles vibrated against the roll of fabric as she tugged at her restraints. Juniper Barns tossed a blanket over her, shrouding her in darkness.

Wait!

A whip cracked.

This wasn't happening!

"*Move,* you lazy animals!"

Lily yanked at the handcuffs and twisted in the nest of blankets.

Think, Lily.

She knew all the thought in the world wouldn't release the bindings holding her captive beneath the blanket.

A few moments later the wagon slowed to a stop and she heard muffled voices.

Reginald!

"It'll have to go on the back," said Chuck. "I'm plumb full up here."

Something thumped into the wagon. *The strongbox.* Regi must be sending the payroll down to The Grove.

"Where can I find the sheriff's office?" Regi asked.

She squirmed and tried to scream, drowning out Chuck's reply. Her muffled screams were lost in the groan and creaks of the wagon as Chuck cracked his whip.

She rocked against the buckboard.

Regi!

Chapter Three

Juniper collapsed into the chair behind his desk, his gaze landing on the revolver he'd taken from Lily. He scrubbed a hand over his face. The rage he'd seen in her emerald gaze ignited a sick feeling in the pit of his stomach. Her pretty green eyes had blazed with hell's fury before he'd tossed the blanket over her. He had a notion that when not encumbered by a head injury, Lily Palmer was a force to be reckoned with.

Not unlike her father.

He remembered the ol' man-hunter quite well. Though rumored to be ruthless in his occupation of bringing in some of the most infamous criminals in the territory, Red Palmer had actually seemed a decent sort of fellow. Juniper had spoken with him several times over at the general store and in the saloon. On many of those occasions he'd mentioned the wife and daughter he had stashed up in the mountains.

Juniper had never been forced to shoot someone he'd been cordial with—until the night Red went after him like a loco steer. He'd never faced a more terrifying adversary. He sure as hell hadn't expected to live beyond that night. Part of him still wished he hadn't.

Would he ever outlive his reputation as a gunfighter?

Not likely. The last four years of being a lawman had afforded him some peace, putting his infamous reputation to good use, or at least giving folks pause about approaching him. He'd been trying to build an honest life for himself—but none of it mattered. Watching the mention of his name turn the sweetness in Lily's smile to undiluted fear brought him back to what he'd always be.

A no-good gunslinger.

He was so damn tired of fighting the past. Juniper closed his eyes, silently praying that Lily Palmer would take his advice.

"Good afternoon."

Juniper opened his eyes as a little man in a bowler hat and ruffled suit stepped into his office.

"Reginald Carrington," he said, rushing toward the desk, extending his hand.

"Sheriff Barns," Juniper said as he stood and shook the man's slender hand. His last name, dainty grip and frilly white shirt explained a lot. "I take it you're the new owner."

"Of sorts. We arrived a short while ago and I seem to have lost my charge."

"Your charge?"

"My partner, actually. Lily Carrington."

"Lily *Carrington?*"

"Yes. She insisted on being present for the inspection and must have taken a notion to have a look around on her own. Quite like Lily, you see. She's very involved in all of her projects. The boy from the mill suggested I'd find her here." The man's brows pinched inward as he glanced around the office.

"She's not here," Juniper said, the sick feeling in his stomach turning to a ball of flames. He wondered if this dandy was her husband. "She's on the ox wagon headed down the mountain."

"The wagon that just left a short while ago?"

"Yeah."

"You must be mistaken. We stopped the driver. Lily wasn't with him."

"She was, you just didn't see her because, uh…she was on the buckboard. Under a blanket."

Reginald's dark eyes grew wide. "I beg your pardon?"

"Women aren't allowed up here. She was unconscious when—"

"Good Lord!" Reginald said in alarm. "You knocked her out?"

"Of course not. That was how I found her. She had stepped into the path of a lumber hoist."

"Is she all right?"

"She seemed all right." Other than wanting him dead. "When she woke up she didn't say anything about being a Carrington. She just said her name was Lily. I sent her down the mountain the best way I could without causing a ruckus with the men."

"If she allowed you to send her off without a fight, she was far from all right! Lily is hardly some docile flower."

"I noticed." Juniper rubbed at the tense muscles in the back of his neck. "Believe me, she was fighting mad. Did I mention she was handcuffed under that blanket? And gagged?"

Reginald blinked several times, his expression seeming frozen in place. "You accosted the owner of this camp and sent her—"

"The *who?*"

"Your *boss,* Sheriff Barns. Lily *is* L. P. Carrington. Lily… Palmer…Carrington."

His slow, clear pronunciation didn't make the announcement any less of a shock. "Oh, hell."

"Indeed." Laughter tickled from Reginald's throat. "You poor man. Don't think for a moment I'll be able to save this situation. Lily controls everything, and her wrath could make the devil tremble."

Somehow Juniper didn't doubt it. Cursing, he reached for his hat. "Can you ride?"

The dandy snapped straight as though pricked by a pin. "Of course I can ride. I wouldn't have kept up with Lily all these years if not."

"If that means you can keep the devil's pace and stay in a saddle, you can come with me."

Outside he motioned toward the brown-and-white mare tethered beside Scout, his chestnut stallion. "You can take Günter's mount. You'll likely have to raise the stirrups."

Reginald didn't hesitate, stepping up to the horse to make necessary adjustments.

"She your wife?" Juniper asked as he slung into his saddle, the notion refusing to take hold in his mind.

Reginald glanced up from a stirrup. "Heavens, no. Lily's my second cousin."

"Then how is she a Carrington?"

"By birthright, Sheriff Barns. Her mother was Rose Carrington, youngest of four siblings to inherit the Carrington fortunes, a quarter of which went to Lily after Aunt Rose's death." He mounted the mare with reassuring ease. "A moment with Lily should convince anyone that she's a Carrington through and through."

"I don't think so," Juniper muttered as he spurred his horse. Reginald had clearly never met Lily's daddy.

They beat a fast trail out of camp. As they rode down the wide road cut into the mountainside, gunfire echoed across the sky.

What the hell?

Juniper met Reginald's startled gaze. Both men reined in their horses, listening to an echo that sounded no farther than the next bend in the winding road.

"Hey, Reginald? Why did you stop the wagon?"

"To send our strongbox down to The Grove."

Juniper's heart clenched. "You put the payroll on an unarmed wagon?"

"Surely not! We sent our guard along."

A single armed man? Juniper urged his horse onward, praying the gunfire they'd heard had been warning shots, and that Lily was safely hidden beneath the blankets.

When the load of logs came into view the team of oxen were at a standstill. Chuck was nowhere in sight.

"Chuck!"

"Over here!"

The old teamster stood on a thin strip of tall grass at the side of the road. As Juniper rode close, he noticed a man lying on the ground beside him.

"Poor feller's dead," said Chuck. "Was a goddamn coward what shot 'im."

"This man didn't have his gun drawn?" Juniper asked, spotting a rifle and revolver lying in the grass not far off from the stranger's boots.

Chuck turned his head and spat a stream of chaw. "We knew there was too many of 'em. Dobbs tossed his guns down right off. They got what they was after, weren't no call to shoot 'im."

"Where's Lily?" Reginald shouted, reining in beside the wagon.

"Reckon she's still on the buckboard."

"She's not here!" He turned his horse in a full circle, his eyes wide with terror as he glanced up and down the mountainside.

Juniper looked back at Chuck. "You didn't see them take her?"

"They had me facedown in the grass. I didn't hear no mention of them finding her, so I figured she was still under the blanket."

Juniper's horse leaped back onto the road. Pulling his rifle from a scabbard at the side of his saddle, he fired off three shots, the blasts echoing across the mountain as he set off in the direction of the bandits.

"What was that for?" Reginald shouted, riding up beside him.

"To let them know I'm coming for 'em. *Wait here.*"

"She's my cousin! I'm going after her."

He didn't waste time arguing. They raced down the wide dirt road. A mile farther, Juniper rounded another bend and spotted a figure off in the brush.

Lily.

Her wrists were cuffed in front of the bulging mass of her torn skirt. She inched forward, struggling to walk despite her bound ankles.

He pulled up on the reins as relief plowed through him.

They must have dumped her into the thick brush. Dirt and stickers coated her dress. Dried grass clung to her tangled hair. Narrowed green eyes burned into him.

"Lily!" shouted Reginald. He reined in beside her and jumped from his saddle. "Oh, thank God."

Measuring the rage in Lily's eyes, Juniper wasn't quite ready to thank the heavens. She shouted through the roll of fabric in her mouth, and Reginald took a cautious step back.

Juniper dismounted beside him. He held up the key to the cuffs. "You want to—"

"Hell no, man." Reginald took another step back. "You're the one who tied her up. You can let her loose."

Opting for the least lethal position, Juniper stepped behind her to remove the gag. "I'm sorry about this, Miss Carrington," he said as he loosened the knot on his handkerchief. "Things would have gone differently if you'd told me who you were from the start."

The moment he pulled the bandanna away, she spun toward him in a whirling flutter of fancy green fabric.

"You're fired! Do you hear me? *Fired!*"

"Uh…sweetness? I wouldn't do that just yet."

Juniper bypassed her hands and crouched down to undo the binding around her booted ankles.

"He's fired now! We need to find a *real* sheriff!"

"Lady," Juniper said as he straightened, stuffing the second bandanna into his pocket. "I'm as *real* as it gets up here. If I didn't govern your camp, you wouldn't have a logging company left to speak of because your employees would have shredded it to toothpicks after the second pay hold."

"Uncuff me!" she shouted, holding up her hands.

"I don't know," Juniper said, not trusting the lethal glint in her eyes. "I do that and you're liable to back-shoot me."

"Front, back, sideways. I'm not choosy at the moment!"

"*Lily.*" Reginald clamped a hand onto her arm, clearly fearing she was about to attack him.

"This whole situation could have been avoided," said Juniper, his own temper hanging on by a thread. "What were you thinking to bring a cash box up to this camp with only a single armed guard? Why wasn't I notified? And why the hell didn't you tell me you were L. P. Carrington?"

"You shoved your handkerchief into my mouth before I had the chance, binding me up so that I couldn't even protect myself!"

"*I saved your life.* If you had identified yourself to those men, I doubt they'd have let you off this mountain. You're lucky they dropped you on your ass before they figured out who you were, or you'd likely have ended up like your gunman."

Her eyes flared. "Mr. Dobbs? What about him?"

"He's dead."

She sucked in a sharp breath. Her gaze darted toward her cousin.

"It's true, love. They shot him."

"Miss Carrington, I don't think you understand the dire circumstances you've created here. How did you expect to be greeted after asking your men to work for free, when they'd already been waiting on back wages?"

"The company went bankrupt, we were trying to… We came to…" Her voice trailed. She seemed lost somewhere between horror and utter confusion.

Juniper almost felt sorry for her. Other than wanting him dead, she'd obviously had plans to ease the financial strain McFarland and her subsequent pay freeze had placed on the crews. The men had plain tired of waiting. No doubt they'd heard a pot of money was on the mountain and had set out to claim what they believed to be rightfully theirs.

"Give me your hands," he said.

She held out her wrists without question.

"How's your head feeling?" he asked as he released the first cuff.

"It's okay." The second cuff fell open and she pulled her hands away, rubbing at the tender skin behind her short gloves.

He turned from her and mounted his horse. With only two mounts, she wasn't likely to find her riding options suitable. He didn't know Günter's horse well enough to trust Reginald riding double. Scout wouldn't balk about the extra weight. Used to carting his sisters around, he wouldn't shy away from Lily's flapping skirts. Juniper reined in close beside her and leaned down to grip her slender waist. She shrieked as he lifted her.

"Easy, boss," he said, forcing her stiff legs to bend as he pulled her securely onto his lap. "It's a short ride back to the wagon."

To his surprise, she didn't fight him. She gave a slight nod and quickly averted her gaze. He glanced down at the amber-gold crown of her head, and the grass and twigs poking out from the mass of hair that swirled around her shoulders. The shoulder-to-cuff seam in her green jacket had ripped open, revealing a pink scrape on lily-white skin. Just about every surface of the fancy dress had a rip or snag. The tender skin beneath likely bore bruises from such rough handling.

Guilt festered inside him.

"Miss Carrington, I wouldn't have put you on that wagon had I thought you'd be in danger."

Lily shut her eyes, anger and humiliation clashing inside her. "You're still fired," she said, the tremble in her voice adding to her distress.

"Of course I am."

His gentle tone increased the fine trembling of her body. She tried not to notice the heat of his chest against her shoulder and back, or his muscular thighs all but cradling her backside. Every shift of movement was a startling reminder that Juniper Barns was very much a man.

She angled her head slightly, unable to help herself from stealing a glance at him—a handsome rogue who had an entire community fooled into believing he was a man of law-abiding morals. He glanced down and she quickly looked away from the chilling clarity of his blue eyes.

"Did you get a good look at the group of men?"

Dear God, she did not want to talk while sitting on his lap.

His arm tightened about her waist, stiffening her spine. "Lily?"

"Just the one who took me," she said in a biting tone. "Dark hair, dark eyes and a red handkerchief—clearly a multipurpose tool for *outlaws*." Her tongue still dry from the red handkerchief he'd stuffed into her mouth, she glowered up at him. "A moment later I was belly down across his legs and all I saw was moving mountainside. When someone shouted out that a woman had been taken, he was told to dump me. He did just that, after a bit of groping and foul language."

The indignation of it all sent a sting into her cheeks, along with a delayed lash of fear. Everything had happened so fast, she hadn't been able to truly comprehend the gravity of being abducted, defenseless against her captors.

"Did you hear his name?"

The chilling quality of Juniper's low tone drew her gaze. The cold rage in his pale blue eyes increased the chill of her body. His reaction unsettled her, though she couldn't say why. Perhaps because she'd have expected someone of his nature to find amusement in her mistreatment.

"I didn't hear any names," she said, looking away from him, all too aware that she sat in the arms of her father's killer. "A series of gunshots drew the attention of the others. There was a bunch of shouting. All I saw was a flashing glimpse of horses before I was tossed into the brush."

"Your warning worked," Reginald said, riding beside them.

"Thank God for that much." Juniper spurred his horse into a faster pace. His tight hold increased Lily's outrage.

It was his fault she'd been taken in the first place!

Had he bothered to talk to her before gagging her and tying her up, he wouldn't have had to save her!

A short while later the wagon came into view, the oxen now facing uphill. Chuck stood at the front of the team, fastening a harness. The large deputy hoisted a roll of blankets onto the load of rough-cut boards. When she realized Mr. Dobbs was wrapped up in them, tears stung at her eyes.

Juniper reined his horse in beside the team of oxen, and for a moment she didn't mind the security of being surrounded by his strength.

"Sheriff," said the deputy, his expression glum. "I heard the gunfire. Chuck was just telling me what happened."

Chuck climbed up to his wagon seat and lifted the reins, seeming impatient to be on his way.

Juniper's hands closed around her waist, hitching Lily's breath. "They got off with the payroll cash box," he said, slowly lowering her to the ground.

The moment her feet touched down she stumbled forward and found her balance. Her gaze stuck on the body Günter continued to tie down.

"Why did they take the woman?" Günter jumped from the wagon and swiped the back of his arm over his wide sweaty brow.

Rage simmered in Juniper's blood as Lily's accounts played in his mind. "Can't think of any reason that isn't worth hanging for. Once I find out who grabbed her, he'll be charged with assault and kidnapping. Chuck, did anyone tell you a cash box was on this wagon?"

"Nope. That feller said he had a locked box he needed delivered to The Grove office." Chuck motioned to Reginald as he stepped beside Lily.

Juniper's narrowed gaze moved between them. "This is a fine mess you've gotten us into."

"If you hadn't shipped me off like a hog trussed for roasting, Reginald wouldn't have been left to make decisions without me!"

"I'm sorry, Lily," said Reginald. "We had the files we needed. Grimshaw went over the documentation and gave his approval. He and Mr. Dobbs agreed the payroll should be put in the safe kept in The Grove as soon as possible. They thought it'd be safest to send it down on the wagon, so as not to attract attention."

"Grimshaw couldn't have read any written orders," Juniper said, knowing now how word had likely gotten out about the cash box. Jim couldn't read, and Juniper figured any number of men could have overheard them talking at the millhouse. "Chuck, did you recognize anyone?"

"They all had their faces covered like a buncha stage robbers. With all of 'em shouting to get on the ground, it was hard to hear any one voice. Had to be near fifteen of 'em. They come right over the side of that mountain," he said, motioning to the incline across the road. "They knew the money was there. Started fighting over how to open that locked box before they got it loaded. Heard a mention of John's place. Reckon his woman's hurtin' pretty bad."

Juniper bit back a curse. That meant Calvin had

likely been with them. His widowed sister and her five children had been waiting for the last of John's wages.

"Who's John?" asked Lily.

"A good man who believed this camp would come through for him," Juniper told her. "So he kept working when others left, even though the smaller crews compromised their safety. It cost him his life. His wife and their five children have been waiting on the last of his wages for two months. What exactly did you expect these men to do while you got all your pretty little ducks in a row?"

"To have some understanding. I sent notices—"

"Notices won't buy much at a mercantile, Miss Carrington. Plenty of these men have families who depend on that income to make ends meet. To buy *food* and keep roofs over their heads."

"Surely they have some savings set aside for—"

"Savings?" Lily Palmer Carrington was burning through his patience like fire through a haystack. "Most of your employees have never stepped foot in a bank because they've got nothing to put there. They work to get by, *Miss Carrington.*"

"I realize—"

"No, you *don't.* You've got no business being out here. *You belong in San Francisco.*"

"Do not tell me where I belong! *You* are the one who belongs…in…"

"Hell?" Juniper supplied. "Right beside your father?"

Her green eyes flared with rage. "How dare you!"

"Enough!" Reginald stepped between them. "Lily, what's going on?"

Her lower lip slid between white teeth as her gaze moved between Juniper and her cousin.

"What's the matter, Miss Carrington? Didn't you fill Reginald in on your plans for revenge?"

"Lily?"

"If I'm cartin' this poor dead feller back up to camp," said Chuck, "I need to get goin'. I want to be down this mountain before nightfall."

Juniper turned to Günter.

His deputy splayed his hands wide in question. "You tell me. What do we do?"

He needed to get away from this woman before he lost his temper or, worse yet, she found another revolver. "See the Carringtons back to camp so they can make arrangements for their man and collect their belongings before being escorted to The Grove. Go straight to the kitchen and have Cook tell you which men didn't show up for dinner. That could help us narrow this down. Then meet me at Frank's livery. If I'm not there, he'll know where to find me."

Günter gave a firm nod. He turned toward Miss Carrington. "You wish to ride on the wagon?"

She glanced at the horse Mr. Dobbs had been riding, then leveled those shrewd green eyes on Juniper. "Where are *you* going?"

"To recover the cash box. I think I know what will likely be the first stop of our Good Samaritans."

"Good Samaritans?"

"In *their* minds, though I admit they've gone about it all wrong."

"They shot my guard and stole my money!"

"They took what they believed you owed them, Miss Carrington."

"What we owed an entire camp, not one group of thugs. How can you defend murderers? Though I suppose I shouldn't be surprised," she added, crossing her arms as she glared up at him.

Juniper glared right back. "Only one man pulled that trigger, and he'll be found and charged with the crime. I'll get your money back, Miss Carrington."

"Not without us, you won't." Lily strode toward Dobbs's black horse, and Juniper had to clench his jaw to keep from swearing.

"Let the man do his job, Lil'," Reginald said, a blessed voice of reason.

"I plan to make certain he does." Her tiny form swung into the high saddle in a most unladylike fashion, and with an ease that shocked him. "We can't move forward until the payroll is recovered and properly distributed." She tucked the excess folds of her fancy skirt securely beneath her slender white knees, then shifted in the saddle as though reacquainting herself with what had once been familiar.

"Which is why we're riding along. Reginald."

Her stiff-backed tone put a pinch in Juniper's spine. He glanced at poor Reginald. The man's weary expression threatened to dash the last of his hope. "What are my chances of talking her into staying at the camp?"

Reginald shook his head. "I always knew she'd be the death of me," he said in a whimper, and started toward his horse. "I just thought it would take a little longer."

Glancing back at Lily sitting stiffly in the saddle, Juniper knew it wasn't the dandy's death she had her heart set on.

It was *his*.

Chapter Four

Juniper kept Scout at a hard pace. The Grove was close, a small settlement nestled into a lowland mountain valley where squatting oak trees, tall grasses and bursts of wildflowers replaced the towering pines of the higher elevations. Lily and Reginald rode a few paces behind him, their horses hot and lathered.

Juniper had no intention of hunting down a hostile band of men with these two in tow, certainly not with a gunman on the loose. Lily's temper wasn't enough to keep her safe if bullets started flying. Problem was, he had nowhere to stash them. Folks in The Grove weren't likely to greet the Carringtons with warmth and hospitality. The entire community had suffered from the recent pay hold.

Two parallel rows of rooftops marking the settlement came into view, and Juniper's mind raced for a solution. He'd met all the residents of this town at one time or another, having served as their local sheriff for nearly two years before he'd moved up to the high

Sierra camp. In the past few years he'd spent his days beating the trail up and down this mountain.

Juniper veered off the wide stretch of road. Below, individual rooftops fanned out on either side of the shops on the main strip. Homes spotted the uneven hills tucked into the mountain crevasse. Descending a high stretch of ground, he caught sight of a cluster of residents gathered beneath the narrow awnings of the main strip, spilling out into the street.

Spotting his approach, the dense crowd scattered like a clutch of spooked chickens, rushing off in all directions. Not his usual greeting.

Something's definitely up.

His gaze swept the deep valley, searching the passes in and out of town. Thick foliage covered the steep ridges spiking up on three sides, offering ample shelter and few outlets. He truly doubted the band of timbermen had stuck around for his arrival, knowing he was in pursuit and that a man lay dead up on the mountain. Then again, if their intentions had been relief for the community rather than greed, he should find them passing out wages at McFarland's office. Somehow, that didn't seem likely.

Experience told him that no matter what their initial intentions had been when they'd descended upon that wagon, the moment their hands had been on the money, greed had kicked in. If they'd taken a mind to keep the loot for themselves, the township posed as great a threat as the law. The stolen money was rightfully the townspeople's. Juniper's impending approach would be a good excuse for them to keep riding—only if they'd managed to rally support from those they'd come into contact with, convincing them that their sheriff was the greater threat. Not a position any sheriff wanted to be in.

He pulled up on the reins and glanced back at his meager posse. The sight of Lily barreling down on him brought an abrupt shift of focus—and damn near took his breath away. Her hair flowed out behind her like a shimmering mane. Attraction prowled through his body, tensing his muscles as she came up beside him, her squared shoulders and raised chin giving off a flare of confidence.

Even snagged and scuffed, she stood out in these mountains like a swan in a duck pond.

There's no way to hide her, to make her blend in. Reginald wasn't much better in his ruffled shirt and brimless black hat. What the hell good was a hat that didn't even shade your face? Both reined in beside him, exhaustion clear on their faces. He imagined neither were used to spending hours on horseback, much less keeping up the rigorous pace he'd demanded.

"Mr. Barns—"

"Stay beside me," he said before Lily could get another word out. "I want you both tight on my flank." He urged Scout on, giving no time for Lily's rebuttal. They murmured behind him before moving into position, their horses just visible from the corners of his eyes.

In a town usually humming with activity, the streets

were nearly deserted. Folks peered out through open doors and shop windows. Only the general-store merchant stood in the entrance to his shop, twisting one upturned end of his fancy mustache.

"Afternoon, Sheriff," Deke Winton said with a wave.

"Deke."

Juniper rode on toward the livery, which marked the far end of town. Frank would know who'd been in and out of The Grove. If the men had ridden out, they'd likely taken fresh horses.

On the second block the wide doors to Jonas's blacksmith shop were shut tight, a sight he'd never seen before in the middle of the afternoon. A nagging chill wormed up his spine. More than likely, Jonas's last clients had been a band of timbermen needing help with a locked box.

"On my flank," he repeated, Lily and Reginald falling out of his peripheral vision. Both closed in.

Juniper wasn't pleased to see the sheriff's office locked up, shutters drawn. He wondered if his deputy had caught wind of the trouble or was off on other business.

Reaching the center of town, he slowed. He glanced past Lily's mount and honed his gaze on the small white house located on the edge of town.

"Mr. Barns, would—"

"Pipe down," he said offhandedly, cutting off Lily's question as his gaze swept the yard and nearby fields of tall grasses. He didn't see any sign of visitors outside

Widow Donnelly's home, but that didn't mean they weren't lurking about.

He continued toward the livery.

Residents who were usually quick to greet him peered through windows. Those who'd ventured out onto the boardwalks ducked back inside as he approached. He stopped in front of the large stable.

"This is a livery," Lily said from beside him.

Her pristine pronunciation coupled with the bafflement buried in her crisp tone brought a grin to Juniper's lips. "Sure is. Our horses are done for today. We'll need fresh mounts." He swung out of his saddle and began to quickly remove the pack of leftover supplies from his trip into the high country.

"Should I presume we are about to embark on another of your *brilliant* schemes?"

A quick side glance at her pursed expression told him to focus on removing his saddle if he wanted to keep a hold on his temper. He usually had the patience of a priest, yet one look at Lily's cold stare and slender, arching eyebrow snapped at his nerves.

It's your guilty conscience, he told himself, knowing he'd made a rash mistake sending her down the mountain in the wagon the way he had.

"I would think you'd have apprehended half the town by now, being so quick to use handcuffs and handkerchiefs with me."

"Give the sheriff a break, Lily," Reginald said in a dull tone. "He did rescue you."

Lily dismounted and turned her sour expression

toward her cousin, her hands fisted against the alluring curve of her hips. "From the situation he put me in!"

Juniper quickly averted his gaze from her shapely body, telling himself he'd liked her far better while she'd been unconscious.

She needs to get off my mountain.

"An honest mistake by the sound of it," said Reginald. "Though I can't imagine how you'd neglect to inform him you own the lumber camp."

"Hush," Juniper ordered, glancing around for anyone within earshot as he moved in close between them. "Do you two still not get it?" he asked in a harsh whisper. "The name Carrington has brought these people nothing but further hardship."

"But I—"

"I know," he cut in. "You're here to set things right. Until you do, I suggest you keep your lips pinched tight. Am I understood?"

Lily drew herself up, making the most of barely five feet—hardly a sign of compliance.

"We are due a briefing, Mr. Barns, as I've found your judgment to be severely lacking thus far."

"Sheriff Barns." Frank stood at the open end of the barn, his thumbs hooked behind his suspenders.

"Afternoon, Frank," Juniper said, walking past Lily. "Our horses need a cool down, and I'll be needing three fresh mounts. Or have you been cleaned out?"

"Figured you'd be coming down the mountain like a

flash of lighting," he said, sounding surprisingly chipper. "I've got a few left. Saved the best of my stock for you."

"I am obliged. They all rode out, then?"

"A dozen mares rode out in two directions nearly twenty minutes ago."

"Can you name the riders?"

Frank's gaze skated past them. Juniper glanced over his shoulder and noted the growing number of townsfolk making their way back out onto the boardwalk to have a look at their visitors.

"I'd rather not," he said.

Juniper gave a nod, figuring he'd bide his time. "Think I'll stop in and see Emma."

"That's a real fine idea," Frank agreed, telling Juniper that Calvin had indeed gone to see his sister, Widow Donnelly.

"I appreciate your cooperation, Frank."

Cooperation? Lily gaped up at the supposed sheriff, unable to believe he'd forgo further questioning simply because the man preferred not to answer. Mr. Dobbs had been killed. Juniper should be demanding answers!

"Where's Deputy Griggs?" he asked.

"He rode out this morning," said Frank, his gaze moving slowly over Lily. "Said he'd received a wire from a U.S. marshal looking to bring in that highwayman who robbed the stage last month."

"Let's hope this marshal can stick around," said Juniper. "This is Miss Palmer and her cousin Reginald."

"Good day," greeted Reginald.

Lily simply stared up at Juniper, his choice of title having caught her off guard. It had been years since anyone had referred to her as Miss Palmer.

"Miss Palmer," said Frank, "I sure hope they didn't hurt you none."

Realizing Frank was staring at her dress, she glanced down and was reminded of her tattered state. "I appreciate your concern."

Juniper's long arm curved around her shoulders. "She's a little the worse for wear, but otherwise fine. We'll be back shortly for those horses." He wheeled her around, giving her no choice but to follow his lead or be muscled off the ground.

"I'll wait here," Reginald offered, slumping onto a crate outside the wide double doors of the stable. He swabbed a silk handkerchief over his sweaty brow.

Juniper glanced back at Frank and tipped his head toward Reginald, as though silently asking the livery man to keep an eye on him. Frank gave a nod before Juniper started down the street, his hold on her shoulders forcing her to keep up with his long strides.

"Mr. Barns—"

"*Sheriff* Barns," he corrected, the irritation in his gaze suggesting he'd noticed her refusal to use the title. As far as she was concerned, he was no longer the sheriff of Pine Ridge.

"I'd like to know how you intend to catch up with

those men much less recover my cash box when you allow your questions to go unanswered."

"All in good time," he said, an easy grin sliding across his lips.

She shrugged off the weight of his arm. "You are wasting time. You're intentionally allowing them to get farther away."

He tucked her right back against his side as they turned a corner. "If Frank had anything other than a general direction to give me, he'd have said so. Don't suppose you noticed the local blacksmith had his shop locked up tight when we rode through town?"

No, she hadn't. Nor had he offered any insight to his plans or observations!

"If that lock box was opened," he continued, "I truly doubt Calvin would have left without giving a cut to his sister. With any luck, Emma will know where they were headed, and we'll start rounding up any prematurely distributed payroll."

"*Prematurely distributed?* You say that as though no crimes have been committed!"

"If no crimes had been committed," he said, his tone low and biting, "you'd already be up at camp packing your gear. You have no idea how badly this community needs that payroll. Do you really think I'd allow them to steal from the citizens I've sworn to protect?"

Judging by the reactions of the townspeople to Juniper's arrival, they were terrified of him. His barbaric treatment of her thus far confirmed his use of tyranny and intimidation.

"Must you drag me along as though I'm your captive?"

"Like the rest of these citizens, you're under my protection."

She stopped beside a yard with a white picket fence and pulled away from him. "I do believe I fired you, Mr. Barns. I prefer to seek the assistance of another sheriff."

His slow smile nettled at her frayed nerves.

"Sorry, darlin', you're stuck with me. I don't work for you down here. You're in *my* territory now. Down here I *am* the law."

A manipulator of the law was more like it. A common outlaw posing as a sheriff. *Utter madness.*

He turned away from her and walked through the open gate of the picket fence, heading for the tiny white house at the center of a small yard.

"Where are you going?"

"Exactly where I said I'd be going. To see Emma Donnelly."

He shuffled up the steps and rapped on the door, forcing Lily to hurry after him or stand in the street like a vagabond. The door opened as she reached his side.

A tall and rather attractive woman greeted them, her dark eyes flaring wide at the sight of Juniper. Looking up at Mrs. Donnelly's sweeping honey-wheat hair tucked into a neat bun and her modest black dress,

Lily became startlingly aware of her own tattered appearance. Her hair trailed down her back in a mass of tangles, the torn waistcoat revealing her white chemise and a flash of pale skin.

Mrs. Donnelly glanced cautiously at Lily before looking back at Juniper. "Sheriff Barns," she said, her smile clearly forced. "It's…good to see you."

"Hello, Emma," Juniper said, smiling gently.

The flutter in Lily's stomach made her wonder if he intended to charm the information out of the pretty widow.

"I'm afraid this isn't a good time," she said. "I'm in the middle of preparing supper and have the baby to feed soon, so if—"

"I won't stay long," he said, sliding a boot over the threshold. "We had a problem on the mountain today."

The frown already pressing into her brow deepened. "Oh?"

"Mrs. Donnelly?" Lily said, budging Juniper's shoulder out of her way. "I'm—"

"This is Miss Lily *Palmer,*" Juniper interrupted, all but scooping her into the tiny house as he stepped inside. "She's with the reform committee and is here to help straighten out the back wages."

A partial truth, she thought. Her gaze landed on a rug at the center of the room. Multicolored braided rags made into coils created a large oval on the wood floor. Very similar to a rug her own mother had owned. Beyond the few furnishings in the front room, four wide-eyed children sat motionless at a kitchen table covered with flour, pie plates and other baking dishes. The sight put an ache in her chest, reminding her of a warm kitchen, conversation, her mother's laughter.

A boy around the age of nine or ten held a potato and a paring knife. His three sisters appeared to be between the ages of seven and three, the youngest with a smudge of flour on her chin and nose.

"Hi, Juniper," chirped the little flour-smudged girl. She beamed a bright smile at him.

Lily glanced at the man beside her, failing to see the benefit of hiding her true identity from this woman and her children.

"Hello, Calley," he said. "I see you're all helping your mama with supper."

The girls smiled. Their older brother remained stiff and stoic, his concerned gaze moving between Lily and his mother.

"Who wants a peppermint stick?" Juniper asked, holding up a coin.

"I do!" the girls shouted in unison. All three abandoned their tasks, surging up from their chairs.

"Kersey," said Juniper, "would you walk your sisters down to the store?"

The boy looked to his mother.

"Do as Sheriff Barns asks," she said.

"I just need to talk with your mama for a moment." Juniper offered one of his warm, hypnotic smiles as he held the boy's wary gaze.

"All right." Kersey pushed back from the table. His

worried expression didn't change as he took the hand of his youngest sister.

"That's a good man," Juniper said, thumping the boy on his shoulder as he led his excited siblings to the door. He tucked the coin into Kersey's hand.

The boy's lips twitched with a grin. "Thanks, Juniper," he said softly, and followed his sisters outside.

Masterfully done, thought Lily. Juniper Barns wasn't short on cunning.

The door slammed shut, initiating a bleating cry from the cradle just beyond the sofa.

"What's all this about?" Mrs. Donnelly asked rather sternly as she bent over the cradle. Lily caught a glimpse of the plump, pink-cheeked infant wrapped in the blue blanket before the widow hugged him to her bosom, rocking him gently the way mothers did, instantly silencing his cry.

"We need your help, Emma. A guard was killed today and money stolen."

Mrs. Donnelly gasped, her arms tightening around her baby. "*Killed?* They didn't sa—" Her words cut off as though realizing she was about to say something she shouldn't. "I didn't know."

"I know you didn't," Juniper said, his tone soothing. "I'm sure Calvin didn't want to worry you. He did come to see you today, didn't he?"

Tears welled into the woman's brown eyes. "They're good men, Juniper, trying to fend for their families."

"I know that. As long as the money's recovered and everyone cooperates, the only men facing charges will be the gunman who killed the guard and the man who assaulted Miss Palmer."

Lily could hardly believe his audacity, to make such assumptions. They would *all* be facing charges!

"Oh, my gracious." Mrs. Donnelly's wide gaze landed on Lily's skirt. The state of her attire left little doubt that she had indeed been assaulted. Her initial attacker stood beside her, posing as a sheriff.

"Are you all right?" the woman asked.

"Quite well," Lily assured her. "Thank you. As Sheriff Barns has said, we need to recover the stolen funds."

"They just want what was owed to them."

"And we have every intention of distributing the wages, which are now missing."

"This whole town is waiting on their pay, Emma," said Juniper. "Everyone will get their wages. But it has to be done properly. We have to get that money back."

Tears spilled across Emma's cheeks, twisting the ache in Juniper's heart. He hated having to press her for information. This family had been through so much heartache in the past few months.

"Did they say where they were headed?"

She nodded, sniffing back more tears.

Juniper knew how much it cost her to implicate her brother.

"A man was with him," she said. "Calvin called him Chandler."

"You didn't recognize him?"

"No. He wasn't a pleasant fellow. He kept shouting at Calvin and scaring the children."

Two men by the name of Chandler had been working in Calvin's crew. Cousins, if he recalled correctly. He hadn't had any skirmishes with the two men, yet the name now pricked at his mind in a way that told him he should know more about them.

"They must have known you weren't far behind," she said.

"They knew," he said. "I was told they took off in two directions."

"I'm not surprised. Chandler and another man were arguing something awful outside the house. Some of the men wanted to divide the money and ride back up to camp, so as not to draw attention by missing work. Others sided with Chandler, wanting to lie low, refusing to divvy up the wages until they reached a place called Flat Ridge."

Chandler. The name clicked into place. Juniper was well acquainted with the land where boulders and flat-topped ridges dominated the terrain. He'd also known a Chandler family, their homestead not but a few miles from grazing lands owned by the Double D Ranch. Jed and Ben had suspected them of stealing cattle on more than one occasion, and if memory served, one of their boys had been killed a few years back during an attempted stage robbery.

Adrenaline rushed through his veins as he began visualizing every known route across the sixty miles between The Grove and the Double D Ranch. He'd have a safe place to stash Lily while he went after her money, and his family would welcome the visit.

"Which party did Calvin ride off with?"

She shook her head. "I don't know. They were still arguing when they left the yard, after some of them raided all that was ripe in my vegetable garden," she added bitterly.

"Did you see the other men?"

Again she shook her head. "I kept the children in the bedroom until they left. Cal wasn't in the house longer than it took for him to unload some parcels and Chandler to drag him back out. He said he'd be back when he could."

Calvin was young and likely believed the money would eventually get into the hands of the folks who needed it, but Juniper had a hunch the Chandler boys had other plans in mind. He glanced at the meager food supplies Cal had brought his sister. Potatoes, a few paper parcels of dried goods, none of which would last a family of six a full week. His gut burned as he looked back at his friend's wife. He'd eaten at their supper table more times than he could count. But none of that changed the job he was sworn to do.

"Emma, the money Cal gave you, I have to take it back."

"I made sure it was no more than what John was owed."

"Once it goes through the proper channels, you'll get it back. But right now you're holding stolen money."

She drew a ragged breath, then turned away and walked into her kitchen. Reaching overhead, she took a tin canister from a cupboard and withdrew a leather pouch. Her steps seemed to drag as she crossed the short distance to Juniper.

Fresh tears filled her eyes as she watched him tuck the money into his shirt pocket, and Juniper cursed everything Carrington. All of this could have been avoided had the payroll been handled properly.

"Tonight will be our first decent meal in a week."

Lily shifted uncomfortably, the thought of Mrs. Donnelly's children going hungry tearing at her conscience. She was tempted to tell her to keep the wages.

"I intended to come here today before all this happened," Juniper said. He tugged a small canvas sack from his pant pocket and tucked it into Mrs. Donnelly's hand.

"Juniper." She shook her head. "I can't take your money. You've already—"

"It's the very least I can do," he said, holding her hand on the pouch. He reached up with his other hand to stroke her cheek, brushing away a trail of tears.

Watching the gentle glide of his thumb on her smooth skin, Lily barely restrained a gasp.

"We look out for our own up here."

Chills rushed across Lily's skin as she stared up at the man who'd just spoken her father's words, his compassionate gaze staring into the widow's vulnerable glossy eyes.

"John would have done the same for my family," he said.

Mrs. Donnelly shifted the infant sleeping in her arms and tucked the money into the folds of the blanket. "Thank you, Juniper."

He gave a slight smile, and Lily could just imagine the intimate ways he'd allow the lonely, grieving widow to repay his generosity. Rage flashed through her, curling her hands into fists. It was her place to look out for the families of her employees, *not his.*

"I'll personally make sure you receive his back wages," said Lily. "As well as a pension to help you recover from your loss."

"A pension?" Mrs. Donnelly glanced questioningly at Juniper.

"His wages for the rest of the year," Lily clarified.

Mrs. Donnelly's pretty features slackened. "I…I don't know what to—"

"Miss Palmer is full of helpful solutions," said Juniper.

The angry edge in his voice drew Lily's gaze. She imagined he wasn't so appreciative of her generosity, alleviating Mrs. Donnelly's need to rely on his type of *kindness* to provide for her children.

He took her by the elbow and turned her toward the door. She caught his quick glare before he looked back at Mrs. Donnelly, a gentle smile replacing the flash of anger he'd shot in her direction. "We'll be in touch with all the particulars."

Mrs. Donnelly followed them to the door. "Juniper, Miss Palmer, thank you both so much. I hope you can recover the rest of the money without further violence."

"I'll do my best," said Juniper, stepping out onto the porch, his hand locked around Lily's arm like a steel band. "If you have any trouble, just send word to me. I'll be by to check on you in a few days."

She nodded, sniffing back tears as she closed the door.

Juniper half dragged Lily down the steps. "Clear your conscience on someone else's time."

The moment they stepped through the gate, she pulled away from him. "Listen to me, you—"

"No." He spun on her, his hands slamming down on his hips, his shoulders blocking the sun as he towered over her. "You're going to listen and listen good. That woman has suffered enough heartache without being sold more empty promises."

"My promises are not empty! And why didn't you want her to know who I am?"

"Because your face would be stinging from the door she'd have slammed shut. A few weeks ago she was telling me what she intended to do to L. P. Carrington if she ever saw him."

"Oh, really? Do you *visit* Emma often, Mr. Barns?"

His eyes narrowed. "What the hell is that supposed to mean?" he asked, his tone low.

"I just—"

"Her husband was a friend of mine. I sat on that porch with him the night Calley was born, and smoked cigars. Half the men on that mountain are friends of mine," he said, pointing toward the steep rise of trees. "Don't you dare start pretending you give two cents' worth about their fate!"

"I do care! I've invested a great deal into this company. I just thought it was awfully generous of you to offer your own money."

"*Generous?* When you consider she's got five kids to feed and I have no one, it's hardly generous. I'd say it's nothing short of common decency."

What would a gunfighter know of common decency?

He turned away from her and jammed on his hat. His long, brisk strides made quick work of the dusty, pitted ground. Once again Lily was left to scurry after him.

"What do we do now?"

"My family's ranch is about ten miles from Chandler's homestead. By the time we get to the Double D, we'll all be in need of a warm meal and clean bed. I'll need time to scout out Chandler's property before rushing in."

"Your *family?*"

The escalating pitch of her voice told Juniper she was about to balk at him again.

"You told me your family was—"

"My *foster* parents," he clarified, pausing at the

corner to glare down at her. "And before you ask, *yes,* they knew about my life in Missouri, and they took me in anyhow."

She blinked up at him with those big green eyes, seeming rather disappointed at not having caught him in a lie.

The moment Juniper turned the corner onto the main road, his annoyance with Lily fled.

"Ah, hell."

Half the town had gathered outside the livery. Angry shouts rose up with the name Carrington. Günter was backed against the stable at the center of the mob, gun in hand. Reginald, no doubt, cowered somewhere behind him.

Chapter Five

"Oh, dear," Lily said.

"Do not open your mouth in front of them," Juniper warned as they hurried toward the livery. "Do you understand me?"

His question was met by silence and he stopped, refusing to take her farther without an agreement. "Promise me, Lily. *Not a word.*"

"Fine," she said, her forehead creased with worry.

Perhaps she was finally starting to realize the true danger of their situation.

"Sheriff's coming!" a man called out.

"It's Barns!" shouted another.

The focus of the crowd shifted, a good three-dozen angry expressions turning as he and Lily approached. Hostility rolled off them like a heat wave.

Lily inched toward him.

Sweat trickled down Juniper's back. He moved his left hand closer to his gun and tucked Lily securely against his right side, wishing all the while he could tuck her into his back pocket.

"What's going on?" he called out over the buzz of whispers.

Abel Williams pushed his way to the front, his mouth drawn into a grim line above his thick black beard. As he'd been one of Jim Grimshaw's hardest-working log drivers, Juniper wasn't surprised to see him spearheading the riot. "We heard someone had the gumption to take what's owed us, and this dandy is trying to take it back!"

"You heard wrong," Juniper said, taking his stance before the herd of riled men. "Reginald came here to *give* you your pay. The men who stole his cash box are the ones keeping you from your wages. Don't suppose they slowed down on their way out of town to give you a cut?"

"They was running from *you,*" Abel shouted.

"Why the hell would they do that? I want my wages, same as everybody else. Neither me nor my men have taken a cent from this town in months."

"Some of us got families," shouted another man.

Behind them, Günter discreetly ushered Reginald to safer ground inside the livery.

"Tabs are runnin' high," Deke complained, taking an obstinate stance beside his friends. "So high, we can't afford to give no more credit."

Juniper was well aware of the strain on everyone's finances. Trying to keep the peace during the past few months sure as hell hadn't been a picnic. He was beyond exhausted and just as mad as the rest of them. But anger wasn't going to solve anything. "Y'all might want to keep in mind that Carrington could have cut bait and started anew, and to hell with the money McFarland owed us. Instead, arrangements were made to make good on those back wages."

Lily stared up at Juniper, surprised by his insight. It was true, of course. She could indeed have closed the mill and reopened without the hindrance of back wages and hostile employees. Reginald's warning nagged at the back of her mind.

"That don't change how we been treated," shouted Abel.

"No, it doesn't. I agree, we've waited long enough, but it's sure as hell not worth taking innocent lives over. One of Carrington's men was killed today."

"He must have drawn on them," said Deke, the men around him murmuring their agreement.

"Not by Chuck's account. Carrington's man tossed down his gun straightaway, yet someone saw fit to kill him anyhow. They left here with two months' worth of wages. That kind of loot messes with a man's mind. Are you willing to trust those men with your pay? *Abel?*"

"I ain't thought about it like that," Abel admitted.

Juniper let his gaze slide over the crowd. "How 'bout you, Deke? Will? Marcus?"

Men who'd seemed ready to burn Reginald at the stake now appeared rather chagrined.

"Y'all know I'm on your side in this. We want to get The Grove office stocked and running again. We're working to do just that. Y'all go on about your business and let Carrington clean up McFarland's mess."

"I aim to give Carrington a piece of my mind first," Abel stated, his wide stance suggesting he wasn't going anywhere.

Lily inched closer to Juniper.

"Your grievances have been noted," said Juniper. "Now walk on."

"Who's the woman?"

Lily felt a change in Juniper's stance. Watching his fingers flex above his gun, she stiffened and glanced back at all the curious gazes now gaping at her. Suddenly the air was too thick for her lungs.

"Miss Palmer is not your concern."

The chilling calm in Juniper's voice raised the fine hair across Lily's skin.

"She's one of 'em though, ain't she?" Abel persisted. "Don't see why we can't get some answers. Like why the hell we got to wait a whole 'nother month for wages we should'a been paid weeks ago!"

"There'll be a time for that. This isn't that time."

"I say it is," the other man growled.

"For the last time, *disperse*."

The tight ranks of men seemed to loosen, men falling back, moving off to the side, everyone but the man at the center.

"And if we don't?" Abel asked with a sneer.

One tug and Lily was standing behind Juniper, staring up at his broad shoulders.

"Now, that's just too sad to think about, Abel. We already have too many widows in this town."

Lily stifled the urge to wrap her arms around Juniper, in fear that he'd draw his gun. She wasn't quite sure if she feared for Juniper or the group of men.

"Just walk on," he said.

Mumbled voices grew louder, and men began to file off, walking back into town.

"Dammit!" shouted Abel as Deke dragged him along with the others. "Whose idea was it to hire a gunslinger as a sheriff, anyhow?"

"Think it was yers," said Deke.

They knew? Lily was surprised.

Juniper's arm snaked around her, drawing her back against his side. His gaze didn't waver from the main road as the men returned to their shops and homes. Juniper looked a different man from the pleasant sheriff she'd awakened to in the jail cell. Oddly, she felt protected beneath the weight of his arm.

"Are we—"

"Hold that thought," he said, his arm tightening around her as he guided her toward the livery.

Anxious to be out of the street, she hurried along beside him without complaint, stepping into the dim lighting of the stable. The strong, musty scent of horses and straw bathed her senses. Günter stood at the far side of the barn, his gun still in hand.

Reginald leaned forward, peeking around Günter's

massive frame. Relief eased his tense expression at the sight of them. "Please tell me we're leaving."

"We're leaving," Juniper replied, guiding Lily through the hay-strewn corridor. *"Frank?"*

"They're ready, Sheriff." The livery master stepped into view from outside. He stood farther out, near the exterior corrals, holding the reins of three saddled horses.

Juniper didn't slow his stride until they stood beside one of the two chestnut mares. "Up you go," he said, his hands engulfing Lily's waist before she'd even come to a stop.

"Mr. Barns!"

"I keep telling you, darlin'," he said, dropping her into place, "it's *Sheriff* Barns." Juniper flashed a tight smile, masking the mess of nerves putting a serious twinge in his spine. Having watched most of the men head into the saloon, he doubted their flimsy sense of reason would last long once they all had a few shots of whiskey in them. They needed to get as far as they could away from town before sundown. There was just enough daylight to get them within a day's ride of the Double D.

"Günter," he said, glancing back. "Give me your gun belt."

His deputy tugged at the leather strap hanging at his hips without question. They had spares locked up at the sheriff's office. Juniper took the holstered gun and handed it to Reginald.

"Head straight down that path," he instructed, pointing at the narrow trail leading up to the main road. "Once you hit the main road, keep heading northwest. I'll be right behind you."

Reginald didn't hesitate. Cinching the gun belt tight, he kicked his heels against his horse's barrel and set off down the path worn into the tall grass.

Lily sat stiff in the saddle, her distrust clear as the vibrant green of her eyes.

"Catch up with Reginald," Juniper instructed. "I'll be right behind you."

"Why—"

"You'll have to trust me, Lily," he said, and smacked the horse's haunch.

The mare leaped forward, knowing the trail by heart, giving Lily little choice but to hold on. Her startled words faded as the horse took off.

"What did Emma say?" asked Günter.

Watching Lily take control of the mare, Juniper feared she might turn back and demand answers he wasn't yet ready to give. He watched her until she'd caught up with Reginald. Both disappeared through the trees lining the road.

A breath of relief broke from June's chest. He pulled off his hat, shoved a hand through his sweaty hair, then tugged the Stetson back into place as he met Günter's gaze.

"Group's being led by the two Chandler men. They're headed for a homestead not far from the Double D, up in those flat-ridged hills. You remember how to get to my folks' place?"

"Sure."

"Meet me there tomorrow, an hour after sundown," he said as he mounted the bay stallion Frank had outfitted with his saddle and supplies. "At the north fork at the base of the ridge, where we started roundup last spring."

Günter gave a sharp nod. "I know the place."

"I'll ditch the Carringtons with my family." Juniper's horse shifted, anxious to take the trail, powerful muscles flexing beneath his light golden coat. Juniper tightened his hold on the reins and hoped the large bay was ready for an open run. "You know anything about the U.S. marshal that Griggs went off to meet?"

"No. First I've heard of it."

"See if you can track them down and get that marshal to help us out. Tell Deputy Griggs to get back to his office. If he leaves his post again before I return, he's fired."

"I'll pass the message," said Günter.

"Where's the rest of Carrington's men?" Juniper asked, realizing just now that they were missing.

"All three of them insisted on staying at camp." Günter shrugged. "They said Miss Carrington would want them to keep working. Their carriage driver is on his way back to 'Frisco with their fallen man. Grimshaw said Mathews was with him when the Carringtons arrived with the cash box. He's not in camp now."

No telling if Mathews had stayed with Chandler or

headed back up to camp. Right now his concern was the men still on the run.

"Before you go after Griggs, find Jonas. Arrest him and recover whatever he was paid to open that strongbox. I want a list of names."

"You want me to file official charges against him?" asked Günter.

"Just lock him up for now. We need a reason for any others with stolen money to turn it in. Get the word out, no one receives wages until every dime is recovered." A touch of his heels and his stallion bounded forward. "See you tomorrow, an hour after sundown!"

"I'll be there," Günter called out. *"Good luck!"*

Juniper shoved his hat down tight, thinking he needed more than luck.

Juniper's parting words echoed through her mind, mocking her as she raced to keep up with Reginald.

You'll have to trust me, Lily.

She *didn't* trust him. With each stride of her horse, she wanted to turn back. But Regi hadn't given up his lead, his horse kicking up dust a few yards ahead of her.

Why hadn't Juniper ridden out with them? Surely they'd have been safer staying together.

Rounding the next bend in the road, Regi drew up sharp, his horse nickering as it stumbled to a stop before a fork in the road, the wide path splitting into two trails. Both appeared to curve west, but with the tall scrub and dense foliage, they couldn't see but thirty yards of each path.

Regi glanced back at her, his eyes wide with panic. "Did he say which way?"

"No." Her heart clenched as a rush of fear crowded her throat. What if this was a setup and all his bravado in town had been for show? Without guidance, they'd be easy targets if that mob decided to hunt them down.

"To the right!" a voice bellowed from behind them. She turned to see Juniper bearing down on them.

Relief slammed through her.

The sound of hoofbeats told her Reginald had set off again. Lily's gaze remained transfixed on the man charging toward her like a dark warrior. A tingling rush of sensation rose up low in her belly. She released a hard breath, trying to expel the startling burst of elemental attraction. Her gaze moved beyond him, searching for Günter. Nothing trailed Juniper but his cloud of dust.

Why was he alone? Wouldn't he have brought Günter if they were going after the cash box as he'd said?

Juniper reined the large bay horse in beside her, swirling dust high into the air. "We don't have time to dawdle."

"Where's Günter?"

"Rounding up reinforcements," he said before riding past. "Let's move."

"Just a moment!"

To her surprise he slowed and glanced back at her. "What is it, Miss Carrington?"

"If no one is after us, why are we riding as though we're fleeing for our lives?"

He guided his horse around and rode in close beside her. "We're not out for a Sunday ride. Your bandits aren't cantering through these hills. Best chance for taking them by surprise is to make up as much ground as possible. *Now let's move.*"

He circled her before again taking off down the trail. Lily's horse charged after him without prompting, nearly whipping her from the saddle. She quickly righted herself, digging her boots into the stirrups. It was far too late to worry about scuffing the fine leather. Her entire ensemble would be reduced to scraps before this trip was over.

Over the next two hours the mare beneath her followed Juniper's lead, slowing when he slowed, picking up speed when he urged his horse into a harder pace. With each new rise of grass and trees, she hoped to see signs of a cattle ranch, but only saw more of the same—rolling hills, rocks and oak trees. A few times they reached a high point giving a view of the wide valley to the west, spanning out to the coastal mountains barely visible on the distant horizon.

Regi stayed close beside her, holding up surprisingly well. Rigid in his saddle, he hadn't uttered a single complaint. Too often Lily's gaze strayed to the span of Juniper's shoulders. Knowing who he was should have stamped out any frivolous attraction. But it didn't.

Every time he glanced back, tagging her with those pale blue eyes, her body was crowded by an awareness she'd never felt in the presence of any man. She kept remembering the smiling face she'd awakened to at the lumber camp, his warm, throaty laughter. Ribbons of heat twisted up from low in her belly as nerve endings she'd never been aware of shimmered to full life.

She shifted in the saddle, not at all comfortable with her body's reaction.

Juniper slowed in front of her. His gaze tracked the setting sun before moving across the dirt, short grass and surrounding trees. He stepped down from his saddle.

"We're stopping for the night."

Lily reined in beside him. "I beg your pardon?"

A quick glance didn't show a homestead anywhere in sight. Lily stood in the stirrups, ignoring the ache in her thighs as her gaze swept across the land. She saw nothing but miles of rolling hills and massive oak trees casting shadows across the tall spring grasses.

"You said we were going to a ranch."

"We are." Juniper began releasing the ties holding a pack behind his saddle. "But as you can see, the sun is about to set."

"And you expect us to stop and just…*sleep on the ground?*"

"That's generally how it works, Miss Palmer. Unless you have a tent tucked into another hidden pocket on that skirt." He turned away to place his gear on the ground, and she swore she saw a spark of amusement in his gaze. "Be thankful it isn't raining."

Beside her, Reginald groaned as he stepped down from a stirrup. Their cunning sheriff knew quite well they were not accustomed to enduring such long rides or sleeping out in the open.

"You did this on purpose," she said.

Juniper looked up from the saddle he'd set next to his pack. "Did *what* on purpose?"

"Dragged us off into the wilderness when we could have spent the night in The Grove."

"I'll take the ground over The Grove," said Reginald, busily releasing his saddle. "I haven't forgotten their lack of hospitality."

"But he knew we'd be left out in the open come nightfall."

"My only intention was to get you out of that town before tempers flared up again, and to ride as far as possible before sunset. We've made good time so far. I apologize if our progress poses an inconvenience to tonight's sleeping arrangements, but every hour of riding counts when you're tracking bandits."

She glanced toward north, the direction they'd been riding the past hour. A deep yearning to believe him warred with a persistent distrust. "Will they keep riding through the night?"

"Not unless they plan to kill their horses and go the next forty miles on foot."

"Forty miles?" The thought of another full day of heavy riding intensified the ache in her muscles and the burning of blisters beneath her leather gloves.

"Yes, ma'am. I like a warm, soft bed as much as the next man. I've been without sleep for nearly three solid days. When we reach my family's ranch tomorrow afternoon, you won't find anyone more appreciative of a warm meal, a hot bath and a clean bed."

"By tomorrow afternoon I won't be interested in clean beds and warm baths. I'm not planning a week-end stay on your foster parents' ranch. I want to re-cover my money and get back to The Grove. Are you certain the thieves are headed this way?"

He stepped up to her horse and began uncinching her saddle. "You were standing right beside me when Emma told us where they were headed."

"I wouldn't know one flat-topped ridge from another or where to find them. Why didn't you tell me it was a two-day ride?"

He shot her an annoyed glance as he folded the cinch over her saddle. "Had we started out in the morning, a full day's ride would get us to the Double D. We didn't start out in the morning. I haven't misled you."

"You sent us off alone for a reason. We have every right to know what's going on with this investigation. What did you discuss with Günter you didn't want us to hear?"

"What exactly do you think I'm hiding from you?"

"How should I know? For all I know, you could be leading us in the opposite direction. Manipulation is a skill you've mastered. You're a man of many faces, Mr. Barns, using each facade to bend people to your will."

He tossed her saddle aside and strode toward her, his hands on his lean hips, just behind the pearl grips of his guns. "The hell I am."

"Oh, please. You know what you're doing. I was practically simpering in your hands inside that jail cell, and *I don't simper!*"

His eyebrows shot up, his eyes alight with mirth. "Is that a fact?"

"Until I found out who you really are," she amended. "At which point you became an overbearing brute. Neither of which was the compassionate man I saw in the Donnelly home, or the hardened killer who stood before me outside that livery."

His shoulders shifted. "What can I say? I'm a complex sort of man."

"You're cunning is what you are, I'll give you that."

"Glad to hear you have some faith in me."

"*Faith?* How can I possibly have faith in the man who killed my parents and stole my life!"

"I've been trying to *save* your life all afternoon! I'll recover your stolen money and get you back where you belong as soon as possible."

"Where I belong?" Rage flared, narrowing her gaze.

"I own L. P. Carrington Lumber. The camp is now *my* property. If you believe your manhandling will put me in my place, you can think again."

"I apologized for—"

"I decide where I belong!" Lily shouted over him. She shoved her windblown hair away from her face and tugged at the shoulder of her waistcoat now hanging near her elbow. "I may be scuffed and blistered, which I'm sure delights you no end, but I'm staying in these hills until I've secured my lumber camp!"

Golden eyebrows pinched inward. "Why would you assume I'd enjoy your displeasure?"

"Because of *what you are.*"

Juniper stared into eyes seething with contempt. Her continuous accusations chipped away at his pride. "I'll assume you're not referring to my being a sheriff."

"No, I am not!"

"Well, then. Of course you'd assume I'd take advantage of grieving widows, bind you up to be abducted, then send you riding all over the countryside just for the hell of it. Why did you insist on coming with me when you clearly don't trust me to protect you, much less uphold the law?"

"Do you really think I'd put the future of this company in the hands of a gunslinger? Am I supposed to assume a man who once killed for sport somehow has morals? Seems to me a man of your character and uncanny charm would seek out a position of power and seclusion, *just as you have.* It happens to be the misfortune of Pine Ridge that you chose them."

Her quick, precise depiction of his character stripped away the barrier he tried to keep between his pride and the past. The frustration winding inside him snapped.

He was so damn tired of living like this. He was sick to death of running. *And from what?* Someone like Lily, a daughter seeking revenge for a life he'd taken? Juniper couldn't blame her—he'd admired Red Palmer, until he'd found himself caught between the red-haired giant and death. Once again, he'd dodged death and saved his own life, but at what cost?

Lily Palmer embodied the truth he tried to deny, the guilt that hammered at his conscience. When he looked at her, he saw the wave of pain and anger his choice to live had caused. Had the outcome been different that evening, he'd have left this world without causing a ripple of hurt. No one would have mourned the loss of his life.

A chill slid through his soul, the swift drain of emotion leaving nothing inside him but an empty void.

Had he just stood still his foster parents wouldn't have to shield their children from the danger he'd brought into their lives. Lily wouldn't be standing before him filled with rage and despair.

Who was he to stand in the way of true justice?

He lifted a gun from his holster and held it out to her.

Lily's green eyes surged wide. "Wh-what are—"

"You came here to kill me." He thrust the grip into her hand. *"Get on with it."*

She took a step back, but Juniper advanced on her, wrapping her hand around the gun. "It's what you've been waiting for, Lily. To shoot me. To avenge your father."

"I came to shoot the man who gunned my father down in cold blood!"

Juniper splayed his hands. "You found him."

Lily glanced down at the pearl grip, cold against her palm, and wanted to believe she had. "I can't shoot the sheriff of Pine Ridge, now can I?"

"You fired me." Juniper plucked the tin star from his vest and tossed it into the dirt at her feet. "I'm nothing but a heartless gunfighter with a bullet overdue."

His blank expression and unblinking eyes put a chill beneath her skin. "You're still a lawman."

"Don't go changing your story, Miss Palmer. I'm a killer, a deceiver, a defiler of good women. Now's your chance to balance out this world."

"Sheriff Barns…" Panic swelling inside her, she glanced past him to Reginald, watching wide-eyed a few yards away.

"Might as well call me June." He reached out and dragged her hand up until the revolver pressed against the front of his shirt. "I can't outrun the past, Lily. You can solve all our problems."

The intensity of his steady gaze frightened her. Tears pricked at her eyes. Her hands trembled beneath his. She tried to lower the gun but his grip held fast.

Staring into eyes as vast and empty as a summer sky, she felt the life-draining grief tugging at his soul, cold fingers reaching into her chest. She'd seen the same malady prey on her mother—the empty distance in her mother's gaze as Lily had watched her soul dry up, leaving only pain and exhaustion to ravage her last days.

"Just pull the trigger, Lily."

"Stop it!" She jerked her hands down, away from his hold.

The gun bucked in her grip, the blast ringing in her ears. Juniper's face twisted with pain. He curled forward and reached for his leg.

"Son of a bitch!"

Horrified by the smoking hole in Juniper's boot, Lily dropped the pistol.

Chapter Six

"You shot me!"

"You told me to!" Lily shouted back.

"To *kill* me, not *maim* me!" Gritting his teeth, Juniper dropped onto his butt and tugged at his boot. Hard language fell from his mouth as his boot slid off.

Lily's breath stalled at the sight of his torn and bloody stocking. He peeled away the cotton, revealing a bloody trench running down the outside of his foot and a good nick out of the flesh at the base.

Air hissed through Juniper's teeth as he dabbed the gash with the crumpled stocking.

"It's little more than a scratch," she said, relieved to see all five of his long toes still intact.

Juniper glanced up, his sky-blue eyes snapping with anger. "It burns like hell! You prefer torture to a quick death, is that it?"

"If you didn't want to get shot, you shouldn't have shoved a loaded gun into my hands!"

"She has a point," Reginald said, watching the entire

exchange from a safe distance. "Lily's the last person I would hand a loaded pistol."

"Reginald!" she said, completely insulted.

"Your temper isn't a secret, dearest." He walked toward them, pulled his silver flask from his jacket and held it out to Juniper. "You need this more than I."

"Thanks."

"This is hardly a time for him to be hindered by drink," she insisted.

Juniper glowered at her as he unscrewed the cap, then leaned over his foot. Air hissed through his teeth as he drizzled a clear stream over the trail of blood.

Lily cringed, knowing it must sting. She'd never have guessed he'd use the alcohol for his wound.

"Reg, can you grab a clean bandanna from my left saddlebag?"

Reginald rushed toward the saddles piled near a tree and quickly retrieved the red bandanna.

Lily watched silently as Juniper tied the fabric around his foot. Blood instantly darkened the cloth. He pulled on his soiled stocking and carefully slid his foot back into his boot, gritting his teeth the whole time.

She hadn't meant to shoot him. Yet once again he'd caused a calamity and made her appear to be the one at fault!

He stood and limped toward the horses. He gathered all three by the reins and started walking toward the trees. "There's coffee in my pack and water in my canteen. If either of you manage to start a fire, keep it small. Those men are probably on lookout. We don't want to send up smoke signals to give away our location."

"Where are you going?" Lily called after him.

"To find some supper before you change your mind and decide to roast me over a fire." He limped into the dense cluster of oak trees, leaving her alone amid the seemingly tranquil chirping of birds—

"Lily?"

—had it not been for Regi standing stiffly behind her.

"Don't," she said, refusing to face him. "I'm truly not in the mood to be lectured."

"I'd say you're in need of far more than a lecture."

Warily, she turned toward her cousin, knowing he had every right to be furious with her. His disheveled state increased the lump of regret swelling inside her chest. The hair usually slicked back against his scalp draped down each side of his narrow face like black curtains.

"I knew coming up here was crazy business," he snapped. "It was never about surveying the camp. *You knew he was up at that camp.*"

"I didn't know he was the sheriff," she said with exasperation. "How could I have guessed a gunfighter would be a sheriff?"

"What does that matter? Have you lost your senses?"

Quite possibly.

"How could you come up here to face the man you believed to have shot your father and *not tell me?*"

"He *did* shoot my father, and I never intended for you to come along."

"When have I ever left your side?" Regi demanded.

The answer to his question stripped her defensiveness. Whether it was a quarrel with the family or problem with their company, she could always count on Regi. He was always there to back her up. But this was different. This had nothing to do with the Carringtons.

He sat heavily onto the ground beside their supplies. "You should have told me," he insisted.

Exhausted, she sank down beside him. Yes, she supposed she should have.

"How could you keep something like that from me, Lily?"

She strapped her arms around her raised knees, reluctant to answer him. "You'd have tried to stop me."

He blew out a breath and leaned against the tree. "Considering today's events, I'd have been right to do so."

She shook her head. "I would have come. I had to."

"Yes, but if you had discussed your intentions with me, we may have derived a better approach at least, a plan of action. You may be ruthless in business, but you're hardly barbaric enough to simply walk up to a man and shoot him. Had you actually brought a gun I would…"

Lily cringed; heat rushed to her cheeks.

Regi's eyes shot wide. "You brought a gun? *Lily, what were you thinking?*"

Juniper had stated her thoughts quite clearly. She'd wanted to confront a killer she believed was long overdue for a bullet. It had never occurred to her that Juniper Barns could be anyone other than the remorseless outlaw she'd created in her mind.

She hadn't anticipated a cunning sheriff willing to put his own life in danger to fix a mess she'd created. She hadn't expected to be so affected by his warm smile or devastated by a grief she sensed ran as deep as her own.

I don't really know anything about him. She only knew he wasn't anything like she'd envisioned.

Why should any of that matter? Her father was dead, and Juniper was still wreaking havoc on her life.

Although…if Juniper was to be believed, she'd also never truly known her own father. When she got right down to it, she wasn't so certain she knew herself. *Lily Palmer.*

When had her true name become so insignificant, foreign to her own ears?

I never wanted to be a Carrington—yet her nerves rattled each time Juniper spoke her birth name. She no longer recognized herself.

The faces of Emma Donnelly and her children surfaced in her mind. An entire town hated her. Had she really caused them all such hardship?

Notices won't buy much at a mercantile, Miss Carrington.

She shut her eyes, her mind spinning in a tangle of confusion. Juniper was causing her to doubt *everything!*

Fighting the burn in her eyes, she forced herself to take deep calming breaths. She couldn't fall apart. She'd dragged Regi into this. And Mr. Dobbs... She had to set this right.

After a few moments she realized she was trembling from more than anxiety. She glanced up at the sun descending through the trees. They needed a fire. Soon it would be too dark to find wood.

She pushed up. "Help me by gathering up some firewood."

She crouched beside Juniper's supplies. Opening what appeared to be a canvas bag, she discovered it was a tarpaulin wrapped around a long dark coat and cooking supplies. A leather strap held a small coffeepot and tin cup inside an equally battered tin plate. Releasing the leather, she removed the cup, pulled the lid off the pot and found a box of matches inside a small strainer.

"Where do you expect me to find firewood?" asked Reginald.

"On the ground." She tucked the matches into her skirt pocket and glanced up at Regi. He hadn't moved. His blank expression reminded her that he'd likely never scavenged for firewood in his life. "Don't suppose you know how to make coffee?"

"Of course I do," he said, slowly getting to his feet. "I call for a servant or stroll down to a coffee shop."

That settled that. She set the tin and coffeepot aside. She didn't care to drink coffee, much less know how to make the bitter brew. She frequently made her own hot chocolate—the thought made her stomach cramp with craving and hunger. Her chocolate and silver pot were tucked into her trunk up at the camp.

A howl called out from the distant darkness already blanketing the east. The hollow bark renewed several times before fading into the twilight.

Song dogs, Daddy would say, *calling up the moon.* The memory sent a chill over her skin.

"Lily," Regi whispered. His wide eyes shifted side to side as though he expected a coyote to jump out at them. "There are *wolves* out here."

"Coyotes," she corrected, a smile breaking free. "They're a long ways off."

"It didn't sound a long way off," Regi protested. "Barns shouldn't have left us here unarmed!"

"You're wearing a gun, Regi."

He glanced down, seeming surprised to find the holstered revolver riding low on his hips. "Good grief. Any attempt to fire that thing would likely leave me in the same condition as our sheriff."

Laughter shook her chest, easing the strain on her body, and her spirits. What would she do without Regi?

"Come on," she said, hooking her arm through his. "We'll find some firewood together."

A short while later she struck one of Juniper's matches and touched the flame to the dried grasses she'd pressed into tight clumps.

"You've done this before," said Reginald. He sat cross-legged on the other side of the small fire pit, his waist now free of the gun she'd tucked into Mr. Dobbs's old saddlebag.

"It's been ages." Her father had been adamant about teaching her skills of basic survival—starting a fire, hunting game, firing a gun. Holding her hair back, she blew on the twinkling embers racing across blades of grass, the soft crackle of brush giving way to ribbons of fire beneath carefully placed branches.

"My God."

She glanced up. Regi watched her with wide eyes and a wry grin.

"What?" she asked.

"I just remembered what you looked like when you first came to San Francisco. Some kind of *wild thing.*"

"I did not."

"You don't remember?"

She remembered being miserable, frightened and homesick. No one had asked her if she wanted to be carted across the country to California. Men in dark suits had merely shown up and taken her, depositing her with relatives no more familiar to her than the tall buildings and noisy streets surrounding her aunt's massive house. She'd only wanted out, to return to the security of her home on the meadow in the tranquil mountains she loved, to the parents she desperately missed.

"You were like the wolves pacing their cages at the zoo," said Regi.

"I was *mad*."

"You were vicious."

They'd all treated her as though she truly were some zoo exhibit. The mere memory tightened her jaw with anger, resentment washing through her. Relatives had come by to gape at her, spewing their rude remarks, spoken as freely as though discussing the weather: "Poor dear Rose, seduced by a treacherous rogue. What a waste her life had been."

Lily's urge to flee had been like a fever in her blood. She'd tried countless times, only to be caught by a servant or policeman on the streets and dragged back to Aunt Iris's mansion. The snap of her aunt's hand fan echoed through her mind, followed by her harping orders to correct her speech, straighten her posture, use the proper spoon...

The old crone.

Lily's mother had been far younger than her brother and two sisters. Rose had been the only one of the three daughters to bear a child. It wasn't a wonder. Iris and Camilla were every bit as sour as her mother had been sweet. Lily had a hard time believing any man could love the wilted widows, or that the two sisters had ever taken pleasure in anything other than their own meanness and terrorizing their house staff.

Her old uncle Alder and his four grown children were equally unpleasant. They'd all had their plans for her—to marry her off to a suitor of their choice so they could squander away the remaining quarter of the Carrington inheritance.

Lily had taken refuge in the mansion libraries and her schoolbooks as she'd prepared for the day she would come of age and spoil all their plans; daily doldrums were dispelled only by visits from Reginald. "So you're the blooming abomination," he'd said the first time he had stopped in unannounced, dropping into the overstuffed chair beside her, a dog-eared copy of some fictional fantasy under his arm. "They say you were raised by wolves, you know? I read a story once about a wolfboy, a fascinating tale. Would you like to hear it?" She'd denied his offer, and he'd told her anyhow.

"You were never frightened of me," she said, grinning at the memory.

"Yes, well, you know what they say? Misery loves company. You were the only creature more miserable than I."

Neither of them had been able to find an ounce of solace around the family, which likely forged their bond in friendship and business. In a lot of ways her relationship with Reginald was easy, comfortable, predictable.

"You're my best friend."

"I'm your only friend, Lil, and you don't even trust *me*."

"Yes, I do."

A side glance conveyed his disbelief.

"This didn't involve you, Regi."

"Didn't involve me? Then why am I sitting here in the dirt?"

"I just meant that it had to do with me, my life before…before becoming a Carrington."

Hearing those words unsettled her.

"You've always been a Carrington, Lily."

No, she hadn't. She used to be a Palmer. Like a dark spot on the family tree, the Carringtons had done their best to stamp out every trace of her father's existence.

"Did you know my father?" she asked. Regi had been about five when her mother had left home.

"No. I never saw much of Aunt Rose. But the family story is legend. Aunt Rose running off in the middle of the night with her 'outlaw lover.' The scandal kept the parlors humming for years."

"Just because my father wasn't born to wealth did not make him an outlaw."

"Perhaps, though he did heist one of the most sought-after heiresses on the marriage market."

"My mother loved him."

Regi shrugged and began drawing shapes in the dirt with a stick. "She must have. She gave up everything to run off with him. From what I'd heard, she lived in squalor."

"We did not! We had a lovely house."

Reginald arched an eyebrow. "Which he built himself, I gather?"

"My mother was *happy*."

"Then it must be true what they say, that love is blind. A cabin in the wilds of Missouri is not my idea of a lovely home."

What did the Carringtons know of love? She'd seen no trace of it since she'd been taken from Missouri, not the kind of love her parents had shared. "We may not have had a grand house, but Mother took pride in our home. She wanted for nothing. We had a wonderful housekeeper to help with cooking and household chores. Geneva wasn't a nameless servant. She wanted to keep me when Mother died."

"And yet you were placed with Great-aunt Iris." Regi grimaced. "Luck was not raining down on you that day."

As far as Lily was concerned, Aunt Iris was neither better nor worse than the rest of the blooming Carrington clan. None of them could replace her mother. Rose Palmer had been soft-spoken and gentle. She'd been the tranquil center of their family; nothing ever seemed to rile her. Though she could scold quite well, her daughter and husband alike, especially when her father fretted over money.

"Red Palmer, a fool's fortune cannot buy my happiness." Her mother had spoken those words many times.

Had she been referring to her inheritance—the

fortune Lily had built her life around? She suddenly wondered if her parents would approve of the life she'd chosen. She'd been so focused on taking over Carrington Industries, she'd all but forgotten about the world beyond her mansions.

Her gaze collided with the bare-chested man walking silently from the trees. His shirt tossed lazily over his shoulder, bronze skin and gilded hair flickering in and out of twilight and shadows as he neared their clearing, the night quickly falling in around him.

Not quickly enough.

The vision moving toward her shed new light on the man steadily destroying her senses. His damp wavy hair hung over his eyes. Barefoot but for the bandanna tied around his left foot and his pants rolled up to mid-calf, he appeared rather sweet, disarming and wholly inviting.

As he approached the fire, Lily's gaze slid from curly wisps of hair on his firm chest to the ripple of muscle above his belt. The hard surface flexed with each slow stride. A violent stir of sensation swept through her. She crossed her arms over the sudden, startling ache in her breasts.

Sweet mercy.

"Good God, man," said Regi. "You've caught a feast."

Only then did she notice the line of fish he held in one hand, his boots and hat in the other. She'd been far too busy gaping at his half-clothed body.

Thankfully he and Regi were too preoccupied to notice her visual detour.

Juniper set his hat and boots aside, then dropped to his knees across from Lily. He tossed his shirt over his hat and pulled a bundle of sticks from his back pocket. His damp hair hid his eyes as he focused on the fish and began shoving the long sticks into the ground around the fire.

Lily's gaze locked on a jagged scar just below his left shoulder, the welted flesh stretching from his collarbone to midshoulder.

"How did you manage to catch all those?" asked Reginald, leaning in to watch him.

"Practice and patience."

Firelight glimmered against another spot on his right upper arm, a circular pucker of scared skin.

A bullet wound.

"How clever," Regi said. Inspecting the fish, Juniper slid the open mouths over the sticks arranged around the fire pit, creating a teepee of fish over the low flames.

"This is it for supper," he said. "My food supplies are depleted from my trip into the high country. A small bag of coffee is all I have left."

"Coffee and trout is far more than I expected," said Regi.

A smile bowed Juniper's lips, which collapsed the moment he glanced at Lily. She swallowed, feeling as though he could see right through her. He stood and turned away, flexing dark skin over a muscular torso.

Fighting a flash of tingling sensation, Lily drew up

her knees. She rested her forehead on her folded arms and tried to block him out. *What's come over me?*

Tomorrow she'd get her strongbox, make peace with the lumberjacks and sell the blasted camp as Regi had suggested. For the first time in her adult life, she couldn't win. For the first time, she wasn't sure she wanted to win.

Chapter Seven

"Miss Palmer?"

Lily glanced up at Juniper standing directly in front of her. He wore a gray flannel shirt and had pulled on his boots. She grimaced, knowing his foot must hurt. His ever-present revolvers shone in the firelight.

"Aren't you hungry?"

She blinked and realized he held out a cup and plate.

"Starving," she said, reaching for the dented tin. "Thank you." She set the cup beside her and positioned the plate on her lap. Two shriveled black eyes stared up at her. Was she supposed to just pick up the whole fish and bite into it, skin and all?

Juniper released a hard sigh and crouched low before her. Firelight glinted on the knife he pulled from a scabbard on his belt. A few quick flicks of his wrists left four fillets on her plate.

"Thank you."

"You're welcome," he said, turning away.

Regi sat beside her, holding what appeared to be a

fish lollypop. Undaunted by its unappealing exterior, he pulled back the crinkly skin and broke off a piece of white meat.

It dawned on her that she held the only plate. She glanced at the cup of steaming coffee. "I don't want to take the only cup of coffee."

"There's more in the pot," said Juniper. "After you finish yours, I'll pour one for Reg."

Juniper reclined against his saddle and tried to focus on his meal, while subtly watching her. Lily tugged at her green gloves, plucking one finger at a time before tucking the folded leather into her skirt pocket. She stared down at her plate and he half expected her to demand some silverware. Finally, she broke off a large piece of fish and popped it into her mouth. Her eyes closed as a shiver went through her.

Juniper forced himself to look away. *She must be half-starved,* he thought as he began picking at his own fish.

A few moments later a soft smacking sound drew his gaze back to Lily, just as her mouth closed over a slender fingertip. He stopped chewing as a second finger touched lightly on her pink tongue. He damn near stopped breathing.

Focus on the pain in your foot, he silently ordered, reminding himself that her pretty pink tongue had a razor-sharp edge. He shouldn't be getting hot and bothered over L. P. Carrington.

She's not a Carrington, his mind shot back.

He tossed a fishbone into the fire.

She's Red Palmer's daughter.

Having licked her fingers clean, she reached for the tin cup.

She's something else, he thought, watching her scrunch her nose as she took a small sip.

A grin unwittingly curved his lips. "Don't tell me you're a tea drinker."

She peered at him. The fire illuminated her long amber eyelashes. "I prefer hot chocolate, actually."

He chuckled and shook his head.

"What?" she asked.

"I wouldn't have pegged someone so sour as having a sweet tooth."

"And I wouldn't expect a gunfighter to be a lawman."

"*Touché,* Miss Palmer."

"Must you continue to call me Miss Palmer?"

He sure as hell did. He needed the reminder. "It's who you are," he said mildly. "Lily Palmer. Isn't Carrington just your business front?"

She didn't bother answering him, but turned toward her cousin. *"Here,"* she said, passing the cup to Reg. "I'll only be wasting the coffee."

Juniper crossed his ankles, propping up his throbbing foot. The shift of tight leather over his wound sent a bolt of pain clear up his leg.

My own fool fault. He wasn't sure what he'd been thinking, to hand Lily his gun. His choice years ago to live might have changed her life, but being raised in wealth and privilege wasn't exactly a hardship. She hadn't been shipped off with an abusive uncle who'd let her go hungry, forcing her to fight for her life or die in the street.

When he thought about it like that, the guilt twisting inside him made him mad as hell. Instead of focusing on a company in turmoil, she'd held their pay and taken her sweet time packing all her fancy dresses and polishing her daddy's gun. Men had died on account of her pay holds. Hell, men were still dying! Hadn't he wanted to have a few choice words with the San Francisco bigwig who'd been making life on the mountain a living hell?

And there she sat, in her fancy dress, steel in her spine, arms locked over her chest as though she lorded over these lands. *A spoiled, pampered princess.*

"Why are you meddling with such foolish things as lumber camps anyhow?"

Her green gaze tagged him from across the fire. "I—"

"Why haven't you been married off?" he shot in.

"I beg your pardon?"

"You're nice enough lookin'," he said with a shrug. "When you're not all scuffed up."

Her hand went to the drooping sleeve, drawing his attention to the graceful curve of her dainty shoulder, the supple soft skin he'd rather not have noticed and an attraction he damn sure didn't want.

"I'm unwed because I choose to be so."

"True enough," Reginald agreed. "There was once a time when prospective suitors lined the block."

"Must have been before they got a dose of her shrewd mind and sharp tongue," Juniper said in a whispered yet perfectly audible tone.

Lily's eyes flared.

"Would you look at all those stars," Reginald said, clearly trying to change the subject.

"My guess is," Juniper said, holding Lily's hostile gaze, "any man with the sense God gave him would dodge the risk of frostbite and beat a hard, fast path to safety."

The strangled noise coming from Reginald sounded suspiciously like suppressed laughter.

"Sorry, Lily," he choked. "Carrington women do seem to be cold by nature."

Lily gaped at her cousin. "I'm not cold! I simply choose to focus on building my business. I have nothing to gain by tying myself to a man."

"Spoken like a virgin," said Juniper.

"How dare you!"

"Had lots of lovers, have you?"

Lily could hardly believe he could casually ask such an outrageous question. Heat flamed across her cheeks. "The fact that you think I'd entertain such a—"

"Actually," he said in the same neutral tone, "my point is that you likely *don't* entertain. You've got to give a little of yourself to find real pleasure with someone. Women like you get more of a thrill from watching men squirm. Only a wealthy miser would want a woman who's got her drawers cinched so tight she can eat coal and spit diamonds."

"Now see here," Reginald started.

"You have more nerve—"

"No, I don't," Juniper interrupted, his steady gaze burrowing into her. "I just see through yours."

Startled by a sudden burn of tears, Lily stood and rushed toward the darkness, anxious to be away from Juniper's penetrating gaze.

Juniper watched her go, his pulse pounding in his ears.

He dragged in a deep, calming breath before glancing at Reginald. "Did I go too far?"

"Undoubtedly."

"Good." He knew he had. *Hell.* He'd never spoken so rudely to a woman in all his life. He'd also never encountered a woman who nettled at his control with such efficiency. The ache in his foot had him short-tempered. The ache in his pride wasn't helping matters. And the ache in his britches made him downright cantankerous.

"In all fairness to Lily," said Reginald, "she truly does have a brilliant mind."

"I'm not inclined to disagree with you."

He wasn't ready to *agree* with him, either. So far Lily Palmer Carrington had been nothing but a pile of pretty trouble bound in bad memories and a lifetime of regret.

"What was that business of giving her your gun really about?"

Sheer stupidity.

His reasoning told him Lily had every right to hate

him, but he didn't want to listen to reason. He didn't want to listen to any voice that allowed her to only see the bad in him.

Juniper shoved his hands through his hair. "Temporary insanity?" he offered, certain the woman was driving him out of his mind.

"Lily can have that effect on men," Reginald said in a mournful tone.

Juniper glanced at the man sitting to his right. While Reginald appeared relaxed, Juniper hadn't missed the change in his posture after that last barb toward Lily. He'd been ready to come to his cousin's defense.

"She can be stubborn and difficult," said Reginald, "but she's really not all bad."

Neither was he. Not that it mattered. She was bent on seeing him as nothing more than a ruthless killer. One of her accusations had nagged at his mind after he'd reached the river.

How can I possibly have faith in the man who killed my parents....

It wasn't the first time she'd accused him of killing both her parents. "I didn't *orphan* her," he said to Reginald. "I never even met her mother."

"Aunt Rose died of influenza a few weeks after her husband's death. For Lily, it may well have felt like one endless wave of tragedy."

Both her folks in just a few weeks? A ripple of hurt washed over Juniper.

"She was brought west after Aunt Rose's death.

Quite begrudgingly. I do believe the attorneys who fetched her all suffered bite marks and bruises."

Juniper could just imagine. He wouldn't expect any daughter of Red's to be docile. The meek and mild didn't survive up in the wild country where he'd chosen to raise his family.

"She put up a fight for months," said Reginald. "It must have been frightening to be uprooted from the only home she'd known and dumped off with complete strangers."

"Was her mother estranged from the family?"

"Aunt Rose wrote off the Carringtons when she eloped with her outlaw lo—uh, Red Palmer."

"Family didn't approve?"

Reginald's snort suggested not. "I'm sure she was expected to marry a suitor befitting her social status. They tried to find her, but she clearly did not want to be found. The only correspondence came fifteen years later, a letter from Rose's housekeeper informing the family of her passing and of Aunt Rose's wish for Lily to remain in Missouri. Of course the family wouldn't permit it, Lily being an heiress and all."

"Of course," Juniper mocked. "Never mind a woman's dying wish."

"Believe me, Lily has spent her adult life making sure they regretted that decision."

The thought of Lily harboring such anger unsettled him. Having her around his family might not be the best plan. He couldn't have her spouting her opinions about him around Jed and Rachell and their children.

They wouldn't stand for it. And he surely didn't want them feeling as though they had to defend him. Lily wasn't likely to be swayed on the subject, especially after he'd been so rude a few moments ago.

Damn. Where was his head? How could he expect her to hold her tongue when he behaved no better? Reginald seemed to fare pretty well with her. Surely the woman could be civil if she put her mind to it.

"The two of you seem to get along okay," he said.

Reginald's lips slanted with a wry grin. "We understand each other, I think. We spent much of our youths together."

"Masochistic, are you?"

His smile widened. "To be raised in a Carrington home is no kindness. I'd have been bored to tears without Lily. She intrigued me. She didn't fuss or pout at her mistreatment. *She planned.* The day she came of age was the most exciting day of my life. To see my father and grandfather rendered helpless, the realization that two of their least-favorite people had outsmarted them written across their faces... We were positively drunk with power that day."

"I take it you had your own problems with the family."

"Oh, God, yes. Family wealth isn't the blessing it would seem. When you're made to feel beholden for the air you breathe, it's *bondage.* Lily gave me my freedom. More important—my dignity. She could have destroyed the family's finances. Corrupt accountants had managed their funds for too long. Lily's unspoiled shares were all that kept them afloat. Instead of doing as our relatives feared, she forged her company and rebuilt their fortunes from the ground up. She's made the entire Carrington clan quite rich."

"They must hold parades for you both on Sundays."

"Surely not," he said with a tittering chuckle. "But their brimming bank accounts tend to shut them up. Everyone but my father and grandfather. Though impotent of any real power, they still sit on the board of trustees. Mostly to annoy us, I think."

"And the two of you do as you please?"

Reginald groaned and rubbed at his temples. "We *work,* Sheriff Barns. I assure you, no employee of Lily's sits around on his laurels. Nor is she one to lounge about and simply delegate." He stared at Juniper intently for a moment. "I'd wager you and Lily are much alike."

"You think so? Must be our sweet dispositions."

Reginald grinned. "Likely," he said, surprising Juniper. "Lily can be stern, but she does try to be fair. You seem to share her natural tendency to dominate, which comes from a confidence that's engrained in you. I do believe this is the first time I've ever seen her confidence shaken."

She wasn't the only one. When it came to Lily, Juniper felt about as confident as a rabbit in a rattlesnake den.

"She never talks about her parents, but after today I gather she hasn't gotten over the loss." Reginald yawned as he leaned back.

"You don't have to lie in the dirt." Juniper stood and went to retrieve the tarpaulin. He grabbed up his range coat, shrugged it on, then took the heavy canvas and his only blanket back to the fire. He tossed the blanket to Reginald.

"You'll have to share that with Lily."

"Should I go after her?" His uncertain gaze shifted toward the hills, which were slowly brightening beneath the glow of a rising full moon.

"She'll be back," Juniper said, and flapped out their bedding for the night. She didn't have anywhere else to go. Unfortunately, he didn't have anywhere else to send her.

Reg had been snoring for a solid half hour before Juniper gave in to worry and pushed to his feet. A light breeze had kicked up, chilling the evening air. He figured she might be stubborn enough to sit out in the cold all night, just to be away from him. Not about to let her roam through the night with coyotes and cougars, he started in the direction Lily had fled.

He walked through milky hues of moonlight spiking through the dense foliage of oak trees. A few yards out, the soft moonglow spread across a wide meadow littered with boulders. Atop the highest stone, her form stood out against the night like fine porcelain against black velvet.

Lily sat on the large boulder, her arms bound around her raised knees, gaze fixed on the starlit sky. Her auburn hair glimmered beneath the full moon. The soft light glistened against tear-streaked cheeks.

He paused, hesitant to intrude. Now that his temper had settled, he couldn't shrug off the responsibility he felt for the hurt he'd caused her.

She spotted him and quickly looked away, wiping at her tears.

"A clear night," he said, continuing toward the pile of rocks.

Her gaze shifted back toward the stars. She tightened her arms around the bulk of her skirts.

Ignoring her unwelcoming reaction, he stepped up onto a low boulder and reached her high perch in a few swift, painful strides. He sat beside her and eased back onto his elbows. Crossing his ankles, he propped up the boot that felt a few sizes too small.

"Beautiful, isn't it?" he said, glancing up at the clear view of constellations.

"Yes," she said in a clipped tone. "I didn't invite you to sit."

"My apologies. Foot hurts like hell."

From the corner of his eye he saw her gaze shift to his left boot.

"I suppose I was deserving of your ill temper," she said a moment later.

"No, you weren't." He dragged in a deep breath. No matter how deserving he was of her scorn, they had to find some kind of truce. Vindictive as she seemed, he didn't put it past her to upset his family. He just couldn't have that.

"I was rude and out of line," he said. "I apologize."

Lily glanced at the seemingly relaxed man reclined beside her. Her chest tightened with a sense of caution…and a touch of fear. The fact that her fear had little to do with Juniper and everything to do with the chaos of emotions raging inside her only served to increase her caution.

He gazed up at the stars, but Lily sensed he wasn't as relaxed as he appeared. If he weren't bothered just as deeply by her presence, he wouldn't have a hole in his boot.

"What do you care about, Lily?"

She stared at his upturned face. "What kind of a question is that?"

"A serious one," he said, meeting her gaze. "I can see you're successful and ambitious. You invest a lot in what you do. You said you're of a business mind."

She couldn't tell if he intended further insult.

"There has to be something more that drives you to work so hard," he said mildly. "Family, security…?"

She frowned, knowing she had little interest in either. The moment she'd come into her inheritance, her security had been sustained. She'd used it to turn the tables on the Carringtons—or had she *become* a Carrington? A greedy, insensitive, powermonger.

I'm not like them…am I? She didn't sit around waiting for her bank accounts to be filled. She worked hard.

To what end?

In the past hour of staring into the night, all she'd

been able to see had been the somber eyes of the Donnelly family, Davy Grimshaw's small hands holding such heavy equipment and the angry faces of her employees demanding to be treated fairly—all of them directly affected by her decisions.

She'd always been good with numbers—numbers made sense. She had a knack for analyzing accounts, checks and balances, and finding the weak points. She'd never given much thought to what those numbers ultimately represented, or who her decisions affected. She simply made adjustments until her profit increase reached a sufficient level, or she could increase a value before selling. McFarland's lumber company had been more of a personal vendetta, but even so, she'd been fairly sure she could turn the lumber camp into a profit—for L. P. Carrington Industries.

You have never tried to please the masses. Regi's laughing voice echoed back at her. *Sorry, Lily, Carrington women do seem to be cold by nature.*

"I want to make a difference," she said. She had the money and resources to create positive changes.

"A difference in what?" asked Juniper.

Everything. She'd saved the Carringtons from certain ruin, providing riches they hardly deserved. Why not benefit those who actually had a hand in building their business? Yet to say as much to Juniper… She didn't care to cast light on more of her errors.

"You ask a lot of questions," she said.

His easy smile reawakened the startling flutters in her belly.

"Part of my profession, I suppose."

"Strange. I always imagined you'd be the silent type."

His eyes flinched. "The quiet killer who kicks puppies for fun?"

The truth in his question made her wish she could suck the words back into her mouth.

"It's all right," he said. "We both know a thousand tomorrows can't change even a second of the past."

No. It couldn't. Suddenly she found there was so much she longed to change. It was rather unfortunate business that it had taken her father's killer to bring her such clarity.

She looked away from his bright eyes and wished the moon wasn't quite so full and that he'd get off her rock. "If you wouldn't mind, I climbed up here to be alone."

"Actually," he said, leaning forward, folding his long arms over his raised knees, "I need to ask a favor of you."

"*A favor?*" She stared into the intent blue eyes now mere inches from hers.

"It's about my family. Jed and Rachell, they're my foster parents. They have three children. April's eleven and May's twelve."

It was hard enough being in his presence, but to delve into his personal life was more than her frazzled nerves could tolerate. "I really don't care to hear—"

"The girls know a little about my ugly past," he continued, talking over her, "but Isaac, he's not quite eight. He doesn't remember why I had to leave. I'd like to keep it that way as long as possible. So, while in their presence, I hope you can refrain from referring to me as a gunfighter. It's not something I glorify or something I want my family to feel they have to defend."

Defend him?

It suddenly occurred to Lily that Juniper hadn't made any attempt to defend what he'd done. He'd simply admitted his part in her father's death without a word of justification.

I'm nothing but a heartless gunfighter with a bullet overdue.

When she'd stared into his eyes as he'd spoken those words, she would have sworn he believed them. But a heartless man wouldn't harbor the sorrow she sensed in him. A heartless man wouldn't worry about his influence on younger siblings.

"I realize I have no right to ask anything of you—"

"Fine. Yes," she said, wanting him to leave her be. "I won't say anything."

"I'd sure appreciate it. The Doulans are good people."

"So were *my parents.*"

The words shot from her mouth and were met by sheer silence. He sat beside her, his unblinking eyes searching hers.

Silence stretched.

His lack of response disturbed her far more than any conversation could have.

"I wish I could change what happened that evening," he said at last, his voice a soft rumble on the cold breeze. "But I can't."

"Instead you'll tarnish the only thing I have left of them—my memories."

"That was never my intention. I was brash with what I said about Red back at the camp. My terms were callous. Truth is, your father did the world a service for the number of wanted men he brought in."

"My father was a *salesman*."

"Depends on how you look at it, I suppose. Red Palmer sold outlaws back to the government. He had a solid reputation of going after criminals who made most lawmen think twice before tracking them down. A dangerous profession, to say the least. I'm sorry if you weren't aware."

She shook her head. "You're implying that he *killed* men for money."

"I never said he killed all the men he caught. I don't doubt the ones he shot down were doing their best to bury him first. Red earned his pay for turning in the men he caught. His line of work might not have made for pleasant suppertime conversation, but there's no shame in it, either."

"Is that why you shot him? He was trying to apprehend you?"

"No. I've never been wanted by the law. Red came after me because he wanted a gunfight."

"Why?"

Juniper averted his gaze, knowing he didn't have an

answer that would satisfy either of them, least of all Lily. "I was known as a fast gun. Red believed he was faster."

Lily couldn't fathom her father partaking in such foolishness. A man had to be barbaric and arrogant to do such a thing.

She glanced at the man sitting beside her. Or perhaps he just had to be hard. Moonlight outlined the chiseled contours of Juniper's face and lit up the tips of his blond hair. Remembering the bullet wounds she'd seen in his flesh, her gaze went to the open collar of his shirt.

"How does one become known as a fast gun, Mr. Barns?"

"A whole lot of bad luck," he said, staring down at his boots. "I didn't choose the path of a gunfighter, any more than someone chooses to be in a train wreck. It just happened."

"Shooting people for sport *just happens?*"

His gaze snapped toward her so fast her breath hitched. It did seem a ludicrous question to be asking a man with whom she sat alone in the moonlight, but she'd never been very good at keeping her thoughts from reaching her tongue.

"I've never shot anyone for sport."

"Isn't that the nature of a gunfighter?"

"I don't know. I was a kid trying to stay alive."

The reminder of his age didn't sit well with her. "So you're saying my father was the heartless killer."

"*No.* I don't believe he was."

His instant denial shocked her. "Why would you defend a man who tried to kill you?"

"It's not my place to defend or condemn. Truth is, I'd always liked Red. He struck me as a pious man. We all make mistakes, Lily. Red was no exception. Neither am I."

Her father should have been an exception! Perhaps it was childish to hold him in such high esteem, but she expected more of him. Had she really ever known him at all?

"We should get some sleep." Juniper stood. He stepped down onto the lower rock. Reaching the ground, he looked back at her. "Tomorrow's bound to be another long day."

"I know my way back," she said, needing some time alone to sort out her thoughts. She didn't want to believe Juniper, yet he had no reason to lie to her.

Realizing he hadn't left, she glanced down to find him still standing beside the boulders.

"You don't need to wait for me."

"I don't mind."

"I'm not ready to go."

"Take your time. I don't mind waiting."

"I'd rather you didn't."

"Plenty of wildlife roams these hills. I'd feel better if we walked back together."

"I don't need a personal escort."

His gaze moved over the meadow. His posture relaxed, his fingers tucked into his pockets, he just stood there, silent and patient as a rooted oak tree. She imagined he'd stand there all night without complaint if she chose to stay put.

She tried to ignore him. But it was no use. She couldn't think with him staring over her shoulder. With every passing moment, the breeze seemed to grow colder, until finally she began to shiver.

Releasing a hard sigh, she pushed to her feet. "I think I like you better when you talk."

A smile spilled across his lips, and her stomach somersaulted. He held his hand up to assist her down from the boulder. She glanced at the darkness beyond the surface of the rock and realized stepping down would be a slight more hazardous than climbing up had been.

Reluctantly she placed her hand over his warm palm. Before she had the chance to negotiate her footing, he tugged her forward. She gasped as her hands landed on his shoulders and his hands circled her waist. In the next instant she was standing beside him in the tall grass, dizzied by the rush of movement and bursts of sensation.

She quickly moved past him. Juniper silently fell in step beside her.

"We're limited on heat and blankets," he said when they entered the small clearing. Regi slept near the dying glow of the fire, a thick gray blanket tucked in around him, the canvas tarpaulin stretched out beneath him. Juniper pulled his leather gun belt out from inside his long duster. He sat on the end of the tarpaulin, a few feet from Regi, and set the holster on the ground beside him.

"You'll have to share the blanket with Reg."

Lily stared at the sliver of space between Regi and Juniper. *Dear God.* She couldn't be so close to him.

"Come lie down."

The words had been spoken gently enough, but she sensed the clear order buried in his easy tone.

"I can sleep—"

"You'll sleep right here in between us."

Lily stiffened. "I will *not*."

"In a few minutes you'll realize it gets damn cold out here at night. Unlike the cougars, bears and coyotes that stalk through these hills, you don't have a pelt of fur to keep warm. The warmest, *safest* spot for you to bed down is right here between me and Reginald. But you're the boss. If you want to freeze and take the chance of being dragged off for some critter's late-night meal, you go right ahead."

He eased back onto the flap of canvas, folding his arms beneath his head. "Just don't expect me to wake up and defend you. I'm dead tired."

"For God's sake, Lily," Regi mumbled, "just lie down." He eased up, punched at the jacket wadded up beneath his head and hunkered back down.

Bed down beside Juniper Barns—why the blazes not? Today had already been the most trying, infuriating and exhausting day of her life. The tarpaulin had to be better than the bare ground. She walked slowly toward them and squeezed in close to Regi. Even so, the heat of Juniper's body radiated against her back.

She burrowed beneath the blanket with Regi. The instant warmth eased the ache of her sore body and seemed to increase the weight of her eyelids.

Juniper shifted, turning onto his side, rustling her hair with each of his exhaling breaths.

She wriggled closer to Regi and pinched her eyes tight.

Just go to sleep. Fully exhausted, she was asleep in minutes.

A short while later, a nagging chill penetrated her reprieve. She woke to a chilling breeze filtering through her velvet dress. Regi lay beside her, bound up in the blanket, sleeping like a newborn babe.

"Regi," she whispered. Trembling from the cold, she pulled on the thick wool and nudged his shoulder. "Regi," she whispered a bit louder.

The weight of Juniper's arm landed on her waist. Lily barely suppressed a scream as he pulled her close, sliding her next to him.

"Shh," he murmured, tucking her snuggly against his warmth.

Her heart thundering in her chest, she stared at the shadow of Regi's back. After taking a moment to catch her breath, she tried to scoot forward.

Juniper's arm tightened around her, tucking her more firmly against the length of his body. "It's just the wind," he murmured, the warmth of his lips brushing her ear, sending a tingling surge to the tips of her toes. "Go on back to sleep."

How could she sleep when she couldn't breathe?

As she lay beside him, trying to get air into her burning lungs, she realized she was no longer cold. Shielded from the breeze, warmed by the heat radiating from his chest, she sweltered.

Dear Lord, she was actually sweating. Belatedly she realized she was tucked into his long coat, *with him*.

She trembled from a surge of sensation she'd never experienced from the touch of any man.

I shouldn't be feeling it now! Not while lying in the arms of a man she hated.

He shifted slightly, his arm settling more firmly around her middle. His palm spread wide over her ribs, the tip of his thumb nestled just below her breast.

Her breath fragmented. A rush of shivers shook her. The thought of his hand sliding beneath her bodice—

Good heavens.

Lily flushed, silently mortified by her thoughts and her tremulous reaction.

Juniper didn't move to do any such thing. He simply held her possessively, sheltering her as he slept. Every breath rustled her hair, curling the ribbons of heat spiraling up from low in her belly.

Lily shut her eyes and prayed for sleep, every agonizing moment of consciousness reminding her of something she'd learned a long time ago.

Life could be cruel.

Chapter Eight

Warm and comfortable, Lily burrowed deeper into the solid source of heat. She breathed in the soothing masculine scent. He called to her, his husky drawl adding to the tingles dancing across her skin.

"Darlin'?"

That voice. His image came to her, pale blue eyes, an easy, slanted grin.

Juniper.

"That's right. Hope your dreams are better than mine."

Her eyes sprang open. Juniper hovered over her, though he wasn't grinning down at her as he'd been a moment ago in her dream. His lips were set in a firm line. The soft blush of early morning painted the sky behind him.

"Sun's up," he said. "I need my arm back."

Her ear was resting against the pillow of his arm. Her gaze dropped to the chest nearly pressed to her cheek, then lower still. Shock stole her breath. She had turned beneath his coat, her arm now draped over his waist; she realized he'd been trying to untangle himself from her.

She shot up, nearly clipping his chin with her head.

"Sorry. I, uh…" An instant flush burned into her cheeks. "I wasn't trying to…"

"Stay warm?" he offered.

"Yes, well, not with *you*."

He arched an eyebrow.

Frightfully aware of every warm spot on her skin, she couldn't rightly push that argument. Her body hummed from a volatile combination of reality and dreams. Had she really said his name aloud?

The heat in her face intensified.

Juniper turned away and picked up his gun belt as he stood. He pushed back the edges of his long coat and strapped on his guns. His first step faltered, reminding Lily of his injured foot. He muttered something under his breath, then knelt beside the smoldering fire pit.

Lily released a long, hard breath and pressed her hands to her flushed cheeks. Not even the morning air helped to cool the warmth blazing beneath her skin.

We were just sleeping! The heated swirls twisting low in her belly reminded her that her dreams hadn't been quite so innocent. She'd never felt such a pleasurable stir, not even with Edmond. And he'd had his hands on her bare skin.

Why am I thinking about that?

"I was trying to wake Regi," she explained, more

for her own peace of mind than Juniper's. "And you... you grabbed me."

Juniper was glad she couldn't see the smile seeping across his lips. "Did I?" he asked, knowing full well he had. It hadn't taken more than a whisper to wake him from a deep sleep. He couldn't get back to sleep with her chirping at Reginald.

"You did," she said. "When I tried to pull away, your hold only tightened."

"Tired as I was, I'd likely have cuddled up to a porcupine."

"Yes, well..."

He glanced back and followed her gaze toward Reginald, still curled up in his blanket, sleeping like the dead.

Lucky man.

Juniper would be a long time forgetting the vision of Lily lying in his arms, a smile on her lips as his name tumbled from her mouth in a breathless sigh. The thought that she'd welcomed him into her dreams... His body didn't stand a chance.

I shouldn't even be contemplating such things, he silently scolded.

He rocked back on his heels, watching a small fire blossom and hoping the one in his britches would soon go out. "I must confess, I'd have expected you to fight me off like a wounded bear before lying pliant in the arms of a gunslinger."

"Oh, let's not start that again," she said with exasperation.

Another grin tugged at his mouth.

"And I was hardly lying pliant in your arms—we were *sleeping*."

Sleep hadn't come easy once he'd tucked her trembling weight into his coat. When she'd finally succumbed to sleep, she'd turned in his arms, burrowing deeper into the cove of his body, tormenting him with every sigh. She'd relaxed in his arms as pliant as a sated lover. And he'd sweated bullets, aching to the roots of his teeth as he'd waited for sleep to descend upon him like a dark shroud of mercy.

Once it had, the hours of sound sleep had been worth the initial discomfort. He'd actually slept past sunrise. Now all he had to do was distract her long enough to ditch her at his folks' place, find her cash box and get her tucked back into her San Francisco mansion.

Doable.

"I'm going to check on the horses and get some water."

"I'd love a hot chocolate, should you find a sweetshop along the way."

Juniper glanced back, her request spoken as though he might actually find a sweetshop in the middle of nowhere. "I'll keep an eye out."

Lily glanced at Regi sleeping soundly beside her, wrapped in the blanket he'd hogged for himself.

"Wake up," she snapped, and smacked his shoulder.

Regi surged up, his eyes wide and unfocused.

"*What?* Who?"

"Me, and it's morning."

He blinked and rubbed at his eyes. "So it is." He glanced around and scrubbed a hand over his face. "Where's our sheriff?"

Regi's choice of words did little to help the maddening stir of heated flutters fading into a wave of sheer dread. "He's gone to fetch some water. If you can unwrap yourself from that cocoon, perhaps you can help me saddle our horses?"

"Sorry, love. I hope you didn't freeze."

Lily rather wished she had. Suppressing a groan, she pushed to her feet. She needed a privy, a warm bath and a cup of steaming cocoa, but would have to settle for the privacy of a bush and a refreshing splash of stream water.

"Let's freshen up and then saddle the horses."

The sooner they were on the move, the sooner this nightmare would end.

"Are you ready to admit I was right?" asked Regi, his smirk suggesting she should indeed have sold the camp without opening the first file.

Her expression must have conveyed her answer.

"Right," he said, turning away. "I'll fetch the saddles."

Lily went to Juniper's saddlebags and pulled out one of the bandannas he'd used to tie her up. Might as well get some use out of one, she thought, and turned in the direction of the stream she'd spotted while sitting atop the boulder the night before.

Bright spring grasses covered the countryside amid the sporadic clusters of gnarled oaks. Large clusters of golden poppies and purple lupines swayed with the blades of tall grass, looking very much like colorful kelp beds on a green sea. The early-morning sun felt warm against her skin as she walked up an embankment, toward the growing sound of trickling water. Her sore legs complained with each stride. At the top, grass and flowers spilled over toward the wide stream at the bottom of the slope. Sunlight twinkled like stars on ripples of water rushing over smooth rocks. Her tension eased as she descended into a vision of tranquility.

She knelt at the stream's edge and dunked the red cloth into freezing-cold water. Chills raced across her skin as she pressed the cold rag to her face. Just what she needed, something aside from Juniper Barns to jar her senses.

By the time she made it back to their campsite, she was hardly refreshed, but had managed to at least wipe off some trail dust and had used the damp bandanna to tie back the tangled mass of her hair. Juniper was crouched near the fire, capping a canteen. He stood and held the canvas-covered canteen out to her as she approached.

"Something sweet for the lady," he said.

"Sweet?" She took the canteen and glanced questioningly at Juniper.

"Blackberry tea. I found a bush near the river, and some herbs for the tea. You and Reg can finish off the rest of the berries." He motioned to the tin plate piled with black and purple berries.

An herbal tea sweetened with blackberries? As she opened the cap, a pleasing aroma soothed her senses. She took a sip, which became a deep drink. Still warm, the tea was slightly sweet, mostly tart, and wholly refreshing. Lowering the canteen, she dragged in a deep breath.

"It's good."

"Glad you like it," he said, squatting back down. "That and a handful of berries is all you'll be getting until we reach the Double D." He poured some water from another canteen into his coffeepot, swished it around, then tossed it out before filling the pot and placing the filter inside.

He'd made the tea just for her. Unease winding inside her, Lily slowly twisted the cap back on. She hadn't truly expected him to bring something sweet back from the river. She didn't know if she should be wary or simply grateful.

"Thank you."

"No problem," he said, keeping his gaze on the bag of coffee in his hands.

Unsure how to respond to his unexpected consideration countered by such indifference, she slid the canteen strap onto her shoulder and started toward the meadow. Birds chattered in the trees overhead. A squirrel scampering up the twisted trunk of an oak paused, then raced quickly into the branches. She found Regi beyond the noise and activity in the trees.

He stood on an open field, the two horses behind him already saddled. Bridal and bit in hand, he watched Juniper's horse bite at a clump of tall grass.

"What's wrong?" she asked, noting his pinched expression.

"I don't think he likes me. He snorts and turns his ears down whenever I take a step in his direction."

The stallion was definitely aware of their presence, his ears pricking at the sound of their voices. Lily moved closer, and sure enough, the large bay horse snapped his ears back, but made no attempt to avoid her. If anything, he dipped his big head and lipped the grass at a faster pace.

"He's bluffing," she said, and took the harnesses from Regi. The stallion's brown eye watched her approach, his muzzle moving even faster over the tall grasses.

"You're just enjoying your downtime, aren't you?"

The moment she stopped beside him, he raised his head, his powerful jaw working a mouthful of grass. She reached up and rubbed at the stiff hair behind his hears. His pleasurable response sent a spatter of green dots across her dress front.

"Don't worry," she said with a laugh. "You can't do more damage than has already been done." She lifted the halter toward his muzzle. He took the bit and bridle like a true gentleman. "You've got good manners, don't you, boy? After the way you were worked yesterday, I don't blame you for wanting to avoid a saddle."

"Keep him distracted," Regi said, stepping up to the horse with a saddle blanket.

Now disinterested in the people around him, her new friend went back to grazing. Regi hoisted Juniper's saddle and shifted it into place. He seemed surprisingly spry after the grueling day they'd spent on the trail. He'd also had more sleep than any of them. The memory of how he'd enjoyed Juniper's colorful depiction of her personal life burned into her mind. Regi had actually compared her to her *aunts*.

"Did you mean what you said about me last night?"

Regi fastened the cinch and glanced up at her. "What's that?"

"Your references to me being a cold tyrant."

His dark eyes flared wide. "I said no such thing."

"You told Juniper I was cold by nature."

"A slip of the tongue. I was far too exhausted to have my wits about me."

"I see. You were too tired to suppress your true feelings."

Regi blinked in surprise. "Are you serious?"

"Yes."

"Has Sheriff Barns said something else to upset you?" he demanded, touching the backs of his hands to his hips.

She glanced down at the canteen of tea. "No. I've just been thinking about yesterday, and seeing myself in a new light, I think." *A bright and startling light.*

"Lily, you're hardly a cold tyrant. I wouldn't choose to spend each day in your company if you were. If you tend to be harsh at times, it's only because that's what life requires of you. It's no secret between us that you carry all the responsibility of the company. Do I worry that you spend too much time focused on numbers and not enough on yourself? *Yes.* I harp on the matter quite frequently. None of which changes the fact that you're my dearest friend and about the only relative I care to claim. And who else would put up with my endless prattling about utter nonsense?"

"You don't prattle about utter nonsense, and you were right about the lumber camp. I owe you that apology. I'm sorry for not listening to you, Regi."

His brow creased with concern. "Perhaps I should check that bump on your head."

"My head is fine." The rest of her was in tatters, but what did it matter?

"This is about Barns. I understand your distrust of him. But I do believe his intentions are sound. Last night he was angry and ill-tempered. You did shoot the man. All things considered, I think you're both handling the situation rather well."

Lily nearly laughed, certain all that could have gone wrong most definitely had.

"You'll turn this lumber camp around," he said, offering an encouraging smile. "You've not failed me yet."

She'd also never been the direct cause of an employee's death, nor was she used to such feelings of insecurity. In her own element she hardly ever second-guessed herself or her decisions.

It's easy to be confident when not looking further than one's self.

Juniper stepped onto the meadow, his bundle of supplies in his arms. Just the sight of him sent a charge through her body.

Juniper Barns was an element unto himself.

"Your breakfast of coffee and berries is in camp," he said to Regi. "Better get it before the critters do."

"I'll fight off anything for coffee," Regi said.

"Thanks for tacking up my horse."

"Not a problem," said Regi. "You might want to double-check everything."

Juniper was already reaching for the cinch. His hands moved to the bridle, checking every buckle and clasp. "For a dandy, you ain't half-bad, Reg."

Already rushing toward camp, Regi turned, flashing a smile. "Lily has had some influence on me."

"Keeps you on your toes, does she?"

"Somebody's got to," Regi called back before walking beyond the trees.

The friendly exchange bruised her ravaged ego. Lily turned and walked to her mare grazing a short distance away.

If you tend to be harsh at times, it's only because that's what life requires of you.

Regi's words were little consolation. Her only friend thought her harsh.

Stop thinking about it. Once they recovered her

money she could start to put things right, and Juniper could go back to dominating the mountainside.

She reached for the saddle, her strained thigh muscles burning as she lifted a foot into the stirrup. A groan escaped her lips.

"Are you hurting?"

She turned, shocked to find Juniper directly behind her, his pale blue eyes full of concern. Instantly she wanted to rage at him. *Of course she was hurting!* She spent her days in a cool, cushioned office, not blazing through the hillside on horseback.

"I'll survive."

"Here, let me h—"

"Would you just *stop?*" she spat, stepping aside to dodge his helpful hands.

His shocked expression only made her feel worse and increased her anger.

"I was—"

"Being considerate. I know. *I get it.* Juniper Barns, the dashing lawman."

"I wasn't trying to—"

"And *humble,*" she added, laughter uncurling from her throat. "My God, Prince Charming could take lessons."

She stepped up and shifted into the saddle, ignoring the pain. "All you need to worry about is recovering our money. Can we just do that?"

"Sure," he said, shaking his head as he turned away.

Harsh. Seemed Regi was right, and this was one of those times when life required her to be harsh.

She didn't know how else to react to Juniper, or to the flurry of emotions he caused by simply standing there.

As the day wore on, Lily realized she might have wanted a horseback view the day before, but not at the pace they'd been keeping. In these lower hills every new stretch of land seemed nearly identical to the last; massive ripples of grass were spotted by rocks, oak trees and cattle. By the time the sun began sliding away from its noontime position, her canteen was bone-dry and her energy sapped. With every dragging moment, she knew Juniper Barns would have her eating her words yet again:

"By tomorrow afternoon I won't be interested in clean beds and warm baths. I'm not planning a weekend stay on your foster parents' ranch. I want to recover my money and get back to The Grove."

Sore, tired and starving, nothing sounded more splendid than a full meal, a warm bath and a soft bed. Provided she managed to stay in the saddle long enough to reach the Double D Ranch. It wouldn't have mattered if her cash box dropped from the sky and into her lap at this very moment. She doubted she could ride another five miles to save her life. It wouldn't take more than a good gust of wind to knock her flat on the ground.

Regi rode beside her, his shoulders slumped, looking as worn-out as she felt. Juniper rode a few yards ahead of them, and didn't appear to be fatigued in the slightest. Poised and alert, he seemed ready to tackle a bear or any other danger that might come their way.

A tall wooden arch came into view. A sign hanging above the wide dirt road announced the entrance to the Double D Ranch. Yet she saw no sign of a house, barn or anything else to indicate a ranch nearby.

"It's around the next hillside," he said, motioning ahead of them as they rode beneath the archway.

Lily heaved a sigh of relief. She hoped to have a few hours of rest before Günter arrived. It was time he shared their plan for recovering her cash box. Juniper must have discussed them with his deputy after she'd ridden out with Reginald. She urged her horse on and rode in close beside him.

"Juniper?"

He turned his head, surprise lighting the features shaded by the brim of his hat.

Dear Lord. She clearly looked as weary and ragged as she felt.

"Lily?" he said.

"The thief's ranch is close?"

"You see where that ridge ends?" He motioned to a long rise of flat terrain trailing off into the distance. "And the taller one spiking up just beside it?"

"Yes."

"The Chandler homestead is in the middle of that gap."

Lily nearly winced. Miles and miles of hilly ground stood between them and *that gap*. "How far is that?"

"Likely just over ten miles from Jed's house."

Juniper glanced again at Lily as her tired eyes roved the landscape. He wondered if sheer exhaustion had her relaxed in the saddle and calling him by his first name. She hadn't said but five words to him all day and hardly looked in his direction. He wasn't about to complain. He'd been trying to do the same. It didn't take but a glimpse of her bright hair for him to recall the only other time she'd addressed him so informally. The gentle sway of her body in the saddle only reminded him of those smooth curves pressed flush against him.

He forced himself to look away, toward the ranch coming into view. She'd be safe with Jed and Rachell. His foster parents wouldn't hesitate to invite her and Reginald into their home. Hopefully she'd be tucked into a bed and sound asleep by sundown—giving him the opportunity to recover her cash box.

"Günter will be meeting us here?" she asked.

"Likely late tonight or in the morning."

"Are you sure we should wait?"

We?

She either had more gumption than any woman he'd ever met, or she didn't have a clue as to what they were dealing with. Either way, she clearly wasn't going to make this easy on him. "Lily, I'm not taking you into a den of outlaws, and I don't plan to charge in without some backup."

"What happened to them just being lumberjacks with good intentions? If that's the case, why can't we just reason with them?"

"Those lumberjacks are traveling with men who come from a family of outlaws. I don't know if it was a Chandler who killed your guard, but—"

"Mr. Dobbs," Lily said, her brow pinched in a frown.

"Right. Point is, when tensions run high the loudest voice tends to dominate. Based on what we heard from Emma, that voice is one of the Chandler boys."

"There's more than one?"

"Two that I know of for sure. Cousins."

"When did you learn this?"

"I knew we had two men by the name of Chandler on a cutting crew. I didn't realize they were from the same Chandlers who once lived near the Double D until Emma mentioned the valley with flat-topped ridges."

Lily glanced at Reg, who'd ridden up beside her, before looking back at Juniper. "They could be gone by morning."

"Those men worked a full shift on the mountain, then rode as hard as we did. They're just as worn-out and hungry as we are."

Lily didn't look convinced, her eyes revealing a mind fast at work as she chewed on her lower lip. "When Günter arrives, I want to be included in your plans."

"My plans start with food, a bath and a bit of rest. Hungry and exhausted is no way to start an ambush."

"Are you sure it's wise to take us along?" asked Reg.

"No," Juniper answered with quick honesty.

"We're not lawmen, after all," he said to Lily.

"You convince her of that," Juniper said, "and I'll forfeit my two-months' worth of back wages."

"I want to see them held accountable."

"As do I," said Reginald, "but we all serve our..." His voice trailed off as his gaze locked on the ranch up ahead, a maze of fences spreading out from a massive two-story house and a cluster of outbuildings. "Now that's more like it."

Juniper shared his enthusiasm, increasing their pace, anxious to see his family. They stayed on the main road, riding past the Darby house and beyond a wide stretch of barns and stables, toward the entrance to Jed's home farther out on the open field.

"Who lives in the first house?" Lily asked as the farmhouse disappeared behind the barns and stables separating the two properties.

"Jed's partner and his family." Juniper hoped Ben's son, Jake, was around and in the mood for some late-night possum hunting. He could use an extra gun on his side.

Part of the tension coiled inside him relaxed as he turned onto the path toward Jed and Rachell's house. Coming home always seemed to ease the raw loneliness buried in the shadows of his heart. Jed's place stood farther out from the ranch, another two-story house of similar size. The wide covered porch faced the tall peaks of the Sierras. The only other structures in the yard were a stable and a chicken coop. Isaac stepped from the stable as they rode into the yard.

"June!" Twice the height of most seven-year-olds, he barreled toward him with the size and speed of a bull calf.

"Hey, sprout," Juniper greeted, dismounting in front of the house. "You keep growing at this rate and you're going to be eight feet tall and too big for the barn."

"Won't, neither," he said, laughing as Juniper ruffled his wavy black hair.

"Juniper?"

He turned to see Rachell standing on the porch. Her face lit with a smile as she rushed down the steps.

"It's about time," Rachell said, grabbing him up for a tight squeeze.

He returned her embrace. "Work's been hectic."

"April!" May's voice rang out from somewhere inside the house. "June's home!"

"You gonna stay for a while, June?" Isaac asked from beside him.

His answer was cut off by a high-pitched squeal from inside, just before his sisters raced out the front door. April leaped past the steps in a flutter of plaid skirts, her long auburn braids trailing behind her as she ran toward him.

"June!"

He opened his arms as she launched herself at him. Laughing, he hugged her, then lowered her to the ground. Lord, it did feel good to be home. May was next. Juniper planted a kiss on the top of her head. Her black hair, usually bound in braids, spiraled down her back in loose silky coils.

"What's with the new hairstyle?" he asked, touching one of the ebony candlestick curls.

"May has decided she's too old for braids," said Rachell.

"*Mother.* Don't tell June such things. He and Daddy will lock me in the hayloft until I'm eighteen."

"More like twenty-five," Juniper amended.

Everyone gazed curiously at the guests standing behind him.

Lily realized belatedly that she was the only one still sitting in a saddle and quickly dismounted. She'd been distracted by Juniper's exuberant welcome and the sight of him surrounded by his family.

"Rachell, this is Miss Lily Carrington and her cousin Reginald Carrington. They're the new owners of McFarland's lumber camp."

"Madam." Reginald gave a regal bow. "These lovely ladies must be your sisters."

The girls giggled, and Lily resisted the urge to roll her eyes.

"My daughters," said Rachell. "April and May."

"Ah, the fairest of months of spring," Reginald said, pressing a hand to his chest: "*When the red-cheeked, dancing girls, April and May, trip home to the wintry, misanthropic woods...even the barest, ruggedest, most thunder-cloven old oak will at least send forth some few green sprouts, to welcome such gladhearted visitants.*"

"Melville," said the girl with ebony curls, her gray eyes alight with recognition.

"Melville?" said her sister, her amber eyebrows pinching inward.

"You know, April. The book *Moby Dick,*" her sister explained.

"Oh. Yeah."

April, May and June. The combination sent a shiver across Lily's skin. She glanced at the woman who was clearly Juniper's foster mother. Had she intentionally named her daughters after him?

"Have you had a rough journey?" Rachell asked, her gaze skimming over Lily's ravaged dress.

"To say the least," said Juniper. "We ran into quite a bit of trouble."

"A mountain of trouble," Reginald agreed.

Rachell's eyes widened with concern.

"Juniper's taken good care of us," Lily said, forcing a reassuring smile, glancing only briefly at Juniper's look of surprise.

"We could all use a meal and a warm bath," he said. "And Miss Carrington is in need of a fresh change of clothes."

"Certainly," said Rachell. "I just pulled some bread from the oven and I have plenty of dresses. We seem to be about the same size."

"I'm truly grateful."

"Happy to help," she said with a smile. "Please, come inside. I left supper cooking on the stove and had just started a pot of tea."

"My dear woman," Regi said, following her across the wide porch, "if you have sugar to go with the tea, I may just weep at your feet." The girls giggled beside him.

"I'll take care of the horses," Juniper said from behind them.

Halfway up the steps, Lily stopped. She turned as he took a step back. Despite wanting to be rid of him all day long, she suddenly didn't want to let him out of her sight. She didn't want to be alone with his family.

"I'm not leaving," he assured her. "I'll come inside after I've finished." The gentleness in his tone suggested he recognized her distress. "You go on in and get something to eat."

"Hey, June," said Isaac, yanking on his sleeve. "You got a hole in your boot."

Lily stiffened.

Juniper chuckled and dropped his hat over Isaac's black hair. He draped his arm over the boy's shoulders and started toward the horses. "Another example of why a man shouldn't be dangling guns from his britches."

"You shot yourself in the foot?"

"Pretty much, sprout."

"I want to help!" His youngest sister rushed past Lily.

"Come on then," Juniper called back, he and Isaac already gathering the horses.

April looped her arm through his as all three walked toward the barn.

I really don't want to be here.

Lily dragged in a deep breath and went inside. Her gaze swept over a grand front room beautifully decorated with lace and floral drapes, the deep greens, golds and browns matching the rich tapestry of the furniture. Polished oak tables supported an array of exquisite vases, each filled with fresh spring flowers.

Her mother had always loved fresh wildflowers. Lily had loved gathering them for her from the meadows around their home.

Her gaze moved to a massive stone fireplace taking up the entire end wall. The sound of Regi's voice and the heavenly scent of fresh bread drew her through the dining room, beyond the long table and a wide curio cabinet displaying very fine china. She glanced twice at the crystal chandelier hanging from the high, polished wooden ceiling.

Stepping into a kitchen as grand as any Lily had seen, she realized this was not the home of simple country folk, as her parents had been. Polished cabinets with glass fronts lined the walls. Ornate canisters, an apple peeler and other gadgetry sat on a wide expanse of countertops.

Her overly dramatic cousin sat at a smaller table, his hands in motion as he chattered away with an ease she'd always envied. May sat across from him, her elbows on the table, her chin propped between her hands, listening intently as Regi detailed one of his favorite adventure novels. Regi could make friends wherever he went, whereas Lily preferred to slip in and out without notice.

Rachell turned from the stove, smiling as she held out a cup of tea.

"Thank you," she said, taking the cup and noticing the stylish cut of Rachell's dress. Not some homespun number, but a finely tailored gown.

Ranching must be good.

"Would you like something to eat now or would you prefer a bath first? We have a tub upstairs."

"Could I grab a bite of bread to take with me?"

"Certainly."

She hoped some nourishment and a bath would soothe her frazzled nerves.

"I'm anxious to hear what has happened to bring you so far north with June."

Regi's voice fell silent. He and May glanced up, staring questioningly at her.

So much for soothing her nerves.

Chapter Nine

"I'm always up for a little excitement." Jake Darby tugged off his leather gloves and tucked them beneath the buckle of his dusty chaps. "I got your back, cousin."

The words came as no small relief as Juniper accompanied him into Jed's barn. A few years younger and a few inches shorter than Juniper, the curly-haired cattleman wasn't blood kin, but they'd spent their adolescence working together on this ranch.

"I appreciate the help." There wasn't a man he'd rather have as backup than Jake or his older brother, Kyle. Unfortunately, Kyle hadn't come around much in the past four years. A marriage engagement gone awry had sent his best friend into a life of yondering, and Juniper right along beside him. They'd traveled together for better than a year, having a fairly good time while working odd jobs—until Kyle had chosen an occupation Juniper couldn't follow him into, and had tried to talk him out of. Bounty hunting meant looking for trouble. June tended to find plenty without tracking it down.

"Heard from your brother lately?"

"Not in nearly six months." Jake reclined against the hay bales stacked up just inside the barn. "Last letter came from Montana. Said he wouldn't be writing home for a while and not to worry. He was infiltrating a band of outlaws. How he expects his family not to worry after delivering that bit of information is beyond me."

June grinned. He'd received a similar letter about six months back and thought the same thing. He sure missed the simpler days when their biggest challenge was breaking in new horses or rounding up an ornery bull.

"What I want to know," said Jake, "is why the hell you'd bring your boss lady with you when you're chasing after bandits?"

Juniper sighed. Taking down an ornery bull would be a welcome task over his current situation. "Frankly, she's not an easy woman to ditch. She's not easy to deal with, period."

"Come on, now," said a gruff voice from across the barn. Jed stepped from a horse stall. His foster dad tugged off his hat, revealing sweat-dampened black hair streaked with lines of gray. "The new boss can't be all that bad. I've heard of Carrington Industries and the shrewd, feminine mind behind its success."

Juniper groaned and sat heavily onto a hay bale beside Jake.

Jed grinned as he strode toward him. "Real spitfire, is she?"

"You could say that," he said, raking his fingers through hair still damp from a quick rinse beneath the pump outside. "You know me, Jed. No matter the circumstance, I'm usually the most patient man in the room. But this lady, she makes me...*crazy*."

"She a looker?" asked Jake, his dark eyes sparking with interest. "Maybe you ought to invite me to supper so I can meet this Miss Lily Carrington."

"Not yet. She can't know we're heading out tonight. She's hell-bent on going after her payroll. I'm hoping the girls will distract her so I can tiptoe off the place. As soon as the moon is up, we should have a decent view of the Chandler homestead."

"I bes' get home before my own supper is cold then," Jake said, pushing up and turning to leave. "Meet you on the north rim after sundown."

June and Jed followed him out and started for the house.

"You got enough men riding along?" asked Jed.

"We should be good." Juniper knew Jed wouldn't hesitate to help him out. But he had his family to look after, and Juniper wasn't about to put him in any kind of jeopardy. "Günter should be bringing a marshal and any other lawmen he can round up on the way here. I'm counting on you to keep Lily from following me into a den of outlaws."

"Most women would avoid such hostile situations."

"She's not 'most women,'" Juniper said. "She's the

most domineering, outspoken, opinionated woman I've ever met."

"Reminds me of another spitfire," Jed said with a grin.

No. Rachell might be headstrong at times, but she trusted Jed. Lily didn't trust him any further than she could toss him across the yard. He shuffled up the front steps, reluctant to reveal her connection to his past. Having Lily at their supper table would be disconcerting enough without disclosing that bit of information.

"I better go wash up," Jed said as they stepped inside, and headed for the stairs.

Juniper removed his gun belt and tucked it on a shelf above the door just as he used to do during the years he'd lived here. In the dining room the table had been set. Rachell's bright voice carried out from the kitchen, along with the voices of his sisters. He breathed in the soothing combination of Rachell's baked bread and fresh flowers. She'd given him everything he'd missed out on as a kid, a home full of warmth, commotion and laughter. Seven months without a visit had been too long.

Having scrubbed up at the pump outside the stable, Juniper went to retrieve a pair of old boots he'd left with some other clothes and personal items up in his room. Isaac raced down the steps.

"Did you clean up for supper?" Juniper asked.

"Yeah. Mama had me fill all the washbasins in the rooms on account'a that funny feller's still takin' a bath. Long as he's been in there, he ought to be clean enough for a whole month."

Juniper grinned and headed up the stairs. He pushed open the first door on the left to the bright glow of a lit oil lamp. Too late to catch the door, it floated open as his gaze locked on Lily near the center of his room. Bent forward, she was gathering the long length of her hair with both hands. Her clean floral scent invaded his senses.

A lily that smells of lilacs.

She straightened and looked into the mirror above the chest of drawers. A line of hairpins protruded from her mouth. Even as she reached up, twisting her hair, the full burgundy skirt touched the floor. He doubted she was a full five feet to his six and a half.

Focused on coils of gold and copper curls, her *beautifully* determined expression was trained on the top of her head. Tiny curls sprang free at her hairline as she began poking in hairpins. His gaze trailed down her slender neck. Black lace poked up from a high burgundy collar.

She made the modest gown damn appealing. The fitted waistcoat molded to the swell of her full breasts and showed off her tiny waist. A scalloped lace trim at the bottom lay neatly against her narrow hips.

The clatter of hairpins hitting the dresser snapped his gaze back up. Her green eyes tagged him in the mirror.

"Juniper?"

"Sorry to bother you," he said, walking into the room. "I just need to grab a pair of boots."

Lily turned and watched him walk to the tall wardrobe on the far wall, still startled by catching his heated gaze in the mirror.

It wasn't as though he'd caught her half-undressed, but his presence was nonetheless unsettling.

He pulled a pair of brown boots from the slender cabinet. It dawned on Lily why he'd walked into the room with such casual familiarity.

"This is *your* room."

"Used to be." He sat on the edge of the bed and tugged off one of his boots. "Now I'm just a guest from time to time."

Lily turned back to the mirror. Working quickly, she shoved in the last few hairpins Rachell had given her, but couldn't quite keep her gaze off Juniper. He'd taken the time to clean up. His hair rippled across his scalp in damp blond waves and he wore a blue-and-green plaid shirt she'd not seen before. His second boot dropped to the wood floor, and she noticed his left foot had been wrapped in a thin ivory bandage.

"How's your foot?" she asked, turning to face him.

"Better," he said, though his jaw clenched as he shoved his heel into the boot. "Jed makes a salve that helps fight off infection. I'm sure it'll heal up just fine."

Had he told them how he'd really gotten shot or, worse yet, her intentions to kill him? He stood and her gaze automatically went to his waist. She found only the thin brown belt threaded through his dark trousers and a knife scabbard at his side. He wasn't wearing his holster. Lily's gaze slid up the length of him. She was stunned by how very different he appeared without his gun belt.

"You look real nice," he said.

"I, uh, thank you."

He stood there, the faintest hint of a smile on his lips. He looked quite handsome, though she wasn't about to say so. Something about his relaxed posture, the way he looked at her, stirred a wave of emotions both familiar and frightening. Suddenly the room felt smaller. Too small.

"Shall we go down?" she said, and darted for the door.

"Yeah." He grabbed up his damaged boots and quickly put them away before catching up with her in the hallway.

"Miss Carrington," said a low, gruff voice from behind her.

Lily turned and instantly knew where May had gotten her gray eyes and ebony hair. An older man every bit the size of Juniper strode down the dimly lit hall. His long straight hair hung past the broad span of his shoulders.

"Hello," she said.

"Lily, this is Jed Doulan."

"Pleased to meet you," he said. "And sorry to hear

about your guard and the trouble you've had up at Pine Ridge."

"Thank you."

"Can't say I'm surprised. I never did care for McFarland. June's had to work real hard to keep that place from going up like a shooting match."

"The man did put in an effort, late as it was," said Juniper.

"The man's an ass," Jed said flatly. "He couldn't find any common sense if he kept it in a paper sack."

Lily suppressed a smile. "I'd have to agree."

"No sense in us standing here in the hall. I'll follow you two downstairs."

Lily turned and led the way.

"June tells me you have a real mind for business," Jed said as they entered the front room. "Your firm has made quite a name for itself in the past few years."

She glanced back at her host. "You frequent San Francisco?"

"I'm in 'Frisco and Sacramento far more often than I'd like. Someone's got to ride herd over those politicians. If it was left up to them they'd starve every last Indian Nation out of existence."

"To the table," Rachell called out as she placed the roast on the table. The girls came in behind her, each holding a steaming dish. Isaac was making his way around the table with a pitcher, filling glasses with what appeared to be tea.

"There's my little lady," Jed said as he reached Rachell's side. His long arms wrapped around her, all but absorbing her into his much larger body. His lips brushed her cheek before he released her.

The sight pierced Lily's heart with a shaft of pain.

"Behave," Rachell scolded, tapping a finger on Jed's chest. A smile broke through her scowl before she turned away from him.

"I always behave," Jed said, and followed her into the kitchen.

Lily's mind filled with similar images, a set dinner table, her father's playful antics, her mother's radiant smiles, enough warmth in the atmosphere to melt winter snow.

"Lily, you can sit here." April pulled out the chair beside her.

Distracted by the laughter coming from the kitchen, she forced a smile. "Thank you," she said, moving around the table to sit beside Juniper's youngest sister.

Juniper and May sat down directly across from them, and Lily figured she'd give just about anything for a few hundred miles of distance. To hell with the mouth-watering meal spread across the table—all she needed was the solitary safety of her office and a soothing pot of hot chocolate.

Jed and Rachell came in from the kitchen. He pulled out the chair beside May as Rachell set a basket of bread near the platter of sliced beef roast. His wide, callused hand closed over his wife's shoulder, which she covered with her own hand and squeezed before he took his seat at the head of the table, neither looking away from the other.

Realizing she was staring, Lily glanced around at the others. No one else seemed to notice the affectionate couple. All of them were collecting their napkins and talking to one another as they began filling their plates. The cold, hard weight in her chest expanded, sending a chill to every part of her body despite the warmth in the room. It wasn't just the sweetness between Jed and Rachell that pained her, *but everything.* Everyone's ease with one another, the blatant interest and affection shared between them—why did their warmth make her ache inside?

"It appears I'm just in time," Regi said, stepping up to the chair at the other end of the table, drawing everyone's gaze.

Lily sighed with relief, happy to have a familiar source of strength to focus on. His hair was slicked back in the usual style. The rest of him, however, was unrecognizable. He'd clearly borrowed some clothes of Juniper's. The plaid shirt positively swallowed him, ballooned out above the cinched waistband, and the cuffs of the dark trousers had been rolled up several times. Borrowing clothes from the boy would likely have been a closer fit.

"You made it," said Isaac, sitting up on his knees in a chair beside his father. "I figured you'd have pruned up to nothin' by now."

Regi laughed and took his seat.

"Isaac," Rachell said, giving her son a stern glance

from across the table. "Mind your manners and put your feet down."

"Yes, Mama."

"I don't think I've ever been so in need of a thorough scrubbing." Regi collected his napkin from the table and snapped it out before draping the yellow linen over his lap. "I feel like a new man."

"Your own clothes should be dry by morning," said Rachell.

"I do appreciate your kindness." He smiled at Lily and passed her a bowl of steamed green beans. "You look like your normal self again," he said.

She didn't feel anywhere near normal, but said, "Yes." She glanced at the other end of the table and smiled appreciatively at Jed and Rachell. "Thank you so much for having us in your home."

"You're welcome to stay as along as you need," said Jed.

"We will likely be leaving once Günter arrives," Lily said, fighting to keep her tone from revealing the desperation tearing at her insides. She looked across the table to Juniper. "Isn't that right?"

"Günter?" May's posture stiffened. "Günter is coming here?"

"She's sweet on him," April announced, flashing a wide grin.

"I am not!"

"You are, too."

"She is not," Juniper protested. "May's too young to be interested in boys."

"She's nearly thirteen," April said matter-of-factly.

"James Thompson tried to kiss her at the Spring Festival," said Isaac.

May slumped down in the chair beside him, red flagging her cheeks. Juniper's thunderous gaze shot toward Jed.

"Not to worry, son. My baby girl knew just how to handle herself, didn't you, sweetheart?"

"Can we please talk about something else?" May said through gritted teeth.

"She blackened his eye," April helpfully supplied. "Called him a sneaky, white-bellied jackass, too."

"That's quite enough, April," her mother warned.

April dropped her gaze and forked a bite of chicken. "Well, she did."

"And she was right," Jed said in a low tone.

Rachell shifted her narrowed gaze to her husband.

He laughed, ignoring his wife's disapproving glare. "We brought home a pile of blue ribbons from that festival. May and April made a patchwork quilt with Ben and Corin's daughters. Looked like vines of colorful ivy creeping up the blanket. Fanciest needlework most folks had ever seen."

"I did a sack race with Uncle Jake," said Isaac. "But he wudn't so good. Bet we coulda won it if you'd come with us, June."

"Wish I could have. Maybe next year."

His gaze met hers and held. Those pale eyes seemed to reach deep inside her, touching a place in her heart she'd never exposed to anyone.

Lily broke the contact, lowering her lashes.

No. He wouldn't win. She was in control of her life, her emotions. She had survived the loss of her parents, her home, had overcome the torment and ridicule of the Carringtons.

I can handle supper with the Doulans.

Staring at her plate, she methodically took bite after bite. No matter how hard she tried, she couldn't block out the hum of easy conversation. A blend of cheerful voices and delighted giggles ricocheted around the table. Even May perked up once Regi commented on her impressive collection of his favorite authors.

"June got me started," she said. "He was always sending books home to us."

Of course he had, Lily thought, stabbing a green bean with extra force. *Juniper Barns, gunfighter turned savior of the whole wide world.*

It was all she could do to stay in her chair as pain swirled around her. Finished with her meal, she risked a glance at the man sitting across from her. He grinned at whatever May was saying to her mother. He fit in with the rest of them, all smiles and cheer—his family's affection for him as tangible as the food on their plates, all of it reminding her of a time when she'd sat at a supper table and felt the same affection and delight at being part of a family that loved her.

He stole my life.

Suddenly it all made sense, her attraction to Juniper, the chaos of emotions that had plagued her the moment she had entered the Sierra foothills. Every memory of home was like a chink in her armor, letting in slices of old despair, the feeling of helplessness she remembered from her youth as her world had fallen apart around her. By the time she'd awakened to Juniper's sky-blue eyes and tender smiles, her guard had been down, her security breeched.

"Lily, may I take your plate?" April asked as she pushed back from the table.

Startled to realize Juniper was staring back at her, his brow creased with a frown, she turned to April. "Yes. Thank you."

Everyone began collecting dishes and carrying them into the kitchen. Watching Juniper disappear through the doorway with Regi and the others, Lily didn't waste a moment—she bolted for the front door and quietly slipped outside, needing to get away from all their cheerful chatter.

The cool evening air washed over her like a soothing balm as she walked into the growing darkness just beyond the lights from the house. The shadow of mountains against a black sky was still visible in the last bit of twilight. Lily stepped up onto the white fence rail, folding her arms over the top rung as she gazed out at the quiet serenity, miles of peaceful beauty stretching out beneath an open sky—all of it seeming to scream of her injustice.

He'd come here, to a tranquil home, a wonderful family that loved him—gaining everything he'd taken from her. It just wasn't fair!

A small voice inside her told her she was being

childish. Crying over what she couldn't change wouldn't help anything. Her anger over something so trivial was juvenile. But the pain was real—a sense of loss swelling inside her as though she'd lost her parents all over again. She pressed her forehead against her arms as a surge of grief took hold.

This wasn't the time to resurrect old emotions. A few days ago, she'd been strong, independent, afraid of nothing. Until she'd met Juniper, she hadn't cried a single tear over *anything* since she'd been dragged out of Missouri. She wondered now if that was because nothing else in her life had ever hurt so deeply.

She had to find the Lily who could face hardship, insolence and ridicule and *feel nothing*. She shut her eyes and pulled in a deep, calming breath.

"Lily?"

Juniper's masculine voice shattered her concentration.

Not now.

His boots scuffed the ground behind her as he approached.

She stepped down from the fence. One look at his questioning blue eyes and she felt her control begin to unravel.

The concern in his gaze made her yearn to be near him. She turned back to the mountains, telling herself she was some kind of crazy to allow her father's killer to affect her in such a way. No matter how frequently she reminded herself of who he was, what he'd taken from her, still there was a tenderness in Juniper she'd sensed from the first moment she'd laid eyes on him, a sincerity that appealed to her clear down to her soul.

She didn't like it.

"They're serving up pie."

"I don't want any."

He moved in beside her, crowding her space, her thoughts, her sanity.

"You sure?"

"I'm sure I don't want to be here," she said. "I don't want to be in that house. I don't want to see you with your family!"

Her sharp voice echoed back at her on the light breeze. When moments passed and Juniper didn't respond, she glanced beside her. He stood with his back slumped against the fence, his thumbs through his belt loops, his somber gaze trained on her. She couldn't tell if he looked hurt or confused or a little of both. The fact that he was making her care about him at all infuriated her.

"Do you do it on purpose?" she asked.

"Do what?"

"All of it! The dashing smiles, easy charm, the honey-and-hickory voice that makes me want to…to believe in you. To forget what you took from me."

"I'm not trying to upset you and I'm certainly not asking you to like me."

"Yet you make it very difficult for me to do otherwise!"

His lips quirked with a smile. "Sorry."

Tears pricked at her eyes, which annoyed her all the more. "It's *not funny,* you know?"

"I know," he said, his eyes darkening with clear emotion, and suddenly her cheeks were hot with tears.

She turned away from him, but it was too late. Her breath came in short gasps. The moment he was near her, she couldn't find herself, not the Lily she needed to be to keep the chaos at bay—Lily *Carrington.* She'd take being cold and bitter over the storm of emotions surging for release.

"Honest to God, Lily, I'm not trying to hurt you."

He moved toward her, standing so close she could feel the warmth of his body against her back. His presence was like a hair-trigger on the lid to Pandora's box, releasing all the little demons of suppressed sorrow and despair she'd kept locked away in the deepest regions of her heart. To her sheer horror, she couldn't stop the flood of tears, the sobs wrenching from deep inside her.

"Lily."

His warmth closed around her.

"I'd do anything to take back the pain I've caused."

"That only makes it hurt…all the more."

She tried to turn away, but he surrounded her, offering a comfort she'd been denied for so many years. Blinded by tears and frustration, she buried her face against him as grief rose up like a dark cloud. Wave after wave of anguish surged through her, releasing a deluge of tears, until all she felt was raw and open.

Juniper's shirt muffled her sobs. Each sharp breath drew in his distinctive, masculine scent.

Regaining some clarity, she realized Juniper's arms were all that were keeping her standing. He held her close, one hand gently stroking her hair. Sniffing loudly, she found her balance and released her tight grip on his shirt.

Juniper eased his hold but didn't release her entirely. Her cheeks warmed as she stared at the fisted wrinkles that moments ago had been smooth pockets on his shirtfront and the dark tearstains at the center of his chest.

Dear Lord, she'd used him as a giant hankie.

"Sorry," she said, refusing to look higher than the damp spot on his shirt.

His hand slid beneath her chin and tilted her face up. "You've got nothing to be sorry for."

His light tone was a clear contradiction to the turbulent gaze intent on hers. His thumb lightly traced her flushed cheek, sending tingles to the tips of her toes. She shut her eyes and turned her face into his touch, brushing her lips over the pad of his thumb. Ribbons of heat spiraled up from low in her belly.

Why did he make her feel so...*strange?*

"Lily?"

The deep whisper of her name caressed her skin. She smiled against his palm. A *good* kind of strange.

She opened her eyes, her gaze instantly focusing on his mouth. Would his lips feel as pleasing as his touch, *a soothing burst of shimmering warmth?*

He leaned in, and her breath caught. She rose on tiptoe to meet his kiss. The light, fleeting caress of his lips against hers sent a shudder of desire rippling through her. Her breath broke and he tilted his head, fitting his mouth more fully to hers. The first glide of his tongue reminded her why this was all so new to her, every velvety caress teaching her that she knew nothing of true intimacy. She returned the light, fleeting touches, meeting each rhythmic caress until she clung to him, trembling as she kissed him in a way she'd never kissed another man.

She slid her hands up his shoulders, her fingers seeking the silky waves she'd been longing to stroke. The smooth strands caressed the delicate skin between her fingers, which flexed against his scalp in the slow, sensuous rhythm of their kiss.

His breath emerged as a groan, bringing another tingling burst of pleasure. His body shifted against her, the hands gliding over her back, pulling her closer, igniting an unmistakable spark of desire. Lily held on tight, loving every fluid movement of his hands, his body, his mouth.

His lips trailed across her throat, leaving sparks beneath her skin. She tilted her head, arching against him, ravaged by the flood of new sensations.

"Juniper."

The sound of his name registered in her hazy mind, breaking through the wild surge of heat strumming through her body.

What am I doing! She was allowing him to slip past

twelve years of hatred, to awaken a desire she'd never dreamed she'd possess—and *for him.*

"No," she said, pulling away.

She stumbled back, gasping for breath.

"Lily—"

"I've *hated* you," she said, trying to reclaim her thoughts, "for so long."

Juniper couldn't have been snapped back to his senses faster if he'd dropped through ice on a frozen pond. Her words brought him back to where he was, what he'd done, the line he'd just crossed.

"Yeah," he said. "Me, too." He took another step back and released a hard breath in an attempt to slow the violent beat of his pulse.

"June?" April leaned over the front porch railing to glance back at them. "Are you two coming? We're serving the pie. I made it," she added, her grin stretching wide.

"Then you'd better save me a slice," Juniper called back. "I'll be right there."

The moisture shining in Lily's eyes turned the passion that had burned so deeply a moment ago to a sick feeling in the pit of his stomach. What the hell had he been thinking? She'd displayed a moment of vulnerability, uncertainty at best, and he'd jumped on it. The first touch of her generous mouth to his, and he stopped thinking altogether.

"I'm going to bed," she said. "You'll tell me if Günter arrives?"

"I will," he lied.

He watched her scurry toward the front porch, lifting her skirt as she raced up the steps. At first light he hoped to be delivering her money to The Grove and she'd be spitting mad. He'd gotten to know her well enough to be certain she couldn't be reasonable about staying behind. She didn't trust him as a lawman. He couldn't rightly say he blamed her. He'd botched up yesterday, sending her down the mountain the way he had. He'd only been thinking of her safety, but she wouldn't believe that, either.

He hadn't been thinking of her safety a moment ago. He'd watched her over supper, had seen the pain in her eyes when she looked at him. She'd only been seeking comfort, and he'd given in to a craving he'd been fighting since the first time he'd held her in his arms. He strode back to the house knowing there wasn't a pie on this earth that tasted as sweet as Lily's kiss.

And he was a fool for finding out.

Chapter Ten

"You sure you don't need another gun?"

June glanced over his saddle as Jed stepped into the lamplight of the barn. "You're supposed to be my lookout."

"She hasn't come out of her room since she raced up those stairs, and her cousin just turned in, as well."

Juniper dropped his rifle into the side scabbard. "Trust me, keeping an eye on Lily can be far more hazardous than going after outlaws."

Jed's low chuckle carried through the barn.

"No doubt she'll try to follow me if she spies me leaving. She's bound to be flaming mad in the morning, when she finds out I've left without her."

"Not to worry, son. I do have some experience in dealing with unruly females."

"Not like this one."

"You sure?" Jed said mildly, reclining against a stall as Juniper finished tying down his bedroll and supplies. "She seemed rather quiet and gentle during supper."

The reminder stung at his pride. He'd seen the

struggle of emotion she'd tried to hide as she'd sat at the table, but hadn't guessed how hard it had been for her to be around his family.

I don't want to be in that house. I don't want to see you with your family!

"Only reason she seemed docile is because she's so far out of her element she doesn't know up from down." She never would have allowed him to kiss her had she been of a right mind. "Lily ought to be tucked into her big-city office, buying and selling companies the way us common folk barter flour and salt at the market."

"I wouldn't have figured you as one to be bothered by a quick-minded woman."

"I wish it was just her quick mind that bothered me."

"She been trying your patience, son?" Jed asked, a note of humor in his tone. "Carrying a flame for a pretty woman tends to tamper with a man's reasoning."

Juniper glanced up at Jed's sharp eyes that missed nothing. Attraction didn't change the unpleasant reality of their situation.

"I killed her father, Jed. Back when I lived in Missouri."

Jed stared at him a moment before muttering a curse. "Does she know?"

"*Oh, yeah.* That's why she's here. She saw my name on her employee roster, loaded her daddy's gun and hightailed it up the mountain to kill me."

Jed's mouth twitched with the start of a grin. "Can't help but notice you're still breathin'."

"Yeah, well...this ain't over yet." After his behavior tonight and sneaking off like he was, he didn't doubt she'd be gunning for him if she got the chance.

"I'm sorry, son."

Juniper let out a long breath. "Me, too."

"Sweet on her, are ya?"

"Only when she's sleeping or unconscious," he said, though he knew that wasn't really true. She annoyed and allured him in equal turns. After the way she'd kissed him... *Good God*...how could he have known she'd turn to sweet fire in his arms? Her kiss burned through him faster and hotter than any flicker of passion he'd ever experienced.

"I'm not sure I want to know what that means," Jed said with a laugh.

"She has the face of an angel and the temperament of her father."

"You remember him?"

"I remember all of them. None so clearly as Red."

Juniper shut his eyes as memories of that night descended on him like a cold fog. "The man had arms the size of tree trunks, the height of a giant and a gun hand accurate enough to make anyone on a Wanted poster beat a hard, fast path out of Missouri. When I heard he'd been drinkin' and was looking to call me out, I did what any kid with an ounce of sense would do—I scrambled for a place to hide. I thought I was gonna die that night."

"What happened?" asked Jed.

"He found me, picked me up by the back of my shirt, dragged me outside and tossed me into the street. I tried to talk him out of it—but there's no reasoning with a man in a drunken rage."

The images played out like a recurring nightmare in his mind. "He counted. We drew. He fell. Just like all the others."

But that night had been different. When he'd stumbled off into the darkness, the aftermath of staring into the face of death closing in hard around him, a voice had called to him from the shadows: "June? Can I sit with you?"

His silence had been answered by a tender touch, then a comforting embrace. Rachell had been the beginning of his salvation. Her kindness had given him hope when he'd long since stopped looking for a trace of good in his hellish life.

Jed closed a hand over his shoulder. "No one can blame you for a situation that was beyond your control, June. You didn't do nothin' but choose to live."

"Yeah. But sometimes...sometimes it feels like the wrong choice."

"I know."

Juniper glanced up at the stark clarity in Jed's gray eyes and knew he was one of the few who truly understood his torment. Jed had traveled a path marred by violence and bloodshed. He'd also lived a long, hard life before finally burying the demons from his past and taking a wife. Rachell and Jed had welcomed him in, giving him something to care about, only to have it snatched away by a past that wouldn't let go of him. Having to keep his distance from this family, everyone he loved, was a personal hell.

Lily Palmer was that torture personified.

"June, there's not a day that passes when I'm not grateful for the choices you made. If it weren't for you, I'd likely not have my wife or our family. A family you're a part of."

"And I'm grateful."

"I know you are. It might help if you forgave yourself."

A cold laugh uncurled from his chest. "How do I do that?"

"I may not be the best example, son. I let guilt rule my life for far too long."

"I'm too busy with crazy female employers and trigger-happy lumberjacks to worry about guilt."

"So, what do you plan to do with her?"

"Help her get her money back, keep her from getting herself killed, then ship her safely back to 'Frisco."

"Well, as long as you got it all worked out," Jed said, amusement shining in his eyes. "How long do you plan to be gone?"

"Providing we recover the cash box tonight and get it to The Grove office by morning, I hope to be back by late tomorrow night. The following day at the latest."

"I wish you luck, son." Jed reached up and put out the lamp.

"Thanks," Juniper said, leading his horse from the barn. "I've got a feeling I'm going to need it."

Lily's breath felt like fire in her lungs as she inched her way through the side door of the barn, listening to the murmur of Juniper's and Jed's voices as they walked farther out into the yard. It was the words that Juniper had spoken about her father that played in her mind, chilling her skin from the inside out.

I did what any kid with an ounce of sense would do—I scrambled for a place to hide. I thought I was gonna die that night.

He'd run from her father?

He'd told her Red had been the one looking for a gunfight. She hadn't wanted to believe him. Why would her daddy do something so reckless when his family needed him?

There had to be more he wasn't telling. Her daddy wasn't a drinker; she'd never seen him hindered by liquor. Of course Juniper would tell Jed it was all her father's doing. But…why had he told Jed at all? He hadn't been boastful or defensive. She'd heard the change in his tone, the sadness and *fear*.

I thought I was gonna die that night.

Had her father assumed he'd win? That thought only tightened the knot in her chest. She couldn't imagine the terror Juniper must have felt, facing down a man twice his size and three times his age.

She couldn't deal with this right now.

She glanced around inside the barn where slivers

of moonlight seeped through cracks and windows. Listening to the soft murmur of Jed's and Juniper's voices moving off into the distance, she hurried toward the tack stored in the far corner.

He meant to leave her behind.

Was that why he'd kissed her, to send her fleeing into the house so he could sneak off? Surely he hadn't expected her to welcome such an advance, and yet... she had.

Shame flagged her cheeks as she recalled just how welcoming her response had been, the startling surge of passion he'd so easily evoked in her. Pain swirled into rage. How could he take advantage of her in such a cruel manner!

She knew full well he was trying to protect his friends, the men he'd called *Good Samaritans,* the men who'd killed Mr. Dobbs. She couldn't allow that. Not when Mr. Dobbs had died trying to protect the money those men had stolen. She owed it to his family to make sure all the men responsible for his death were held accountable. She hoped his loved ones could find some peace in knowing justice had been served for his murder—which was more than she'd ever received.

Working quickly and quietly, she gathered Mr. Dobbs's equipment and saddled the horse she'd been riding. As she finished, she draped the gun belt Juniper had given to Regi over the saddle horn. The sound of Juniper's departing horse was fading into the night. She stroked the mare's dark coat and waited until she heard the front door close behind Jed.

Slowly she crept from the barn, keeping her eyes on the house as she led her horse toward open pasture as quietly as she could. In the distance Juniper was little more than a moving shadow as he descended over a hillside in the direction of the gap between two rises of flat-topped ridges.

"I hope you're rested," Lily whispered to the mare as she shifted into the saddle. "We have a sheriff to catch."

The moon shone bright overhead, giving a good view of the ridges standing against an onyx sky. Up ahead three horses came into view, shifting in the shadows beneath a cluster of oak trees. Recognizing Günter's horse, Juniper slowed and quickly dismounted.

He staked his horse between the two bearing a D&D brand. His gaze swept over the high flat ridge and surrounding scrub, searching the shadows as he listened for sounds of movement or voices.

He heard neither. Nothing but a light rustle of leaves shifting in a cool evening breeze.

Had they gone without him? He'd said an hour after nightfall and he wasn't late. He'd ridden at a near reckless pace, pushing his stallion as hard as the increasing moonlight would allow.

Walking toward the break in two sheer rises of earth and stone, he moved his gaze over the straight ledge, searching for signs of Jake or Günter spying on the Chandler homestead just beyond the gap. He surely wasn't going to just sit here and wait for them to come back. More than two seconds of idle thought and his mind strayed to where it shouldn't. Emerald eyes, the scent of lilacs, the taste of—

Knock it off, he silently berated himself, his blood stirring at the mere memory of her kiss. The first timid touch of her tongue, and desire had pounded through him, blinding him. Consuming him.

He should have guessed she'd approach passion with the same bold tenacity she'd displayed on the mountain. Touching her had been the first mistake. One moment she'd been a tender flame in his arms, the next the fire of her touch and taste had surrounded him—burning him like a fever in his blood.

"Gotcha," said a low voice.

Juniper spun, his gun breaking free of his holster in the time it took most men to flinch.

The wide grin of Kyle Darby met his stare. "Hey, cousin."

"Damnation," Juniper said in a wheezing breath. He shoved his gun back into the leather and was more than tempted to punch out his best friend.

"It's a sad day when a man can sneak up on Juniper Barns," his friend lamented, slapping a hand against his shoulder.

Juniper returned the friendly nudge, none too gently. "You're lucky I didn't shoot you!"

"I warned him." Jake stepped beside his older brother.

"Only a fool shoots what he can't see," Kyle said

mildly. "You're no fool." He chuckled. "Leastways, not usually. What has you stargazing when you should be on guard?"

"I wasn't stargazing. I was waiting on your brother."

"And stargazing," said Kyle.

Juniper rolled his shoulders against a tension in his muscles nagging at him to take that punch.

"Save it for the outlaws," Kyle advised, his dark blue eyes reading him with an ease that came from years of friendship.

"Where's Günter?"

"Working his way around to the east side of Chandler's place," said Jake.

"We came in early and counted ten horses at the homestead," Kyle informed him. "We're not sure how many they had on the place before the others arrived. Either way, we're outnumbered and figured it'd be best to go in from all four sides."

"It's just the four of us," said Jake.

"What do you mean by *just?*" Kyle broadened his stance. "You and June can go on home and darn socks for all I care. Me and ol' Günter can handle that little band of thieves."

Juniper grinned. It was that cocky attitude that had gotten them both into a number of brawls, despite Juniper's effort to keep them out of trouble. "When did you get home, anyhow? Last I heard you were hunting down outlaws up in Montana."

Kyle's teeth gleamed in the moonlight. "I'm still

hunting." He lifted the side of his long coat, revealing a silver star pinned to the inside.

Juniper stared at the circular insignia in near disbelief.

"You're a U.S. marshal?"

"Figured I'd follow my cousin's good example and go legit."

"You'd think he'd have written home with such news," said Jake. "Getting to meet the president and all."

"Same job, new title," Kyle said with a shrug.

"I can't believe they'd let you near the president," Juniper said in bewilderment.

Kyle laughed. "Would you believe President Arthur knows Jed?"

Juniper grinned. "Yeah. Ain't many folks of political importance who don't."

"My jaw must have hit the table when ol' Chester Arthur asked me how the Doulan family was faring. Apparently they don't pass out stars without combing a man's background. Your sheriff's office could use that kind of efficiency. I take it you never got the telegram I sent to The Grove?"

"*You're* the reason my deputy left his post."

"The hell I am. Deputy Griggs is an idiot."

Juniper didn't bother arguing with him. "After all the trouble we've had, there aren't many men left in those mountains willing to pin on a star, and I need a body in the sheriff's office while I'm chasing hell-raisers up the mountain."

"If you had got my message you'd have understood I was coming up to have a quiet look around. Instead, your deputy greeted me at the ferry like I was the governor of California. I don't know how he recognized me. I must look like a lawman, because he was announcing to the world that I was a U.S. marshal the moment I stepped off the boat."

"Musta been nothin' but women and children on that ferry," said Jake.

Juniper grinned at the barb. With Kyle's straight dark hair and midnight eyes, Griggs couldn't have picked him out due to any family resemblance. The only similar features they shared were height and build.

"Your other deputy caught up with us," Kyle continued. "He came barreling down that mountain road like Paul Bunyan come to life. He tore into Deputy Griggs for leaving his post. You ought to have that big Swede in your sheriff's office. I didn't think there was anyone who could cast a shadow over you, and that boy looks mighty fierce when he's riled."

"Which is why I've needed him up at the camp. In the past couple months most of my trouble has been with the crews up at Pine Ridge. Inundated by pay holds and informative leaflets that only stoked tempers, the men have been so riled they don't know who to fight first."

"Guess the Chandler boys were able to give them some direction."

"It would seem," said Juniper.

"Those Chandlers are everywhere these days. I just

spent a few months up in Montana with Ned Chandler and his buddies. You'll never guess where they were headed."

"Is that what brought you home, the Chandlers?"

"I don't like to leave any loose ends," said Kyle.

"You sure loose ends brought you home?" said Jake. "I think it had more to do with a certain Montana wildflower."

"*Shut up,* Jake."

Juniper arched an eyebrow, Kyle's sharp response piquing his interest. "You have a wildflower I ought to know about?"

Kyle scoffed. "Hell no. I learned my lesson. I don't pick flowers, I just roll in 'em for a while."

Juniper couldn't say he blamed him. He sure hadn't envied Kyle the day he'd stood beside him and Jake, looking out at a church full of expectant faces, waiting for a bride who never showed.

"Why focus on a single flower when all I gotta do is ride through town and have entire bouquets blooming for my touch."

"Careful," Jake warned. "Your head's gonna swell up inside your hatband."

"A snug hat's one thing," said Juniper, "but you go spending time with them indoor bouquets and something else is liable to shrivel up and fall off."

Jake gave a hoot of laughter.

"Keep it down," Kyle grumbled. "Or have you forgotten we're a half mile from the Chandler place? June's the one with flower troubles. According to Günter, the lilies are particularly vibrant this spring."

"I can handle the lilies, it's the Chandler boys I want to know about. I didn't place the name until Emma Donnelly mentioned their homestead in the flat-topped hills. I know there's been stage robbers in the family."

"Just before I checked Ned into a Montana prison, he'd gotten word from Clyde and Billy about a job up in the pines. I don't think he was referring to cutting down timbers."

Juniper muttered a curse. "Everyone on that mountain knew we were waiting on two months' worth of wages."

"A big chunk of change," said Kyle.

"Had I known that cash was coming up the mountain, I damn sure would have had a swarm of armed guards. Even so, I had a hard time believing our guys would shoot a man down in cold blood during the heist."

"Billy and Clyde have done far worse. If they're from the same stock as the rest of their kin, like Ned, which I'm betting they are, finding a pigeonhole and lying low in between jobs is what they do best."

Juniper shook his head. "Desperate as everyone has been for their wages, I doubt it took much carousing to get the rest of the crew involved. They've got honest men caught up in all this."

"You? A bleeding heart?" asked Kyle.

"Lord knows I've spilled more than my share. But

I'd bet my gun belt some of those men didn't want any bloodshed and went into this with good intentions."

"Not to worry, June." Jake started in the direction of the homestead, his dark hat fading into trees and shadows. "We only shoot when shot at."

"Amen, brother," said Kyle. "It's the vermin you can count on to strike first and ask questions second."

"All right then," Juniper said, taking the lead. "Let's go flush 'em out."

The Chandler house seemed to rise up out of nowhere.

Lily, emerging from a dark channel of stone into a thick field of sagebrush, stayed just beyond the yard of the ramshackle house and dilapidated woodshed. The run-down place stood in a small clearing just beyond the high cliffs.

Even in the dim moonlight, the house appeared abandoned, showing signs of long-term neglect— weeds growing from the uneven roof planks, tall grasses almost overtaking the shack. But the house was occupied. She'd smelled fresh wood chips as she passed the old woodshed, and a thin trail of smoke snaked from the stovepipe on the house.

She crept lightly through the dense sage and manzanita, wondering if Juniper had already entered the house. She'd lost track of him quite a ways back, but the channel of stone leading through the gap, just as he'd described, had been easy enough to find. This had to be the Chandler homestead.

Light burned in the single front window. Yet she didn't spy a flurry of activity as she'd expect following an ambush. She couldn't rightly walk up and knock on the door to see if her strongbox had been collected and all the men apprehended.

A low murmur of voices drew her gaze to the corrals beyond the far end of the house and a wide patch of sheer darkness. With the moon at her back, a stone ridge cast a wide shadow, cloaking a broad stretch of ground in the pitch of night.

Suddenly she wondered if the gun she gripped tightly in her right hand was even loaded, something she should have checked before now. Crouched low, she eased into a patch of milky moonlight and opened the chamber.

Fully loaded.

Drawing a silent, steady breath, she raised her gun, not knowing if the hushed whispers were lawmen or outlaws. She eased up, and took a cautious step forward. With her next step a man seemed to materialize out of the shadows, soundlessly appearing before her, his gun trained on her.

She gasped, and looked up into wide blue eyes beneath a brown hat.

Juniper.

He stared at her, his gun dropping to his side.

"Lily?"

His whispered word barely reached her ears. He'd obviously expected to find someone else standing in the brush. Someone other than the woman he'd brazenly kissed as a cruel ploy to leave her behind.

Her finger tightened on the trigger. Maybe he was just who she wanted to have in her sights.

Juniper hardly believed his eyes. Yet there she stood, her pale skin bright in the moonlight, a revolver aimed at his chest. Her glistening eyes narrowed; her gun hand steadied.

Holy hell. She meant to shoot him.

He fought his reflex to raise his gun. *Damn* if he'd take aim against her. He'd sooner take his place in hell.

Her gaze darted past him. Her eyes flared. Her aim shifted, the blast splitting through the evening silence as she shouted his name.

He twisted to see the man who'd been sneaking up on him stagger back, the blood trailing down between his eyes appearing black in the moonlight before he toppled to the ground. His rifle hit the dirt beside him.

A man sprang up from the brush, the barrel of his rifle nearly touching Lily. "You sunuva—"

Juniper fired both his guns, dropping the man nearly as quickly as he'd sprung up.

Gunfire rang out all around the house, his men clearly mistaking the first gunshot as their signal to rush the house. Shadows moved off to the right. Two figures started running toward a south pasture.

"Get down!" he shouted to Lily as he ran after them.

Crashes and shouts came from inside the house as June reached the edge of the yard.

"Don't move!" Kyle's voice boomed amid the ruckus. The sound of pounding hoofbeats told him the two deserters had reached their horses.

With no chance in hell of catching them on foot and his men outnumbered, Juniper turned and sprinted toward the porch. He vaulted up and over the railing and kicked in the door. Two lumberjacks stared up at him, their arms stretched over piles of money.

Jake charged in from the other side, his gun drawn.

Both men threw their hands up.

"Face down," Juniper ordered.

They dropped to their bellies.

"Restrain 'em," he said to Jake.

"Put it down!" Kyle shouted from one of the bedrooms on the right. Juniper stepped inside and saw Calvin, his gaze wild, a pistol in his hands.

"Do as he says, Cal," Juniper said in an easy tone.

The kid's gaze moved between them, but the gun didn't waver.

"You make me break your sister's heart again, and I swear I'll shoot you twice just for the hell of it."

His hands trembled on the gun as he stared at Juniper. The distraction was all Kyle needed to rush him and knock him to the floor.

"Wait!" Cal shouted. "I was just—"

"You were just pissing me off," Kyle said in a growl as he cuffed the younger man's wrist.

"How many we got?" Juniper called out as he stepped back into the main room.

"I got two," Jake said, straightening away from the two men kneeling, their wrists and ankles bound by the same strip of rope.

"Three secured in here," Günter shouted from the kitchen.

With the two dead and two deserters, all ten were accounted for. He had to get back to Lily. He'd need her to identify the man who'd abducted her yesterday. Tension coiled across his back at the thought of bringing her within the view of these men.

"Blindfold all of them," he said to Jake.

"What?" Calvin stumbled in from the bedroom, Kyle at his back. "Why?"

"We'll ask the questions," Kyle said, shoving him to the floor beside the other two timbermen.

"Can you cover this?" he said to Kyle.

Kyle gave him a questioning glance. "Sure."

"Where you goin'!" Cal called after him.

Juniper was already rushing across the rotted porch.

Chapter Eleven

Standing in the tall brush beyond the yard, her pale skin aglow in the moonlight, Lily hadn't moved an inch. Juniper's gaze locked on the fine trembling of her body and the gun still in her grip. Her arms limp at her sides, she stared at the body sprawled on the ground a few yards out.

"Lily?"

She looked up at the sound of his voice, then dropped to her knees, her breath rushing out in a sharp burst. Juniper knelt in front of her and slid the gun from her grip as his arm closed around her. She drew a jagged breath, the all-too-familiar tremors shaking her small frame.

"You're all right, darlin'."

"I… H-he…"

Juniper eased her limp weight against him. "Shh. You're all right," he said, lifting her into his arms as he stood.

Her arms went around his neck and held tight. "I shot him," she breathed against his throat.

Pain twisted through Juniper. He should have been the one to shoot Clyde Chandler. He carried her beyond the back of the house. Not wanting any of the others to know she was here, he continued toward the shed some fifty yards from the house. He eased onto a rough-cut bench at the side of the shed. Her breath came in and out in short puffs. Her tight grip damn near cutting off his air, he reached for her arms.

"Lily?" he whispered, loosening her hold.

"Don't let go," she gasped, pressing more firmly against him.

"I won't," he promised, working to ease her hold so he could help her catch her breath. "But you've got to breathe, darlin'."

Lily shut her eyes and tried to draw a full breath. The image of blood spattering into moonlight forced them back open. Pain racked her body, her lungs rebelling against her attempt to suck air.

"I can't stop…shaking."

"I know," he said. "Focus on those deep breaths. Nice and easy."

She gazed up at him, confused by the simple order as panic swelled up inside her.

"Focus," he said. "Deep breaths."

She dragged in a hard breath. "He's dead," she said on the exhale. She twisted, trying to look back.

Juniper's hand cupped her chin, preventing her from glancing toward the front yard.

"You're safe," he said. "That's all that matters."

Tears streaked hotly across her cheeks. "I nearly…

got you killed," she said, knowing he'd likely have seen the other man if she hadn't distracted his attention.

"But you didn't."

Dear God, her chest felt as though it might burst open at any moment. She kept seeing the man's head rear back, the spray of blood, his blank expression as blood trailed down his face before he toppled to the ground.

Her stomach turned.

"Head down," Juniper instructed. The hand on her back gently eased her forward as he spoke. "Got to keep breathing, sweetheart. Slow and easy."

After a few minutes of focused, steady breathing, her stomach began to settle. Still, Juniper didn't let her up.

"That's it," he whispered, his soothing voice encouraging her to keep taking long, slow breaths.

As her mind began to clear and her nerves settled, she realized she was actually on his lap, her head between her legs, her hair hanging toward the ground. Suddenly, she hated him seeing her like this.

She dragged in another deep, shaky breath and eased back.

"I think I'm okay," she said, using his knee to push up.

"You're still shaking," he said, the arm around her waist keeping her on his lap. His hand slid into the side of her tangled hair, his fingers resting on her neck. She knew he was checking her pulse, the flat line of his mouth suggesting he wasn't satisfied with what he felt.

"Believe me, you're not ready to stand just yet."

"I'm j-just cold," she said, realizing the fact.

"Then I'll warm you up." His arms tightened around her, tucking her against his chest, beneath his chin. His big hands slid over her arms and her back in slow, gentle strokes.

Another shudder racked her body. She shut her eyes, allowing him to rub the chill from her skin.

After what felt like an eternity, his warmth began to seep through her and her pulse settled to match the steady thump of Juniper's heart. Shouts from inside the house drew her attention. She sat back, realizing she was keeping Juniper from doing his job.

"Shouldn't you be inside?" she whispered.

"There's three other lawmen in there to keep things under control."

Lily released a long, shuddered breath.

"Feeling a little better?" he asked, his hand gently stroking her hair away from her face, his gaze heavy with compassion and understanding.

"You've felt like this?"

"More times than I care to recall."

The blend of understanding and regret in his gaze filled her with an instant unease. She hadn't imagined he'd feel such emotion over taking a life. Yet he'd come to her, knowing just how to penetrate the chaos in her mind, to calm the grip of cold fear that had surrounded her. His warm hand moved across her back, and this time the startling intimacy of his tender embrace filtered into her dazed mind.

"If you need to go inside—"

"In due time. I haven't yet lectured you for following me, when you knew damn well I wanted you to stay put."

"Remind me to listen to you next time."

His slow grin caught her by surprise. The backs of his fingers brushed lightly across her cheek, setting off a rush of shivers that owed nothing to fear or shock.

"Count on it," he said, his smile fading as his hand dropped away from her face.

The back door opened, spilling light across a small back stoop. A wide span of shoulders filled the doorway. He wasn't tall enough to be Günter.

"Juniper?" she whispered, sliding her arms inside his jacket, around his waist.

"June?" the man called out.

"It's Kyle Darby, one of ours," he whispered. "Over here," he called out.

The man hurried toward them, and Lily tightened her hold.

Juniper's hand moved reassuringly across her back.

"Two men are missing," Kyle said as he approached. "Best we can figure, the men standing off in the scrub were…" His voice trailed as his gaze locked on Lily tucked against Juniper's chest. "Apparently there were more than bandits hiding out in the brush."

He pulled off his hat, revealing dark eyes and straight

dark hair. "I didn't know you were bringing your girl," he said to Juniper.

"She decided to surprise me."

Lily's cheeks burned. She tried to rise, but Juniper's arms held her firmly on his lap.

"Neither Chandler is inside," said Kyle.

"Then Billy must be one of the two men who got to their horses. Clyde and his uncle are in the front yard awaiting headstones."

Lily turned her face to his shirt, the image of pooling blood and glassy eyes dragging an involuntary whimper from her throat.

Juniper's arms tightened around her. "She got caught between Clyde and me."

"Did he hurt her?" asked Kyle.

"She's just shook up. First kill is never easy on the stomach."

Kyle's eyes widened.

"As far as this investigation goes, I shot both men."

"Understood," said Kyle.

"But you didn't," Lily protested.

"She saved me from a bullet," said Juniper.

"Any one of us would have done the same," Kyle said to her. "Cousin, I do believe I need a proper introduction."

"Kyle Darby, this is the owner of Carrington Industries and the Pine Ridge Lumber Camp and Mill, Miss Lily Carrington."

"*Palmer* Carrington," she corrected.

Juniper raised his eyebrows, surprised by her sudden insistence on the use of her given last name.

"Miss Palmer Carrington," said Kyle, "it's a fine pleasure to meet you." He took her hand in his and drew it to his lips.

"Mr. Darby," she said, sounding a tad breathless.

Kyle flashed one of his fallen-angel smiles and there was no fighting the tension tightening in the muscles across Juniper's back. He had to remind himself Kyle was one for laying on the charm with the ladies—didn't matter if she was young, old, gorgeous or homely.

"I've got to go inside," he said, his voice harsher than it should have been. He stood, shifting Lily onto the bench in the same motion. "I need you to sit *right here*."

"Where are you going?" she asked, her eyes clouding with worry.

"To check on things. Kyle's a U.S. marshal. He'll stay with you."

"It would be my pleasure."

She glanced warily at Kyle standing behind him. "All right," she said, though the hard slant of her mouth said she'd rather stay with *him*. For some odd reason, he found some satisfaction in that reaction. Which didn't make a damn bit of sense once he reminded himself she'd been contemplating putting a bullet through him seconds before Clyde had popped out.

"I won't be long."

"If you'd like," said Kyle, "I can escort the lady back to the ranch."

"No."

Kyle's eyebrows shot up at his quick response.

"I need to see if she can identify the man who abducted her yesterday. I don't want any of them to know she's here, which is why I had them blindfolded."

"Understood," said Kyle.

"You feel up to taking a quick look," he said to Lily, "to see if you recognize the one who grabbed you?"

Her expression instantly firmed, her eyes getting back some of that Lily spark. She gave a vigorous nod.

"All right, then," he said, admiring her determination. "I'll be back for you."

Kyle eased onto the bench beside her.

Juniper forced himself to turn and walk away. With every step he had to tell himself he had no cause to worry about leaving her in Kyle's care. It was the men in the house he needed to worry about. If Kyle could help in getting Lily out of here, he needed to be grateful.

Inside, Günter and Jake stood watch over the six men who'd been blindfolded with dishtowels or shredded linens. He motioned for Jake and Günter to join him in the kitchen.

His deputy ducked through the kitchen doorway, his seven-foot frame hardly accommodated in the small, dank ranch house.

"You find the others?" asked Günter.

"Two are dead and two rode out."

"The Chandlers?" asked Jake.

"Clyde and his uncle need burying. If Billy isn't one of those six, he rode out with the other man. They give the name?"

"Billy Chandler and a man named Mathews," said Jake. "You going after them?"

"They'll keep." He leaned toward them and whispered, "Lily's outside."

Two sets of eyes flared wide.

"She followed me. I need to see if she can identify the man who grabbed her, but I don't want these men to know she was here. I'm going to bring her in, real quiet like. Make sure there's no gaps in those blindfolds."

"I will do," Günter said.

Juniper walked back across the yard, following the low murmur of Kyle's voice. Nearing the shed, he found them sitting so close he could hardly make out Lily in Kyle's shadow.

I'm the one putting her in danger, he told himself. *She'd be better off under the care of any other lawman.*

A cold acceptance settled over him. After he took her inside, he'd send her back to the Double D with Kyle. He'd have Kyle escort her all the way back to San Francisco if need be, whatever it took to get her out of harm's way.

"Are you really cousins?" Lily asked.

"Our family's a lot like one of them patchwork quilts," Kyle answered easily. "Juniper and I may not share any bloodlines, but we're tightly stitched."

"So you're only related to Jed?"

"Nope. But he did raise my stepmother and we've always called him Uncle Jed. When June came along that made him our cousin."

"Claiming me as kin isn't going to earn you any grace with Miss Palmer."

Lily gave Juniper a startled look before he took her by the hand and tugged her up.

"While we're inside that house, you will be silent as a church mouse. Take a quick look at the men and hold your tongue until we're back out here. Do you understand me?"

"Yes."

"Good. Because if you disobey me one more time you'll be cuffed, gagged and on your way back to 'Frisco before you can blink."

He didn't give her a moment to think about those options. He wrapped his arm around her stiff shoulders and ushered her toward the house.

Lily rushed along beside him, wondering what had happened to the kind, consoling Juniper. "I see you're back to being Sheriff Barns."

"It's what you pay me for," he reminded her. He pulled her closer as they approached the steps. "I meant what I said," he whispered. *"Keep quiet."*

Lily had no reason to doubt him, the memory of his handcuffs and handkerchiefs still fresh in her mind. Deep voices filtered outside as he reached for the doorknob. Lily squinted against the bright lights burning in the tiny kitchen. Her open iron strongbox sat on a small table, coins and piles of bills stacked all around it.

Juniper touched his finger to his lips as he guided her past the table. In the front room a row of six bound and blindfolded men crouched on their knees. Günter and a shorter man with curly brown hair stood on either side of them.

Lily glanced at each man. With half their faces covered it was hard to identify their features. Even so, she knew none of them were the man who'd held her on his lap. She wouldn't forget his lips pressed against her neck as he'd made her skin crawl with the filthy promises of all he planned to do to her. They'd been a peculiar red, like rubies or the underbelly of a black widow spider.

"How can a man be arrested for trying to feed his family?" one of the prisoners demanded.

"I got four kids at home," said a robust man near the center.

"What are we waiting for?" A younger man on the end twisted against his restraints. "I want to talk to Sheriff Barns!"

"Don't worry," said Günter. "You will have your chance."

Juniper turned her toward the kitchen and rushed straight to the back door. Lily tried to stop at the table.

"No," he said in a low growl.

"Bu—"

His hand strapped over her mouth and Lily was

wrenched off her feet. She struggled against his hold, which didn't do a bit of good. They were beside the shed before he set her back down.

"What didn't you understand about 'Keep quiet until we were outside'?" he demanded, his hands gripping her shoulders.

"I was going to whisper."

"I said *not a word*."

"Let go of me!" Lily shrugged out of his hold.

"Did you recognize any of them as the man who grabbed you?"

"No."

"What about the man who shot Mr. Dobbs?"

His face clear in her mind, Lily shook her head.

Juniper cursed under his breath.

"I would like to recover my cash box."

"Not happening."

"I didn't come all this way to go back without my money."

He pulled a pair of handcuffs from his belt. "You'll ride back to the Double D this instant or I'll arrest you right here and now."

"You cannot arrest me!"

"The hell I can't. You're impeding my investigation."

"This is my—"

A sharp scratch and spark of light blossomed in the darkness beside her, making Lily jump with fright.

Kyle stood on the shadowed side of the shed holding a match to the tip of a cheroot. The orange glow lit up the chiseled features of his face as white smoke curled out from his lips.

"You two finished bickering?" he asked as he shook out the match.

"Tell him he's being ridiculous."

He took a step forward, his smile bright against the moonlight. "Sorry, Lily. A man don't have to be reasonable when he's fretting over his gal."

"I'm *not* his gal."

"Figurative term. Might not look like it half the time, but June knows what he's doing."

"Gee, thanks," Juniper said.

"Anytime, cousin." He blew a smoke ring at Juniper before turning his smile back to Lily. "I'd be keeping you out of that house, too, and would likely be mad as raging hell if you'd snuck along on an ambush. Soon as his temper settles, I'm sure he'll get around to thanking you for saving him from that bullet."

Juniper simply glared at her. "Don't count on it."

She was fairly certain Kyle's relaxed presence was all that kept him from gagging and cuffing her as he'd promised, and carting her back to the Double D.

"You cannot keep me from what's mine."

"You can pet and count your coins once they're in The Grove office. Right now that money is evidence and under federal protection. Isn't that right, Kyle?"

"Yep."

Juniper shot a quick glare at his cousin, thinking he could have offered a little more support.

"I'd like to at least know what's accounted for," she said.

"I'm just as anxious to get that payroll squared away so you can pack up and get off the mountain for good."

"You keep forgetting I own Pine Ridge. I might decide to relocate there."

"I appreciate the warning. I'll be packing my gear the second we get back. McFarland might have been rock stubborn and stone blind when it came to running that camp, but at least the man had a shred of common sense."

Lily's hands fisted at her sides.

"E-e-easy, June," Kyle muttered under breath. "You're bound to fall in that crater you're diggin'."

Juniper glanced at Kyle but lost the chance to ponder his warning as Lily started for the house. His fingers clamped around her wrist. He tugged her back toward the shed, ready to drag her all the way to the horses on the other side of the cliffs.

"Let go of me!" Lily raged, digging her feet as they reached the tall scrub.

"Dammit, Lily! I'll take you back to the ranch myself if I have to, and to hell with the prisoners and payroll!"

"Then I got here just in time." Jed's gruff voice came from the darkness. All three turned to see Jed emerge from the shadows, leading a tall fawn horse by the reins.

Juniper exhaled a sigh of sheer relief.

"Hey, Uncle Jed," Kyle greeted in a cheerful tone.

"Kyle. My wife will be lookin' to tear strips from your hide once she catches wind you're in the area and haven't stopped by."

"You be sure to tell Aunt Rachell I'm looking forward to a long visit, just as soon as I finish helping June clear out some of the local trash."

"I came as soon as I realized she'd gone," Jed said to Juniper. "She had to've been hiding near the barn just before you left."

Lily didn't dare look at either of them, not wanting Juniper to know she'd overheard him talking about her father.

"Can you take her back?" he asked.

"Whenever you're ready."

"She's ready now."

Lily glanced beside her and found Juniper staring at her expectantly. "I've not recovered the strongbox."

"And you're not going to."

"It's my money."

"Anyone holding that money is a moving target until we get it locked up in The Grove," he said, towering over her. "*I will not have your blood on my conscience. Do you hear me? I won't!*"

Conviction blazed in his eyes, stopping her protest.

"Prince Charming here will make sure your money reaches that safe," he said, jabbing his thumb toward Kyle, "since we both know it's wasted breath to ask you to trust a gunslinger."

Kyle's eyes widened with surprise before he lowered

his gaze to his boots, the tip of his cheroot flaring bright as he took a long drag.

Lily was quite certain she was the only one standing there who'd questioned Juniper's integrity.

"I trust you," she said, forcing her voice past her constricted throat.

"Of course you do. That's why you didn't know who to shoot first, me or Clyde Chandler."

"I wasn't trying to shoot you! If you had told me your plans instead of dumping me off at the ranch—"

"If I thought for a moment you'd have listened to reason—"

"You didn't even try, you just...*distracted me,*" she said, spitting the words out like bitter seeds. "And then you snuck off!"

Juniper's steady gaze bore into her. "So if I'd said, 'Miss Carrington, rushing a house full of armed men is far too dangerous to have you along,' you'd have just stayed on the ranch?"

First of all, he never called her Miss Carrington unless he was feigning politeness while giving an introduction, not that his choice of title would have convinced her to stay behind. Knowing she likely wouldn't have allowed him to leave without her no matter what he'd said, she chose not to answer him.

"That's what I thought," Juniper said, as though he'd heard every thought in her mind. "We both know you're single-minded and stubborn as hell," he said in a matter-of-fact sort of way. "And if you say you didn't have designs on pulling that trigger while I was in your sights, *you're lying.*"

His intense blue eyes having the ability to see through her, she wanted to avoid his gaze. But she couldn't. "I wanted more than anything to pull that trigger," she admitted, "and *feel nothing.* To finally find closure. But I couldn't. When I realized your attention had been diverted from the other man, I…" She shut her eyes and drew a ragged breath, the cold grip of fear closing over her.

"You saved me from a bullet," Juniper said, the gruffness in his voice drawing her gaze. "You put your life at risk." He shook his head, his eyes dark with pain. "I'd rather have been *shot,* Lily, than see you come to harm."

Knowing he meant it, an ache settled in her chest. Several times now he'd put her life before his own. Twice she'd held a gun at his chest, and twice he'd made no attempt to defend himself.

You didn't do nothin' but choose to live, Jed had said to him in the barn.

Sometimes it feels like the wrong choice.

The clarity of those words closed around her like a blanket of ice. He would have allowed her to shoot him. More than that, she was quite certain he would have felt he was deserving of the bullet. For a brief moment she saw the frustration and exhaustion weighing on his spirit, felt it in her own and wanted to reach out to him, as though soothing his hurt would heal her own.

She shivered at the thought. *Madness.*

He averted his gaze and drew a hard breath, reclaiming his composure. "I want you to ride back with Jed."

"Okay."

"The payroll—"

"I trust you to take care of it."

He stared at her for a long moment, his stoic expression unchanged. "Then you'll do as I ask and stay at the ranch until I return for you."

A sudden burn of tears clogged her throat. She gave a slight nod of agreement. She'd endured all she could handle for one night.

"All right, then. Where's your horse?"

She motioned toward the trees and bushes leading into the dark channel between the stone cliffs.

Juniper held his hand out to her. She took it, welcoming the warmth of his palm against hers. No matter how odd it seemed, his presence soothed her tangled nerves, giving her strength.

"I'll take care of it, son," Jed said, stepping forward.

Lily's hand tightened on his.

"I got it," Juniper said, walking in the direction she'd indicated. He couldn't shrug off the responsibility he felt for her. Nor could he stand to send her away with tears shining in her eyes.

They walked slowly through a blend of shadows and moonlight, not following any real trail as they carefully maneuvered around rocks and scrub. "How far away did you leave your horse?" he asked.

"A short way beyond the gap."

Half a mile. "You saw me leave the ranch," he said.

She gave a slight nod.

He couldn't believe he hadn't detected her presence or spotted her trailing him. But then, he'd allowed his thoughts to become preoccupied, *with her.*

"I lost you along the way," she said a while later. "So I just followed the ridge to the opening. I only wanted to be sure all the men were apprehended. I'm sorry if I…foiled your ambush."

The catch in her voice tugged at his heart. "You didn't. Other than you scaring the life out of me, I'd say it went rather well. We recovered the bulk of the payroll and none of my men were injured."

"If I hadn't been there, you could have caught the others."

"Doubt it," he said. "My men were outnumbered. I wouldn't have pursued the others until I knew things were under control in the cabin. Either way, they'd have gotten a considerable lead. As for you getting caught in the cross fire, the whole situation was my fault."

She shook her head. "I should have trusted you."

"I don't see how you could have." Juniper knew better than to expect such a thing. He wished he'd realized sooner that it was his presence that endangered her life. Lily wasn't stupid and he doubted she was often reckless. It was his presence that forced her to make rash decisions.

The thought of her coming to harm because of his past—it would have been more than he could bear.

Lily watched her horse come into view up ahead and felt a touch of disappointment. She glanced down at her fingers laced with Juniper's. His palm was warm against hers, his thumb caressing her wrist in slow, lazy circles, every whispering touch sending a maddening current of tingles throughout her entire body. She was certain he wasn't even conscious of the light caress, which only heightened the surge of pleasing sensation.

The moment they stopped beside her horse, he released her hand. She missed the contact.

His stance widened. His hands came down on his hips, pushing back the long sides of his coat. With half of his face hidden in the dark shadows beneath the brim of his hat, she couldn't see his eyes. The hard set of his jaw told her he was about to say something she wasn't going to like.

Any other time, she would have cut her opponent off with a defensive debate before he opened his mouth, but she was simply too tired, too emotionally drained. So she waited, and wished his hat wasn't hiding his eyes.

"I think it'd be best for everyone if I let Kyle take over."

Lily's breath stalled.

"He can fill in for me until you or the folks in The Grove can hire a new sheriff."

"*No.*"

"It's the best solution. If you were anyone else, this situation would be difficult enough. *Damnation*," he grumbled, tugging off his hat, shoving a hand through his matted hair. "I can't make a move without nearly getting you killed."

"My decision to follow you wasn't your fault."

"The hell it wasn't. If I'd been any other lawman, I seriously doubt you'd have felt the need to be charging up to that house."

He couldn't leave now, not when they were just about to turn things around. He was too influential. "You can't go. You must know how the men at Pine Ridge depend on you. The people in The Grove trust you."

"They'll manage just fine. Kyle's good with town folk. And I'm sure Günter will stay on. Hell, they might even talk him into being the sheriff."

"But I… It just won't do. I'd rather you stayed."

He shifted his weight. His eyes narrowed as he stared down at her. "Can you really trust the man who killed your father?"

The words hit her with the force of a blow. The man who killed her father. Her gaze strayed to his guns. That was who she'd gone up to Pine Ridge to find, the man who'd shot her father. And yet she hadn't truly found him. The Juniper Barns standing before her wouldn't have tried to hide from an adversary; he wouldn't have had to be thrown into the street to face down a gunman.

"A man didn't kill my father," she said, the realization coming to her like dawn breaking across a night sky. "A *boy* did."

The surprise and wash of emotion in Juniper's

expression sent a wave of apprehension through Lily. She knew she'd touched a part of the hurt deep inside him, but she wasn't ready to let go of her anger. Her understanding didn't make up for all he'd stolen from her.

"Lily—"

"I'm not saying I forgive you," she said. "Just because I recognize the difference between the frightened actions of a boy and the will of a man doesn't erase the pain you've caused me. I'm just pointing out that... you're not the kind of man I thought you'd be. I know now that you didn't intend such harm, and well...*that's all*. I trust you to protect my employees."

"That's a lot, Lily. More than anyone else who's hunted me down has ever bothered to see."

Anyone else who'd hunted him down...? She frowned, the reminder tightening the ache in her heart. "Yes, well, clarity doesn't always reveal what we'd like to see. I'm certainly not used to seeing my own errors with such clear distinction," she said, glancing down at her hands. "I've made some bad judgments in my handling of the payroll, but I know I can benefit the men at Pine Ridge. I have the resources. And at the risk of sounding arrogant, I'm good with numbers and finding weak points in a business and ways to fix them. I can make that camp productive. I want to set things right."

"You will."

She looked up, surprised by the certainty in his tone. "Not without *you*. I was up at that millhouse. Jim

Grimshaw won't be swayed on anything without your approval. If you leave, they'll think I ran you off."

"Well, you have fired me several times over the past couple days."

"And what difference has that made?" she demanded. "Besides, nothing's official unless it's in writing."

His lips twitched with a grin. "In that case," he said, tugging on his hat, "I'll get the payroll to The Grove office and pull in the staff. They know who's owed what and will make it available to those still in the area."

Lily smiled. Relief poured through her, shaking her, draining the last of her energy.

Juniper turned away and swung up into the saddle. "Com'ere," he said, reaching down for her.

She grabbed his arms as he lifted her onto his lap. Too exhausted to worry about proximity or propriety, she leaned back, resting her head against his shoulder as his arm came around her. He tucked her skirts beneath her legs to keep them from flapping. His hand spread wide over her hip, holding her securely against him as he guided her horse toward the shack, and she really didn't mind his touch.

"Are you going after the men who got away?"

"Lily," he said in a dark tone.

"I'm just curious."

"We have their identities. Charges will be filed against them. They'll be caught."

"Good."

"Does that mean you're ready to step back and let the law handle the criminals?"

She shifted, allowing her arms to slide around his waist as she leaned more snuggly against him. "Yes. I believe I've had my fill."

His other arm tightened around her, hugging her close, and she was fairly certain his lips brushed the top of her hair.

"Good," he said, the gruffness of his whisper stirring warmth in regions of her spirit so recently awakened, sensations she'd only felt with Juniper.

She wanted to ask him why he'd kissed her earlier this evening. Had he only meant to distract her, or had he been overwhelmed by the same stir of passion that continued to draw her to him?

Then again, maybe she didn't really want the answer. No matter his reasons, she didn't need to be contemplating his kisses, certainly not while enjoying the strength and warmth of his embrace. Right now she needed strength, not passion.

As the lights of the house drew near, Lily leaned up, forcing her exhausted body to cooperate. Only Jed stood outside in the yard. He mounted his horse as they approached.

Juniper reined in her horse and gently eased Lily to the ground.

"Everything okay?" Jed asked, staring her straight in the eyes.

"Yes. Thank you for coming after me."

"Not a problem," he said. "I'm just glad neither of you was hurt."

Juniper dismounted and held the horse steady for her as she turned into the saddle.

"I'll see you back at the ranch in a day or two," he said, handing her the reins.

"You'll be careful?"

A firmness seized his expression. "I'll be careful," he agreed, and took a step back.

Jed rode in close beside her. "Let's get you home, darlin'."

Chapter Twelve

Juniper wasn't sure how long he stood there in the cool night air staring into the darkness Lily had ridden through. He wasn't entirely sure what had just happened, but something had changed between them. He'd felt it in the way she had relaxed against him. The tender way she'd looked at him before she rode out—it scared the hell out of him.

He expelled a hard breath and tried to shake off the shudder of ill emotion. *She's probably still in shock.*

Focus on your job, he silently advised himself as he walked back to the house. The one that had just been reinstated. The best thing he could do for the both of them was to get her off the mountain as soon as possible. With a shooter still on the loose and more men to round up, he had to keep a clear head.

He entered the back door and found Jake in the kitchen peering through a half-opened doorway to the front room. Juniper could hear Kyle's voice on the other side, and figured it was time he gave his cousin a hand.

"Hold up," Jake said in a low whisper before he could push the door open. "Kyle's still getting them warmed up for you."

Juniper leaned in to peer through the gap.

"Understand Sheriff Barns is well acquainted with y'all," Kyle was saying. "I, on the other hand, don't have any such affliction. We do things a little different out here."

Juniper eased the door open just enough to see all six prisoners. Their blindfolds removed, Kyle touched the tip of his bowie knife to Calvin's chin, using the sharp point to tilt his face up. "Sheriff Barns wants to hear you spout names. I'm just as willing to hear you scream for your mama."

Calvin trembled and looked on the verge of wetting himself.

Juniper resisted the urge to groan as he stepped back. "Your brother sure has a knack for theatrics."

Jake choked back a laugh. "We're all damn lucky he didn't turn con." He strode toward the table. "Check out that loot," he said, drawing Juniper's attention to the open strongbox. "I can't believe your boss lady was traveling with all this cash."

"McFarland had put her in a bind."

"I'm not so sure it wasn't the other way around. That little lady is something else," Jake said with a note of humor in his voice.

"Yeah," Juniper agreed, while wondering what he'd gotten himself into. The burning in his gut told him he should have cut bait and run while he had the chance.

* * *

Moonlight touched on the silhouette of six men sitting in saddles. Juniper secured a seventh horse to the end of the line, a double load draped over the horse's barrel.

Jake and Günter rode toward the train of horses. They'd be taking their prisoners to the nearest jailhouse while he and Kyle packed up the payroll.

"Hey, Juniper," Calvin said, looking back at him. "When you see Emma, will you tell her not to worry about me?"

"I might as well tell a river to flow uphill."

Calvin's frown deepened, and Juniper couldn't help but feel some sympathy for him. His hands bound to the saddle horn, his feet tied to the stirrups, the kid was a pathetic sight and still didn't have a clue as to the kind of trouble he was in. Prison life was hard on the toughest of men, and Cal still had a lot of growing up to do. June imagined that was about to happen right quick. Armed robbery was guaranteed to garner a prison term.

"I'll tell her I'll do all I can to get you a reduced sentence," he added. "Lord willing, you'll be home by Christmas."

"That long?"

"Hell," grumbled Fred Sullivan, a man in his thirties sitting on the horse ahead of Calvin. "On account of Billy Chandler, a man was kill't. We'll all be lucky not to hang."

Calvin's eyes surged wide.

"After all this foolery," said Juniper, "y'all better be praying Miss Carrington will feel some compassion for your families and be willing to plead your cases to the judge."

"Bes' pray hard," Kyle said, moving in beside him. "The way I heard it, she wasn't treated too kindly the other day."

"He'yah!" Günter shouted, prompting the train of horses into motion. Jake rode in behind them.

Kyle turned toward their own mounts. A third horse had been loaded down with the strongbox. "We bes' get movin' if we're going to reach your little mountain town by sunup."

"It's not *my* town," Juniper said, feeling more than a little agitated as he watched men he considered his friends being led off to an uncertain fate.

"Uh-huh," said Kyle. "And Lily Carrington ain't your gal."

Juniper sent him a look that made most folks pale in his presence. "She's not."

Chuckling, Kyle mounted his horse. "Get a move on, cousin," he said, opening his carbine rifle, making sure it was loaded and locked before dropping it into the scabbard at the side of his saddle. "All this cash is starting to make the back of my neck itch."

It was nearly nine o'clock in the morning when Juniper and Kyle shut the door on the tall safe in the back room of The Grove office, both men heaving a sigh of relief as the lock clicked into place.

"We'll get started on this straight away." Otis Baker, a stout, balding, workhorse of a man, stood in the doorway. A meticulous accountant, he didn't take guff from anyone. The day Carrington's notices had arrived announcing another pay hold, he had tossed the leaflets onto the boardwalk, loaded his shotgun and made it known that their new employer's empty coffers weren't his doing or his problem—*it had become Juniper's.*

"We can have payments tallied and sorted by late this afternoon," Otis said as they walked into the front room, "and start easing some of the strain on the folks around here."

"Thank goodness." Dory Baker dropped a box onto a long counter and tucked a strand of silvery-gray hair behind her ear before pulling out a stack of files. "The way tempers have been flaring in town, I've been leery to leave my house these past few weeks."

"Some of the money is still missing," Juniper said, "but with so many moved on, there should be plenty to cover the back wages of those still on our roster."

"You got some cash locked up over at the sheriff's office. After Jonas was arrested, folks came forward straight away."

"We'll make sure Griggs brings it over, and we'll send a wire to get one of Carrington's men down here to go over the numbers with you. If need be, me and my men will wait for our wages until the rest of the funds are recovered or replaced."

"You're a good boy, Juniper," Dory said, placing her slender hand on his arm, her blue eyes twinkling.

Kyle's lips slid into a smirk, and June had to fight not to reveal the same reaction. Dory was a tad biased. He'd recruited the older couple from San Francisco two years ago. They'd been longtime acquaintances of Jed's and had just retired from their own accounting practice and were looking to relocate in the Sierras. They'd been extremely helpful in straightening out McFarland's payment system.

"I'm not hurting for cash," he admitted, having built up a considerable savings while working on the Double D. "If my deputies complain, they can come see me about the matter."

"Folks will likely be storming the doors once they catch word we're stocked up," Dory said, her usual smile replaced with a look of concern.

"That's why I'm here," said Kyle. "To help keep everything running in an orderly fashion. Günter should be along by the time you open your doors."

"If we're all settled, I'll head on back to my folks' ranch."

"Are you sure you wouldn't like to rest a while?" Dory asked. "Breakfast is still on the stove at our house and you're welcome to a guest room."

"Not a bad idea," Kyle put in. She'd already offered Kyle a bed to snooze on while the couple readied the payroll.

Juniper had to get back to Lily. "Thank you, but I have other business to attend to."

Kyle walked him out. "You should get some sleep before heading back down into those hills," he said for a second time.

"Won't do any good," he said. He couldn't close his eyes without seeing her, and he wouldn't be able to relax until he was back at the ranch. If he happened to nod off in the saddle, his horse would get him home. "I left Scout over at the livery a couple days ago. He knows the way home without any prompting."

Kyle gave a nod.

"Thanks for your help, Kyle."

"Anytime. And I'm not going anywhere soon, not until I bring in Billy Chandler. Your two deputies ought to be able to handle this town by tomorrow. I'll head up to Pine Ridge and have a look around."

"We'll meet you there."

Kyle gave him a measuring glance. "You're really going to take her back up to that camp?"

"Lily has a mind to settle the camp herself and I have no right to stop her."

"The hell you don't. You're the sheriff. What happened to laying down the law?"

"She's owns Pine Ridge. Only reason she was so cooperative last night is because she was shaken up."

Kyle chuckled and shook his head. "Is that what you think?"

Juniper didn't answer. "I'll give her a day at the camp. Can you contact some local lawmen for me, arrange a carriage and a few guards for her trip home? I want her protected all the way to 'Frisco."

"I'll set it up," said Kyle.

"Lily's my main concern."

"I noticed." Kyle's goading grin tightened the muscles in his neck. "You were guarding her the way my sisters would hover over a new Christmas kitten."

"She's my employer and she was in shock."

"You're sweet on her."

"No, I'm not."

"Give it up, June. You were ready to pound me into next week just for talking to her. I'd wager you've already kissed her."

Juniper tensed and Kyle laughed.

"It was that bad, huh?"

"Shut up," he grumbled, not proud of the lack of restraint he'd shown where Lily was concerned. "I'd feel best if you'd be the one to ride along, make sure she gets back to San Francisco. I know you want to be there when we bring in Chandler, but I'd see this as a personal favor."

"So will I," Kyle said, annoyance replacing his smile. "I'm a U.S. marshal, not a goddamn lady's attendant. You'll *owe me* for that one."

"I'll owe you, then," he said, more than appreciative of Kyle's begrudging agreement. "We'll be in Pine Ridge day after tomorrow. I'll take Lily and her cousin up through the south entrance. Once the men catch word that their pay is ready, there'll be a stampede coming down that main road. I want to avoid any more unwanted confrontations."

"Good idea, so long as your lovely boss won't mind the added hours of travel."

"On that I'm not giving her a choice."

"'Course that also gives you two another day alone. Sure you want that extra day of temptation?"

"There's no temptation. Her cousin will be with us, not that it would matter. When Lily has her wits about her, she hates me."

"Uh-huh. You keep telling yourself that."

Muttering a curse, he turned away from Kyle's annoying grin and led his horse toward the livery so he could fetch Scout. He damn well would!

She hates me. And he had no business wanting anything else from a woman he had nothing to offer but a past full of painful memories.

The grass cold against her bare feet, Lily tightened the belt of the long white wrapper Rachell had lent her and walked farther into the yard. Thin clouds darkened the face of the moon, shielding some of its light. Despite her exhaustion, she hadn't been able to sleep. She'd hardly slept the night before. Visions of bloodshed haunting her every time she closed her eyes, she'd wished for the warmth and comfort of Juniper's touch.

Tired of spending another night staring up at a dark ceiling for hours, she'd come out here to sit on the porch swing and watch the stars for a while…but even the swing stirred troubling memories, images of a life she'd too-long forgotten.

Chilled by the light breeze, she continued across the yard and stepped into the darkness of the barn. She reached for the box of matches she knew was tucked above the eave just inside the doors. She lit a lamp and carried it toward the stall housing the horse she'd ridden from The Grove. "Hello, sweet girl," she said, then glanced up at the lamp hook so high on the post, she wouldn't come close to reaching it.

Using an upturned pail, she stepped up and hooked the lantern's handle into place. The horse nudged her before she could step down.

"Lonely?" Lily asked. She stroked the horse's dark mane. "I've been surrounded by company all day."

As far as she could tell, Jed hadn't told anyone about her venture the night before. His silence didn't ease the emptiness she felt in Juniper's absence. While she enjoyed visiting with his family, their kindness didn't stop the flood of memories that often took her by surprise.

Jed had stayed home the entire day, doing chores around the house and constantly checking up on her, or creating an excuse to kiss his wife. They reminded her so much of her own parents, constantly doting on each other. Sitting in the kitchen with Rachell and her girls, talking and laughing as she helped them peel apples for pies, had brought back memories of sitting in her Missouri kitchen, helping Geneva and her mother with supper. Watching Rachell, full of energy and smiles as she buzzed around the kitchen, had also spawned a trickle of troubling images.

Lily was struck by a sharp contrast between Rachell and her mother. While her mother was always smiling, she lacked energy. Rose Palmer had been easily taxed. As far as Lily could remember, her mother could tolerate little activity, becoming winded by a walk not much farther than across the yard. While she'd enjoyed strolls through the meadows with her husband, she would often come back in his arms.

As a child, Lily had spent little time wondering about her mother's frequent exhaustion, which now struck her as odd. Geneva had always been there to run the house, much like a grandmother, taking care of most of the chores and tending to Mother when she'd needed a rest. A woman of normal health didn't nap several times in a day.

Your mother's a delicate sort of flower.

Her father had said those words often enough. A simple explanation for a child. Lily had a notion her mother had been far more than simply delicate. There had been days when her mother had been too tired to get out of bed at all. Yet she couldn't recall anyone ever saying outright that Mother was sick. Everyone had seemed to simply accept her frailty.

Why wouldn't they have told her something was wrong?

"Lily?"

Startled by Juniper's voice, she turned so quickly the bucket tipped. She shrieked and gripped the stall, spooking the mare.

Juniper was beside her in a flash, his hand steadying

her as she found her footing. She reached out, her hands landing against Juniper's bare chest.

"Oh!" she said, her gaze locking on the firm muscles and golden chest hair revealed through his open shirt.

He took a step back, his expression nothing short of befuddled as he looked from her to the tin pail then back to her. She was too happy to see him to care.

"Lily, what are you—"

"You're back early," she said, unable to fight her smile.

"Did you miss me?" he asked, half joking.

"I was worried."

So was he...*now.* Didn't she realize how incredibly enticing she looked, her pink lips smiling, her long hair swirled around her shoulders, her bare feet poking out from beneath her nightgown? His gaze slid back up, and he found that her toes weren't the only thing peeking out of that all-too-thin veil of white.

Sweet mercy. Staring at the vision before him, he had to wonder if he'd fallen asleep in the bathhouse. Lily's bright smile and appreciative gaze were something he'd only seen in his dreams. The heated stir of his body assured him he was fully awake, and well on his way to becoming fully aroused.

Aw, hell.

"What are you doing out here in the middle of the night?"

She folded her arms, covering the rosy-tipped evidence of her chill. "I couldn't sleep. I trust the payroll delivery went well?"

"It did," he said, reminding himself he barely had the energy to stand as he pulled his lust in check. Remembering the bedroll he'd dropped in the door-way when he'd seen her fall, he went back to get it. "The Bakers said they'd start passing out wages by late afternoon."

Lily stood in front of the clean hay-filled stall he intended to sleep in. He carefully moved past her, released the ties and fanned the wide, striped blanket out over the pile of straw. "I imagine there's some happy folks in The Grove tonight. By tomorrow most of your employees will be on their way to collecting their pay."

"Do you intend to sleep out here?"

He collapsed back onto his makeshift bed, propped his arms over his raised knees as a polite gesture to hide the tent in his britches and stared up at Lily's questioning gaze with a kind of wonder. She had no business standing there in her nightclothes, him being only half-dressed to boot!

"You're supposed to be using my room and I didn't want to wake the bunkhouse. Tired as I am, a bed of hay will be as comfy as any other. I sure didn't expect to find you out here at this hour."

She picked up her pail and took a step toward him. "I was going a little stir-crazy up in that room." She leaned against the edge of the stall. "I thought coming out here might help me to relax."

"I wouldn't have guessed you'd find the musty scents of a barn to be soothing."

"That's because you don't really know me."

"No more than you know me."

She stared at him for a moment, then gave a slight nod. "Fair enough."

The admission surprised him. But then, her outspoken honesty was something he was starting to expect in her. He decided it was one of the qualities he liked best about her. Good or bad, she told it the way she saw it. And while she sure didn't like to be proven wrong, she used that sharp mind to reevaluate, strategize and find new ground.

Which kept him wary, a sense of caution that turned to outright dread as she took another small step forward and placed her bucket inside his temporary bedroom. She sat on the makeshift stool, crossed her arms over her knees and looked at him as though she had real business on her mind.

Sweet God, he needed sleep. A quick scrubbing in the bathhouse behind the bunks had given him just enough energy to grab his gear and walk to the barn.

"I trust my family has been hospitable?" he said conversationally, his mind searching for a way to politely ask her to leave so he could pull off his boots and pass out.

"Yes." Soft pink lips quirked with a smile. "They're wonderful."

Her toes wriggled beneath the veil of white as she

continued to sit there, not seeming in any hurry to leave. She looked about as soft and delicate as a Christmas angel. But there was far more to Lily than met the eye. She wasn't sitting out here just to look pretty and fuel his fantasies.

Damnation. The unspoken questions darkening her green eyes couldn't be worse than her toe-wiggling silence.

"What's on your mind, darlin'?" he asked, unable to keep a hint of dread from his tone.

"Did you see him often? My father, I mean."

Oh, God. He wasn't sure he was ready for this. But he couldn't deny her. "At least a dozen times during the year I spent with my uncle. I didn't want to shoot him, Lily. I liked Red."

She gave a slight nod of acknowledgment. "Did he frequent saloons?"

He saw the worry in her gaze, seeds of doubt he'd likely planted from the fragments of information he'd given. "Not in the way you might think. Red came in from time to time for a drink and a card game. He always kept his wits about him and I never saw him with any of the uh…*ladies.* I'd venture that he stopped by to see what loose-lipped drunk would leak information on an outlaw's whereabouts. My uncle's hangout was a magnet for such riffraff."

"Why did he call you out?"

Part of him had known this was coming, that she'd want answers he couldn't give. He couldn't tell her more than what he'd seen.

"My uncle and his lies had the power to bring out the worst in men. He knew Red was fast and he wanted a gunfight. I don't know what was going on with Red that night, but he seemed in a bad way. At the rate he was drinking and my uncle was talkin', I could sense trouble and lit out of there straightaway."

"What do you mean, 'he was in a bad way'? Was he hurt?"

Juniper had never understood the change he'd seen in Red that night, but looking into Lily's sullen green eyes, he had a hunch. "He seemed sad," he said plainly. "I can't tell you what was going on with him, Lily, because I don't know."

Lily tried to think back to that week, the days before he'd left for what he'd called a business trip. Had he said anything to her? She recalled that Mother had been sleeping a lot and he hadn't wanted to go, to leave them again.

"Mother was sick."

"With influenza?"

Lily looked up in surprise.

"Reginald told me she died of influenza a couple weeks after Red died."

Old pain seeped into her chest. She'd always known that everything she'd been told about Mother's death had been wrong. "I think Mother had been ill for a long while."

"Had she been getting worse?"

"I think so. But she still smiled. After losing

Daddy…" Tears burned at her eyes as she shook her head. "She just gave up."

"I'm sorry, Lily."

"He was a good father," she said, trying to understand why the man she'd idolized her whole life would behave so irrationally.

"I can see that," Juniper said, his rich tone moving through her like a caress. "He raised an exceptional daughter."

"I don't see why being sad over Mother would have driven him to do something so dangerous."

"My uncle had a hand in that. He filled his head full of lies and his gut full of whiskey. When Red caught me he was drunk and fired-up mad. He made a mistake. Or maybe I made the mistake by reaching for my gun."

Juniper wished he had the answers she wanted. Staring at the straw between his boots, he drove his fingers through his hair. Not wanting the see the pain in her eyes, he couldn't look at her. "No matter how many times I relive it, I can't find any answers worth keeping. And I can't change the outcome."

Gentle fingers brushed across his brow, pushing aside his damp hair.

Her touch shocked him, and sent a rippling sensation of sheer pleasure prickling across his skin. He lifted his head and was unsettled by the clear compassion shining in her eyes. He didn't want her sympathy. He didn't want the attraction that hit him harder each time he was in her presence. *No good will come from it.*

"You should go on to bed."

Her fingers stroked his forearm as she stared up at him with a concentration that told him his suggestion to go inside hadn't even registered in her mind. The woman wasn't easily swayed unless she was good and ready to be swayed.

If she knew how deeply her touch was affecting him, she'd likely run for the house and bolt the door.

"What happened to your parents?"

That had been one of the last things he'd expected her to ask. His skin seemed to tighten over his entire body. He glanced back at the small hand gently caressing his arm. The slow slide of her fingertips damn near had him shaking from the strain of fighting an urge to return her pleasing touches.

"Lily, I think it'd be best if we talked more tomorrow." He eased back, pulling away from her touch. He stretched his back and settled deeper into the hay—putting some distance between them. "It's late and I'm beyond exhausted."

The disappointment in her eyes was a blow to his gut. "You know so much about me and I don't know anything about you."

"It won't change anything."

Her frown deepened. Her somber expression made him ache in places he didn't even know he had. He released a hard sigh and said, "I don't remember my mother. She died when I was real young. My father worked for the stage line after the war."

"He raised you?"

"Partially. He was gone mostly and left me in the mission until I was old enough to ride the stage with him."

"He left you in an orphanage?"

"With no wife or family to look after me, there wasn't much else he could do," Juniper reasoned. "I was nine or so when he came and got me for good, said I was old enough to ride along and load luggage."

"You worked on the stage? The stage lines are treacherous."

"They are that," he said, feeling a touch of old sorrow. "But I was young and found it exciting. A few years later I started riding shotgun. Better pay, better seat." The image of him sitting up on the seat beside his pa brought the start of a smile to his lips.

"How old were you?"

"At the end, thirteen."

Her eyes widened.

"I've always been taller than most kids, and folks assumed I was older than my true age. I didn't mind the work, so long as I got to stay with my pa."

"And you shot at men?"

"I protected our passengers and cargo," he said. "Shooting came fairly naturally for me. From the time I was ten there wasn't a competition I couldn't win. I could discourage attackers from a long way off. But on that last run, there were just too many."

"They shot your father?"

"I was taking down as many as I could," he said. "I saw a rider coming up fast on the left. Before I could shift my aim, my pa took a bullet. That outlaw got his ticket to hell a second later, but I was too late. My pa held on. When I'd run out of rifle ammo, he put his pistol in my other hand."

"You fought them off?"

"I shot down every last one of 'em. By the time we made it to town Pa was in bad shape. He died on the doctoring table. Next thing I knew I was being hailed as some kind of hero for saving the passengers. It was like folks didn't notice my pa was dead," he said, shaking his head. "A couple weeks later an uncle I'd never met appeared outta nowhere, ready to claim me. I was sent to live with him and got a good taste of hell."

"Where is your uncle now?"

"He died in a gunfight." June didn't feel up to rehashing how Jed had shot down his uncle while protecting Rachell. "I came west with Jed and Rachell and they took me in."

"You have a wonderful family."

He gave a slight nod of agreement. "Meeting Rachell was one of the best things that ever happened to me."

"It's quite apparent that they miss you. Why do you live so far away from them?"

"Because I care about them. Their love doesn't change who I am or what I've done. Do you think you're the first to come seeking retribution?"

Lily's eyes flinched.

He figured that reminder should abate her curiosity and send her rushing off to bed. But she didn't budge from her perch. Maybe if he got ready for bed, she'd take the hint. He lifted a foot and tugged off his boot.

Lily shot that theory to hell by scooting off her tin pail and plopping onto the blanket right beside him.

"Is that why you became a lawman?" she asked, tilting her pretty face to look up at him.

Juniper laughed to keep from wincing. *Hell.* Clearly, this was his punishment. She was going to torture him.

"I fell into that sheriff job," he said, tugging at his second boot. If he was going to endure her interrogation, suffer the sweet, floral scent driving him to distraction, he'd damn well get comfortable. "I started out at Pine Ridge just like all the others."

"You were a lumberjack?"

"I worked on John Donnelly's crew. Those mountain roads were plagued with bandits. Men had been killed. Some of the timbermen with families in The Grove got real skittish about going home close to payday. When John was expecting his third child to be born and had to get home with his pay, I offered to ride down with him."

"You were robbed?"

He stared at her for a moment before saying, "Not quite."

"You shot the highwaymen."

"I protected my friends and landed a job as sheriff. I told McFarland I'd help with the bandits if he'd set up a new system for delivering pay to the men."

"Mr. Grimshaw mentioned you were the one who set up The Grove office."

Juniper shrugged. "It made sense. A man looking to spend his pay has got to find a township anyhow. By the time we worked out the new system, McFarland was too far in the hole and didn't want to dip into his private coffers to save his own company. He could have, you know? Instead, he let his company slide into financial ruin, and took more than he put in."

"When it comes to Pine Ridge, you are definitely the hero," Lily said reflectively. "And I'm the outlaw."

Instinctively, his arm moved around her. She trembled from his light touch and he realized his error. "We're both just people, Lily, trying to do our jobs best we can. Sometimes the wrong choice seems like the best one at the time. I surely hadn't meant to get you abducted and roughed up by sending you down the mountain. Then again, sometimes what's right feels plain wrong. It wasn't easy to arrest men who'd only been trying to feed their families."

"But they believe in you," she said. "So do I."

The urge to kiss her burned through him, dissolving his restraint.

He'd already made that mistake.

"Darlin', it's late," he said. "We both need to get some sleep."

"I know. But I like being near you."

She said the words so softly, Juniper wasn't sure he'd heard her right.

"Lily, I—"

Her hands slid into his open shirt and across his chest, ending his words in a low groan. She shifted onto her knees, her green eyes a mirror of desire as her hands smoothed over his shoulders, around his neck and into his hair. She tugged him toward her, and he went willingly.

He could no more resist the gentle hands drawing him to her mouth than he could have roped the moon.

Chapter Thirteen

The moment his lips touched hers, Lily let go of everything but the wonderful tendrils of sensation she felt only while in Juniper's embrace. His arms closed around her, crushing her against him. Her knees slipped past his hips, the sudden contact of his body creating instant friction. She'd been waiting for this moment ever since she'd left him standing alone in the moonlight.

Returning his fervent kiss, she couldn't taste enough of him, feel enough of him. The heat of his skin seduced her fingertips as she explored the bunched muscles of his shoulders and arms, pushing his shirt out of her way in the process. Her persistence stalled the hands caressing her back in sweeping strokes.

His frustrated growl vibrated against her mouth as he released her to shrug off his shirt. The sight of his muscles flexing in the lamplight made her breasts ache. More than anything she wanted to feel her skin pressed to his. She grabbed up the bottom of her gown and wrapper and tugged them up, over her head.

"Lily. You…"

She was on fire. The look on his face, a combination of tenderness and desire, was compliment enough. She trailed her fingers across his muscled torso and was shocked by the ripples of pleasure she felt just touching him. The sheer power of Juniper's body was startling, yet she'd never felt more secure.

His fingers brushed her sides, the light touch eliciting a tingling surge that shook her. She'd never experienced this kind of passion, bursts of sweet lightning rippling through her mind, body and soul. She realized she wanted to delight him in the same way, ever so much. But she didn't know how. She'd never felt such a need to be a part of someone. "I want to please you."

"You do." His lips brushed her shoulder. She tightened her arms around his neck and felt a tremor go through him as her breasts pressed against his chest. His teeth grazed her skin bringing another shocking burst of pleasure. He kissed a trail across her throat, each brush of his lips making her tremble.

"Are you innocent?" he whispered against her ear.

The fact that he'd ask such a question after she'd behaved so brazenly made her smile. "No. Just inexperienced. I've never felt like this. Wanting to touch. To be touched."

Juniper leaned back, taking her with him, turning her onto the blanket. His smoldering gaze entranced her. Anticipation bubbled inside her.

"Are you sure about this?"

She only smiled as his lips slowly claimed hers. She'd never been so sure of anything in her life. She welcomed his warmth. His touch. Nothing had ever felt more right. She mapped his arms, his back, smoothing her palms down the firm contoured lines of his body until her hands collided with denim.

She slipped her fingers just inside his waistband and slid them around to the front. Pulling at his button fly, she brushed against the blunt proof of his arousal.

Juniper's breath broke.

"I want these off. I want to feel all of you."

Juniper groaned and lifted her hand away from his hungry body. He knew he should stop this here and now, before they both did something they'd regret. But there was a pleading in her gaze he couldn't refuse, a need he sensed burning as deep as his own. He rolled to the side, tugged at the buttons and shucked his pants in one smooth motion.

He pulled her back into his arms, desperate for her kiss. He melded their mouths, kissing her as though she might dissolve into a dream if he let go. She shifted against him like a living flame as he caressed the satiny swell of her breast and tight peak rising against his palm. Her hands pushed down his back leaving sparks beneath his skin as those slender fingers curved over his backside.

He slid down and drew the velvet tip of her breast into his mouth. She moaned, her body twisting sensually against him. His gaze on the thatch of shimmering gold and amber curls lower still, his hand slid down her belly to the slick heat of her core. At his first gliding touch Lily tensed. Her legs clamped tight, trapping his hand against her moist center, halting his progress.

"Lily?"

The small, gentle hands that had been caressing his back gripped his shoulders. She stared up at him with wide, blinking eyes, as though she'd just woken from a deep sleep, or a nightmare.

"Do you want to stop?"

"No," she said in a pant, though he saw indecision in her gaze. "If you're ready…I can…tolerate the rest."

"Tolerate?" He eased back. *The rest?*

Whatever her past experience had been, her puckered brow suggested she wasn't looking forward to receiving "the rest." Her hands stroked down his chest encouragingly, her tense smile telling him she was ready to face whatever she thought he intended to do to her. Damn if he wasn't touched by her bravery.

He returned her gentle caress, watching her green eyes glaze with pleasure as he stroked her satin folds. He could bring her release without taking her. He refused to take anything else from this woman.

He eased down, kissing her lightly. "I'm not going to take you that way, Lily," he whispered. "So you needn't worry."

"But I—"

Whatever she was about to say was lost in a fragment of breath as he found and circled the slick bud of her passion. Heat welled to his touch. Her head tilted back, body arching, opening to him.

My God. She had such passion in her.

"I'm only going to give," he said, his lips following the graceful line of her neck. "As much as you're willing to take."

Lily didn't understand his words, she only knew he was setting her blood on fire, melting her from the inside out with sharp, shocking currents of heat.

The warmth of his mouth closed over her breast as his caress deepened, creating bursts of sweet lighting. His tongue and teeth teased until her back arched. She twisted against the mounting tension of his double assault. He treated her other breast to the same sweet torment. Pleasure spiked and burst, rippling through her until she cried out.

"Shh," he whispered against her skin.

He expected her to be quiet? She could hardly think with what he was doing to her.

"Juniper?" she said, realizing his lips were making a slow, tingling descent down her body. She shuddered as his breath dusted the vulnerable junction between her thighs.

"Juniper!"

His mouth claimed her in the most shocking way. A lash of intense pleasure impaled her back against the blanket. His tongue caressed and teased, ravaging her body with searing bursts of wild sensation. Every new surge of release coiled a deeper tension. She bucked against his hold. The pressure of his mouth changed, and fire burst and spiraled as her world came apart in wave after wave of shattering pulses.

Regretfully, Juniper released her. Striving to maintain a shred of control, he kissed his way up her flushed skin. Her limp arms reached for him. Lily shuddered as he drew her close.

He'd at least given her passion. Hardly a selfless act, he thought, grinning into her hair. He'd thoroughly enjoyed every heart-pounding moment of it. She nestled closer, the light whisper of her skin against his adding to the harsh grip of hunger still eating his body. Her lips brushed his jaw.

"Did you enjoy 'the rest'?" he asked teasingly, kissing her flushed cheek.

She moaned her approval.

He dipped his tongue into the tender spot behind her ear, smiling as she trembled against him in response.

"Juniper?"

"Hmm?"

Lily shivered as his mouth followed to the curve of her neck, her question escaping her thoughts. She'd barely settled back into her mind. She'd never imagined…anything so powerful.

Easing up, Lily stared into eyes darkened by passion. She shifted more firmly over him. His aroused body rubbed against her core like hot stone, shocking her with a renewed surge of pleasure.

Juniper groaned. His hands closed over her thighs, halting her movement and pulling her fully astride him.

She glanced down at his body pressed to hers, and desire stirred, need coiling inside her. She moved again, measuring, *melting* as the tendrils of pulsing pleasure he'd created with his mouth reawakened.

"Jun—"

He moved beneath her, fragmenting her breath over the rest of his name. The teasing touches left her wanting more of him. She pressed harder, wanting all of him.

"I want you," she said huskily.

Juniper clenched his teeth, the slick heat of her passion threatening to undo him. His body trembled. His muscles tightened, fighting the urge to slam into the tight satin sheath of her body.

"I want to be part of you."

Her words dragged another groan from deep inside him. He threaded his fingers through her hair, drawing her mouth to his. "Then take me," he breathed against her lips.

Lily pushed up, her eyes wide with shock, but surprise quickly gave way to a spark of desire and curiosity.

Juniper couldn't help but grin.

"How?" she asked, and his pulse kicked.

I shouldn't, he scolded, even as his hands stroked the back of her thighs, urging her up. Her gaze hot on his, she eased over him. The first touch of penetration brought an overwhelming sting of pleasure. The tight heat of her body slowly closing over him was the sweetest torture he'd ever known.

Her fingers flexed on his chest. "Juniper?"

He gripped her hips, lifting her slightly then flexing as he pulled her to him, over him, around him. A deep shuddering pleasure expanded between them. Her green eyes widened with surprise, desire blazing as she shared his tremors.

She moved again, an agonizing retreat, a glorious penetrating return. He matched her rhythm, driving her faster, harder each time, until she took all of him.

She was a vision burning into his soul: her skin flushed, every sensuous movement of her body hurling them toward oblivion. Juniper closed his hand over her hips and thrust harder.

Lily arched, the tight sheath of her body convulsing around him. Her broken cries carried his name through the barn. He pulled her down on top of him and took her mouth in a hard kiss, muffling her cries as he turned her onto the blanket. He plunged deeply as pleasure burst through him. Lily's arms and legs closed around him, gripping him tightly as he poured every bit of himself into her, their shared cries of completion lost in their joined mouths.

Spent and panting for breath, he rolled to the side, keeping her pressed against him. She wiggled closer and pressed her face to his neck. Wet tears brushed hotly against his skin.

Had he not felt her smile, he'd have worried he'd displeased her. Her deep, contented sigh dispelled that notion.

"Oh, June."

He blindly reached for the edge of the blanket and pulled it over her. A grin on his lips, he gave in to complete exhaustion.

Juniper woke before dawn to the swooping sound of a barn owl returning from its late-night hunt. The lamp spilled soft golden light over the stall. Lily lay snuggled against him, her thigh tucked beneath his, her arm draped over his waist. Strands of straw clung to the tangled curls of her hair.

Disheveled, wanton and utterly beautiful.

He didn't want to wake her, but he knew he couldn't watch her sleep in his arms much longer without exploring all that feminine softness, awakening her to the intense passion they'd shared the night before.

He couldn't chance them being caught together by any early risers. The last thing she needed was to be found in bed with her father's killer. He was afraid to wake her, dreading the regret he'd surely find lurking in her eyes when realization set in of who she'd actually been rolling with in the hay.

"Lily?" He brushed a light reddish curl away from her face.

She snuggled closer, every shift tormenting his unruly body.

"Wake up, sweetheart," he said a bit louder.

She stretched, the firm pink crowns of her breasts rising toward his mouth, tempting him. She lifted her head from his shoulder and blinked up at him, her full lips tipped with a smile.

"Good morning," he said, reaching up to pick a few pieces of straw from her hair.

"Didn't I fire you?"

Chuckling, he pulled her down on top of him. She never failed to surprise him. He wanted nothing more than to enjoy this last bit of time alone with her. "A few times."

She kissed him lightly on the mouth. "I'm glad you didn't listen to me."

"Should I get that in writing?" he teased.

She made a purring sound, heedlessly stroking her body against his. Her eyes brightened, apparently liking his growing reaction.

"Lily—" Her lips branded his chest.

"You feel wonderful." She loved his warmth, the scent of his skin. "My goodness," she said, the words unraveling in a long sigh. "I had no idea anything could feel so good."

Juniper grinned up at her. "I'd say you *tolerated* me quite well."

Recalling her words from the night before, heat rushed to her cheeks. "I didn't know it could be like

that," she admitted. "No wonder Edmond was so furious with me."

Juniper quirked an eyebrow and shifted up onto his
elbow. "The previous lover?"

"Oh, dear." While she knew nothing of paramour
etiquette, mentioning a man's name while lying naked
in the arms of another was surely in poor taste. "I've
spoiled the moment, haven't I?"

He smiled and leaned up to kiss the tip of her nose.
"Not possible."

She was certain he couldn't have given a sweeter
answer.

"But now that you've piqued my curiosity, who's
Edmond?"

"The man who ruined me."

Juniper's muscles bunched beneath her as surprise
and anger darkened his eyes, and she realized he must
have been thinking she meant by force.

"No, no," she said, patting his chest. "It was all my
doing. Edmond was, um, well-known for socializing
with the ladies, you could say. I was looking to be rid
of my virginity and he was quite willing to perform
the chore."

Juniper was struck damn near speechless. *"Chore?"*
he asked in disbelief.

Lily sat up, the flush in her cheeks brightening as
she grabbed the nearest item of clothing, which happened to be his blue shirt, and held it to her beautiful
blushing breasts, shielding her nudity. "It certainly
felt like a chore to me," she said, pushing her tangled

hair away from her face. "Who better to divest me of my innocence than a professional philanderer? Or so I thought at the time," she added in a whisper. "I will admit it was not one of my better plans."

Understanding her initial unease last night when he'd first touched her brought a rush of new concern. Juniper sat up, his arm curving around her slender waist. Her mouth set in an unhappy curve, she didn't look up at him.

"Was he rough with you?"

She fiddled with a button on his shirt. "Not exactly. I was hardly his first deflowering, and he seemed determined to…well, he didn't want it to be painful." She glanced up at him from beneath thick amber eyelashes. "*It didn't work*. I was woefully naive and I didn't like him touching me. I just wanted it over with."

"Why the rush to be rid of your virginity?"

"My relatives were determined to marry me off. They wanted access to my inheritance by arranging a *suitable* husband, meaning a man they could control. I wasn't having any part of it. Nor had I expected… sex," she whispered, "to be so painful. The moment I was breached I assumed the deed was done and pulled away."

"Before he, uh…"

"That wasn't the worst of it. We were in his carriage, having left in the midst of an opera. I wanted to be seen with him, so that my aunt wouldn't doubt my claims of indecency, which turned out to be an unjust concern. No one in San Francisco could doubt the indecency of our brief affair."

"Why's that?"

Regret became a lump in her throat, stalling her voice. "In my haste to get away from him, I fell out of the carriage, tumbling to the ground in an open ball gown. Edmond landed on his knees in the doorway in an attempt to catch me. His trousers in a heap, the solid proof of what we'd been doing stood out clearly in the lamplight, there for all to see. The opera having just let out, there were plenty of onlookers." She leaned forward, pressing her warm face against his chest. "Startled shrieks could be heard for miles."

"Ah, Lily," Juniper said, his hand gently stroking her hair.

"*It was dreadful.* I wanted so badly for the ground to just open up and swallow me."

"All that to avoid courtship?"

"I hadn't intended on such public humiliation." She sat back, curious about his reaction. Though Juniper had the good grace not to laugh at her misfortune, she saw a touch of amusement in his eyes, which added to her embarrassment. "Good grief, why am I even telling you all this?"

"Perhaps you fear another embarrassing scandal?"

I should. Somewhere deep in her mind, she knew she'd spent the night with a man she'd hated for most of her life, whom only days ago she had intended to kill. All those thoughts faded as her gaze slid across his muscular form. *Scandalous.*

Her lips slid upward in a crooked grin. "You'd be worth the scandal."

Juniper groaned against a hard surge of desire. Her arms curved around his neck, his shirt dropping away as she leaned up and he met her kiss. If they didn't get some clothes and distance between them quickly, he wouldn't be able to think about anything beyond recapturing the intense passion they'd shared.

He broke the kiss and glanced around, nothing short of desperate to find her nightgown. Spotting the discarded item near their feet, he snatched it up, saying, "I doubt you'll feel that way if we get caught in this barn together." He shook out the white fabric and proffered it to her.

"You sure you're not just in a hurry to be rid of me?"

Her lower lip protruded in the slightest, prettiest pout he'd ever seen.

"I'd love nothing more than to hold you right now and repeat 'the rest.'" He stood, revealing just how ready he was to ravish her once again. Her mischievous grin wasn't helping him to do the right thing. "But I wasn't joking about getting caught. Work starts early around here."

Gathering up the bottom of her gown, he held it up to drape over her. "Com'ere."

She stood and he pulled the long nightdress into

place. She slid her arms through the long sleeves, smiling up at him. "You're very sweet."

"So are you," he said, brushing a light kiss across her lips.

"No," she said, a touch of sadness in her tone. "I'm not."

"You are to me," he said, handing her the matching wrapper.

Staring into his sober blue eyes, Lily actually believed him. She smiled and he turned away. She pulled on the thin robe and tied the sash as she watched him dress with brazen appreciation; his long, masculine legs stepping into his Levi's, the soft, worn denim sliding over the tight curve of his backside, lean hips and the rest of his masculinity, which presently didn't fit into his pants quite so easily.

I've truly lost my mind. She'd just spent the night with Juniper Barns…and she couldn't feel even slightly abashed.

Who knew *crazy* felt this good?

Juniper stepped into his boots, saying, "Let's get you back to your room before the house wakens." His arm slid around her shoulders as he guided her from the stall.

Liking the weight of his arm across her shoulders, Lily reached up, taking his hand, holding his arm in place as her other arm moved around his waist. She'd never felt this type of security or ease with anyone. She wondered if he felt the same about her. He smiled down at her as they walked into the moonlit yard, and she was struck by the notion that she'd likely have followed him anywhere. It was a rather pleasant feeling.

What am I doing? She didn't have the faintest notion. As they neared the house, reality began to take hold, her practical mind intruding on a wonderful moment with the man who'd shattered her world twice over, and yet had somehow helped her collect all the broken pieces. Where did that leave her?

He stopped at the base of the porch, his touch falling away from her. The warmth of his side was quickly replaced by cold early-morning air. He stepped back as Lily started up the porch stairs. She stopped on the second step and turned to look back at him. Standing at eye level, she held his gaze for a long moment.

She had no experience with this sort of thing. "Juniper…I don't know what to say."

Her admission sent a pang of regret into Juniper's heart. She wasn't a woman of loose morals, and he'd had no right to lie down with her when he couldn't give her promises of love and marriage. *Hell.* A real gentleman gave the promises and the ring first. Though she didn't seem to expect it, she deserved better. Better than he could offer her.

"How about good night?" he suggested.

She flashed a shaky smile. "Good night, then."

He advanced a step and watched her gaze soften as she realized his intent to kiss her. She leaned into him, her hands touching his chest as he brushed his lips softly over hers. When she eased back, her brilliant smile was another blow. He was sure he'd never known such beauty. The way she looked at him, her eyes bright with affection, it made him ache all over. He wanted to pull her back into his arms and promise all the things he could never give her.

"Good night, Lily."

Taking a step back, he turned away and strode back to the barn while he still had enough sense to do so. He shouldn't have allowed things to go as far as they had, yet he couldn't bring himself to truly regret his actions. He'd die remembering her emerald eyes dark with desire, his name on her lips as passion claimed her.

She knew as well as he that the past few hours didn't change anything. Come sunrise they'd both have their jobs to do, and he… *Hell.*

I can't be sweet on Lily Palmer.

Chapter Fourteen

Leaving Jed and his son to their chores in the barn, Juniper entered the house shortly after sunrise, hoping to find a pot of coffee brewing in the kitchen. The chattering voices of his sisters told him he was in luck. He stopped in the dining room doorway, stunned to find Lily standing between his sisters at the small kitchen table, beautiful as ever with her hair up in one of her twisty hairdos, a dish towel tied around her tiny waist. His body warmed at the memory of holding that little waist in his palms.

He wouldn't have blamed her for sleeping in. Yet there she stood, in her clean and mended green dress, an expression of complete perplexity on her sweet face as she stared down at the can opener she hadn't quite fastened on a can of peaches.

Juniper leaned a shoulder against the door frame, fully enjoying the view of his high-powered boss fiddling with the simple contraption.

"Like this?" she said to April.

His youngest sister gaped at her. "You've never used a can opener?"

"April," said Rachell, her back to the room as she tended the bacon she had sizzling on the stove. "Not all young ladies are schooled in the kitchen. I could hardly boil water when I met your father."

April and May grinned at each other, neither believing a truth Juniper had witnessed firsthand, having suffered through Rachell's earliest attempts at cooking.

"You do it like this," May said, clamping the opener down on the can and giving the handle a single turn.

"Oh. Thank you." Lily took over the task. "I used to help my mother in the kitchen when I was real young. Small tasks like rolling out piecrusts and such. I swear I'd milk a cow right now for some hot chocolate."

The girls giggled and Juniper's smile broadened.

"Once I get home I'm sending you a silver chocolate pot and some of my finest chocolate."

"Will you really?" asked April.

"That's not necessary," said Rachell.

"It's basic survival," Lily insisted, her gaze on the bowl she was filling with fruit.

"June!" April spotted him in the doorway.

Lily glanced up.

"Good morning," he said to everyone, and stepped into the room. "Thought I'd see if you needed any cans opened."

"Very funny," Lily said, her eyes narrowing in mock anger.

"There's coffee here on the stove." Rachell smiled over her shoulder at him.

"I'll get a cup for you," offered May.

"Everything go okay?" Rachell asked.

"Real well," he said. "The Grove office is up and running again, which should settle tempers all over the mountain."

He accepted a cup of coffee from May. "Thank you."

"I hope you're staying home a little longer this time," April said, moving up beside him.

"I wish I could, sweetpea." He gave one of her auburn braids a gentle tug. "The Carringtons need to get back up to Pine Ridge and it's my job to make sure they get there safely. We'll need to head out right after breakfast. Once I get the camp settled, I'll come home for a visit."

"Promise?" she asked, slumping into a kitchen chair.

"Promise," he agreed before allowing his gaze to settle on Lily. She watched him with a fair amount of caution in her gaze.

"How are you this morning, Lily?"

"Quite well, thank you," she said, a smile seeping across her lips. "And you, Sheriff Barns?"

"Mighty fine," he said, returning her smile. He wanted to comment on how alluring she looked in the morning light. The flush rising into her cheeks suggested she'd already noted his appreciation.

"I see our dashing lawman has returned."

Lily jumped at the sound of Regi's bright voice. Her cousin looked from her to Juniper and back again, a single dark eyebrow arched in surprise and silent speculation.

Realizing Regi wasn't the only one staring at her and Juniper with curiosity bright in his gaze, she snatched up her bowl of peaches and turned toward the counter, away from her cousin and Juniper's sisters.

"Hey, Reg," Juniper said. "Can you give me a hand with the horses?"

"Certainly."

"Get some coffee. I'll meet you out there."

Lily listened to the sound of the back door closing behind Juniper and released a silent sigh of relief. *Good gracious.* The man could make her heart pound clean out of her chest with a simple smile.

An hour later, Lily sat at the dining table across from Juniper once again. This time, however, she found it to be a rather pleasing experience. She felt very much a part of the warmth in the room, especially when Juniper's gaze was upon her. She had to struggle to contain the swirls of heat.

When they all stood in the yard, saying their goodbyes, she found she was truly going to miss this family.

"Spill it."

Reginald nearly pounced on her the moment Juniper led the horses off to a meadow for the evening.

Lily straightened away from the fire and took a step back on a bed of pine needles. "What are you talking about?"

"You and your sheriff," he said with exasperation. "What's happened?"

"I don't know what you mean," she said, hoping her cheeks didn't look as flushed as they felt. "He recovered the payroll. You were there when he explained everything over breakfast. The payroll, his reasons for taking this long route through the higher elevations."

Reginald arched an eyebrow. "That doesn't explain the glow in your cheeks or the secret smiles you two have been exchanging all day."

Oh, dear. Had she really been so transparent?

"We talked," she said.

"Talked?"

"Yes. I believe we've come to an understanding."

"Which is?"

Good grief. She wasn't really certain. "That he's the sheriff and we need his help to settle our troubles at Pine Ridge. The men trust him and so far he's accomplished all he said he would."

"You like him," Regi accused.

"What?"

Regi grinned. "Oh, Lily. Your eyes brighten like electric lightbulbs every time he smiles at you."

"So, I like him," she conceded. "So what?"

Regi's grin broadened. "I knew it. Something's happened."

"I hardly think our becoming agreeable with each other—"

"I'm going to head to the river," Juniper said, striding back into camp. "I'll bring back some trout."

"Can I come along?" Lily asked. Seeing Regi's gaze whip toward her, she added, "I'd like to wash up a bit."

"Sure. Reg, once that flame takes, feed another log into the fire."

"You're not going far, are you?"

"Not far," Juniper assured him. "Rifle's behind you, beside my saddle."

Lily fell into step beside him as they walked through a forest of giant redwoods.

"You look petty clean to me," he whispered after they'd walked a ways.

She watched the river come into view and smiled. She wasn't about to admit she merely wanted some time alone with him. "I'm curious to see how you catch fish without a pole."

He jumped down to a lower embankment and turned, lifting her with easy strength. He set her on rocky ground leading to the swift-moving river.

"I'd be glad to show you how," he said.

"Really?"

"Sure." He sat on a boulder near the river's edge and began to remove his boots. She recalled he had come back that first evening with his feet bare, his pants rolled up.

"Are you going into the river?"

"It's the best way to find a prime fishing hole. You may want to take off your skirts if you're coming along."

Take off...*her skirts?*

He looked up from his rolled pant legs and laughed. "It's not a ploy to get you undressed, Lily. Not that it would matter," he added in a low, alluring tone. "I've been picturing you wearing nothing but straw in your hair all day."

"Juniper!"

He laughed again, loving the flush in her cheeks. "You're wearing some sort of bloomers or pantaloons under all those skirts, aren't you?"

"I certainly am!"

His shrugged his shoulders. "You can wait here if you'd rather." He stepped out onto a rock amid the swirling current and glanced in both directions of the river. He likely could find a fishing spot from the shore, but that wasn't his way. He enjoyed trekking through the cool water, navigating over the wide-spaced boulders, surrounded by the hush of the river, the scent of the pines—it soothed him.

The best thing to come out of working for McFarland was having been able to talk the man into selling him this patch of land. McFarland had needed money, and Juniper loved the serenity of these woods, the river—though he often wondered why he'd pushed McFarland to sell the parcel. He'd had money in the bank…and no hope of settling down anytime soon. Still, it felt good to have something, a place to go, even if it was nothing more than ground to camp on.

Deciding it would be easiest for Lily to walk downstream than upstream, he glanced back at her. She stared at him, her arms crossed over her chest, reluctance clear in her green eyes.

"You'll be missing out," he said.

The challenge in his slanted grin had Lily reaching for the tie of her skirt. Telling herself she was positively certifiable, she pushed down her skirt and petticoats and stepped over them. After tossing aside her shoes and stockings, she stepped lightly over rocks and gravel.

Juniper stood a few feet out on a flat boulder. He held his hand out to her as she reached the edge of the stream. "The rocks can be slick."

Lily gripped his fingers just as her toes met the gentle rush of water. A chill jolted through her, stealing her breath.

"It's cold at first," he warned, a moment too late.

"It's *freezing!*" she said, quickly stepping up beside him.

"After a few minutes you'll hardly notice the cold."

"Because our feet will be blocks of ice?"

He only chuckled and stepped onto the next tall stone, keeping her beside him. "After a long day of riding, a walk through the stream is rather soothing, especially since our shooting incident."

Lily glanced down but he'd stepped into the glistening ripple of the river. She shivered at the thought of following him into the cold current.

"I'm teasing," he said. He swung her over to the next large boulder. "My foot is healing just fine." He stepped up and she saw that indeed the pink gash was healing nicely.

"I truly didn't mean to shoot you."

"I know. I didn't mean to scare you into shooting me." They stepped over a few more large stones. "Time to get your feet wet, darlin'."

With that, he tugged her after him into the freezing-cold river water. Lily sucked in a gasp. Just as he'd said, the chill quickly wore off as they walked along through the shallow current toward another patch of rocks where water swirled around them so tightly she wondered how any fish could make it down the river at all. "I thought you were going to fish."

"We are. First we have to find a gentle pool."

"Are you sure there's anything deep enough in this river?"

He smiled down at her. "There's plenty of pools along this river we can dunk into."

"Dunk? I can assure you I will not be dunking for our supper."

His laughter sent tendrils of pleasure twisting through her. The soft light of a setting sun gilded the thick golden waves of his hair as he smiled down at her. *Good gracious, he's handsome.* When he smiled at her like that, she doubted she could refuse him anything, even diving for their meal.

"Is that what you think I have in mind?" he asked.

"I haven't the faintest notion. This is my first time wading for fish."

He laughed again, the warm, throaty sound moving through her like a sensual caress. His thumb brushed over the top of her hand, and Lily found herself very happy to be walking through the river with him, wearing only her waistcoat and bloomers.

"This is the spot," he said as they reached a bend in the river. The narrow, rocky channel opened into a smooth, wide surface of gently moving water. Thick green bushes grew out into the river from steep embankments on each side.

He led her up to a high grassy embankment overlooking a deep section of the river shaded by thick brush growing out on either side, creating a small cove. Lily sat on her knees beside him and peered over the edge at the water nearly three feet below. Juniper opened a small leather pouch behind the scabbard holding his knife. He pulled out a small bundle of carefully wrapped line attached to something black and fuzzy. Looking closer at the long fibers, she spotted a barbed point curving out the bottom.

"A hook!"

"I don't travel without a fishing line," he said, wrapping the length of line around his left hand and letting out some slack between the hook in his right.

"Resourceful," she said, truly amazed.

"Glad you noticed."

He leaned over the edge of the embankment, his gaze on the water. "I prefer using a pole, but that's not always an option." He eased closer to her, and the heat of his body warmed her side. A swathe of wavy golden hair hung lazily over his brow, just above those amazing pale blue eyes. He tilted his head slightly, and the day's worth of stubble coating his jaw captured the evening light and glistened like clear grains of brown sugar. Her stomach fluttered at the thought of nibbling on that sharp jawline and his full lips.

"Watch," he whispered.

Lily couldn't have looked away if she'd tried. Not that Juniper noticed; his whole focus centered on catching their supper. Glancing out at the water, she watched as his fuzzy hook seemed to hop across the shiny surface like a pesky insect. Sure enough, a fish emerged from the brush and shadows, its mouth opening wide as it swam up. Juniper gave a sharp tug and hauled up a wiggling trout. A few deft movements and he was setting the fish aside and held the line out to her.

"Your turn."

Lily leaned back. She hadn't actually been watching his fishing technique. She'd been far too distracted by the smooth lines of his tan face. "Not me," she said, shaking her head. "I'll snag your line."

"I have a spare."

He slid a coil of line over the fingers of her left hand

and set the end with the hook in her right. "Let out some slack and give it a toss."

She peered over at the thick green shrubs growing out on both sides of the shaded cove that now seemed incredibly small. Her gaze shifted to the camouflaged hook, then to the man kneeling beside her. She wasn't about to risk hooking those handsome features.

"The fish aren't going to lunge up and bite you," he teased.

"What about you?"

He smiled. "I won't lunge up and bite you, either."

Lily actually giggled. She couldn't recall ever feeling quite so giddy. She'd also never sat beside a stream in her bloomers or enjoyed anything as much as she enjoyed Juniper's company.

"I meant that I don't want to hook you."

"I've survived worse," he said, and moved closer, his arm reaching around her. His hands gently gripped both her wrists. "I wish I had a pole. I could really show you something."

Lily wished they had a hay-filled stall and the rest of the night to themselves.

Juniper tried not to notice the fine tremble of Lily's body as he guided her arm back. "Release some slack," he said, his voice gruff to his own ears. She released a few coils as he helped her toss the fly to the center of the small pool.

He breathed in the sweet floral scent of her. "Take up some line," he instructed, guiding her wrist as he dragged the fly across the water, though he could hardly think of anything beyond the heat of her slender back pressed to his chest. Luckily the trout were hungry tonight. Their supper swam up and the line snapped taught. Lily's excited shriek had him laughing as he reached for the line she nearly dropped into the water.

They had a half dozen fish in no time. After enduring nearly an hour of Lily's delighted giggles and bright smiles, Juniper congratulated himself on fighting his urge to peel off the rest of her clothing and make love to her right there on the riverbank.

They followed the same rocky path up the river. Approaching another boulder in the fading light, he slid his arms around her waist. "Careful," he said, pulling her close, though she hadn't shown any signs of slipping. Just because he hadn't seduced her didn't mean he'd give up any excuse to touch her. Every minute alone with her was both a torture and a blessing.

Reaching their shoreline, he knelt beside the river and cleaned the fish as she pulled on her stockings and boots, then her velvet skirt and petticoat after petticoat. Finished threading the cleand fish onto the line, his gaze moved over the river and trees. Maybe after he left the camp, he'd move here, put up a small cabin and make a quiet life for himself. There was plenty a man could do in these mountains to make a simple living. Maybe he'd look into trapping.

He stepped into his boots and straightened his pant legs. Lily was all put back together by the time he grabbed the line of gutted fish. Her smile sent a whisper over his skin. It wasn't a flirtatious smile, just a slight tilt of her lips coupled with a warmth in her gaze that made him want to take her in his arms and draw out the passion they'd shared the night before.

She's not for you, he silently reminded himself, and started toward camp.

As Lily walked along beside Juniper, her hand brushed against his, but he made no attempt to hold it. Though she'd been preoccupied with fishing, she now realized that he hadn't even tried to kiss her. Not once.

"I enjoyed the fishing lesson," she said, clasping her hands together.

He smiled down at her. "Me, too."

The light of a campfire glimmered from the darkness up ahead, and disappointment began to fester inside her. She wouldn't get any more time alone with him.

"Took you long enough," Regi said as they walked into camp. He sat beside a tall fire, Juniper's rifle across his lap.

"Do we have any firewood left?" Juniper asked, looking at the massive bonfire Regi had constructed.

"It was getting dark."

Juniper shook his head and walked toward their supplies. He supposed he should be thankful Reg hadn't burned down the forest while they'd been gone.

"You actually caught fish," he said, sounding surprised.

"Lily caught half of them."

"Did you really?" he asked, his eyes flaring wide.

Her nervous smile caught Juniper's attention. "I did," she said.

"Lily, can you pull out the basket and plates Rachell packed for us while I fry up this fish?"

"Sure." She went to fetch the supplies, and Juniper thought he saw a touch of sadness in her expression as she looked at him. Wondering at her sudden change of mood, he strode toward a packhorse loaded with supplies.

By the time they'd eaten and had spaced three bed-rolls around the dwindling fire, he couldn't deny the sullen change in Lily's mood. She was upset about something. Although she'd been conversational with him and Reg, she'd hardly looked him in the eye for the past two hours. Reclined on his own bedding, he subtly watched her sitting on her side of the fire, her gaze never lifting above the flames as she sat cross-legged with her blanket wrapped around her shoulders. It wasn't long before Reg curled up in his bedroll and snored softly.

Juniper stood to put the last log on the low fire. As he did, Lily rose and quietly moved to sit on his bed-roll. He smiled as he eased down next to her. Not about to make a move, he waited to see what she wanted.

Somber eyes stared up at him as she seemed to search for words.

"Is something wrong?" he asked.

"No. Not really."

He heard questions brewing in her mind.

"To be honest," she said a moment later, "I'm wondering why you haven't made any attempt to kiss me since early this morning."

Juniper nearly groaned. As much as he liked her flat honesty, at times it was hard to take. "Believe me," he whispered, "it hasn't been easy resisting the urge. I'm not about to assume that our tumble in the barn entitles me to such liberties."

"Oh." She frowned. "I rather thought it did. I suppose this kind of awkwardness is customary after a, uh...*tumble,* did you call it?"

Hell. He'd upset her. "I didn't mean that in a negative way."

"How did you mean it?"

"Just that...I've never had an affair with an employer or with a woman who's so engrained in my past."

Lily kept hearing the implication that he'd had similar relations with other women. *Well of course he has,* she reasoned. It was the realization that he'd intended the distance he'd kept between them all day that troubled her the most.

It's not as though he's courting me. "A tumble," she breathed, the word feeling vastly inappropriate for what they'd shared.

Juniper hissed a curse. "It was more than that." His arm slid around her, pulling her close. "Honestly, Lily, I've never had an awkward moment with a woman because I've never cared enough to worry about the next day."

"I make you worry?"

"Hell, yes, you make me worry." His fingers grazed her cheek. The intensity of his gaze made her tremble. "The last thing I want to do is hurt you."

She believed him. She also knew there likely wasn't any way around it. He'd given her so much…leaving was going to hurt.

"I enjoyed today," she said, brushing her fingers over the back of his hand.

He turned his palm to hers and laced their fingers. "So did I. And tomorrow we'll be in Pine Ridge."

"Exactly. *Tomorrow.* Can't we have this last bit of time together?"

His gaze shifted warily toward Reg sleeping beside the fire. "You're referring to kisses and a bit of cuddling, right?"

"Yes," she said, laughing as she leaned into him. "Unless you'd rather not. I'll understand if you—"

His mouth brushed over hers, ending her words. The possessive caress of his tongue stealing across her lips shattered her breath. He took her mouth in a bone-melting kiss…nothing rushed, just the slow sensual mating of their mouths.

He lay back and she moved with him, following him down, stretching out on top of him, melting against him, savoring every stroke and texture as she returned every touch. His hands caressed her from her shoulders to her hips. His kiss became teasing bites on her lower lip, sending shivers dancing across her skin.

"Just so we're clear," she said in a breathless whisper, "you can do that to me anytime you feel the notion."

"You can be sure I've wanted to just about every second since I woke up this morning." His hands continued their slow, sweeping caresses. "But I'm not about to give anyone up at that camp the impression that there's more between us than business. Once we get to Pine Ridge, you're the boss and I'm the sheriff—that's it. I don't want you to think I've taken advantage of you."

"Considering I've made all the advances, I can hardly accuse you of taking advantage, and I'm quite familiar with professional conduct." She laid her head against his shoulder as she stared up at a starlit sky beyond the dark tips of towering pines. "In fact, it's all I've known for so many years, I forgot how good it feels to just be…" *What?*

"Yourself?" he offered.

"I suppose," she said, though she knew that wasn't exactly true. "Or at least who I'm supposed to be."

"Which is?"

"Lily Carrington."

He pulled her closer, his hand coming to rest on her hip. "Is she so different from Lily Palmer?"

"Yes," she said. "I believe she is."

"I don't see how."

"That's because you didn't know me until this past week. I don't think I really knew myself. I'd truly forgotten how my life used to be, all the things I used to care about. I've been so caught up in who I was supposed to be, I forgot about everything else. I never realized I'd suppressed so many memories.

Good memories. How very strange that I'd find them because of *you*. But I suppose you know just how it feels to shut a part of yourself off. I've seen you when you change."

"Change how?"

"When you turn cold and closed off. Like when we were standing in front of that mob. You're not the same person you are now."

"Maybe so, but it's a part of who I am."

"Do you like that part of you?"

Juniper glanced down at her upturned face as she gazed up at the night sky. He'd never pondered any such thing, and wasn't sure he wanted to. "I suppose not," he said.

She shifted over him, folding her arms over his chest. "I've decided I'm going to change it, the part of me I don't like."

"Simple as that, huh?"

"Simple as that," she said.

"You think I should change, too?"

"No. I'm quite fond of you the way you are," she said, kissing him softly. "It's not as though you don't have reason to be armed. You're a sheriff, after all. Though I do prefer you when you're just Juniper."

Just Juniper. He wasn't sure that anyone outside of his family had ever seen him as just Juniper. The fact that Lily did was something like a miracle to him. Deep down, he knew he didn't deserve to have her looking at him with trust bright in her eyes. He didn't deserve the sweetness of her kiss. He didn't deserve it, but he *needed* all of it, more than he'd ever needed anything in his life.

Chapter Fifteen

Thunder boomed overhead, echoing through the small upstairs office of the sawmill. Lily sat at Jim's desk, a pencil in her hand, another tucked cutely behind her ear. Her gaze traveled from the ledgers to the papers spaced across the desktop as Johnson, one of her accountants, talked with the speed of an auctioneer.

Standing on the stairwell, Juniper couldn't tear his eyes away from her. Prim, stylish, attractive as all hell. When she turned on the *boss* attitude, there wasn't much a body could do but stand back. The moment she'd walked into that office, her men had started hopping. The three accountants swarmed around her, giving their detailed analysis of the mill, answering her questions, producing notes and charts at her request without a moment's hesitation. The five of them huddled around the desk, all seemingly unaware of the downpour battering the roof. The light rain that had started this morning had become a full-on storm. Getting Lily back to her cabin in a relatively dry manner was going to be tricky.

He'd taken a few moments to meet all three of her sharply dressed accountants while Lily freshened up when they'd first arrived. He got the clear sense that they were rather protective of their pretty, young employer. A lot of good it had done them or Lily when she'd flittered off to wherever she pleased with *a gun in her pocket*. He grinned at the memory. He saw now how she'd gotten away from them. She rode roughshod over the lot of them. He doubted there was a man who could control her.

And rightly so, he thought, watching her lips flatten, her eyes darken with concentration as she pored over some papers her man Allen had set before her.

Having changed into a sleek black dress with fine gray pinstriping running down the long fitted jacket and trim skirt, she looked like a million dollars of high-powered intelligence. Her hair shimmered beneath the oil lamps burning bright on the wall above her, reminding him of the way her hair had glimmered across the hay while her eyes had glowed with passion.

A lump formed in Juniper's throat. A wad of pride, he supposed. Watching her, he realized just how far out of her element this rough-cut lumber camp office truly was, and how Lily Palmer Carrington must shine in the fancy boardrooms of her San Francisco office.

Fairly certain his presence had been making her nervous, he'd left her alone with her men much of the morning, leaving Günter on guard. He and Kyle had been asking around about Chandler and Mathews.

So far, none of the men they'd talked to had seen or heard any news since the robbery. Chandler was one more reason he couldn't wait to get Lily off the mountain. Tomorrow morning the carriage he'd sent for would arrive and he'd be sending her home under Kyle's protection.

She'd gone through hell in the past week because of this camp and had arrived this morning with a burning determination to save it. She didn't just give off a bossy attitude. There was no denying her prowess and skill, something the men working with her recognized and respected. It showed in their attentive replies as she double-checked their numbers and cross-referenced their carefully calculated profit projections.

I've decided I'm going to change it, the part of me I don't like.

He couldn't imagine what she'd want to change. If this was the other side of her personality she'd been referring to, Lily Carrington impressed the hell out of him. The thought that she saw herself flawed in some way gnawed at his conscience. He hoped he hadn't put such notions into her head. He'd been damn hard on her in those first few days and had made some harsh comments in regard to her business practices. He wondered if that was why she tended to watch him out of the corner of her eye if he was in the room.

Jim stomped toward the door, his expression miserable, his shirt drenched with sweat.

"Relax," Juniper said to his friend as he stepped out onto the landing. "She's got it all under control."

"Yeah," Jim muttered, "and once her group of fancy men let her know I can't read any better than she can chop down a redwood, she'll throw me out on my ear."

"That's crap. This place would fall apart without you."

"I know that and you know that, but people like them Carringtons…" He shook his head. "You wait and see."

"I think she can do this company some good."

"What's good for the account books ain't always good for the rest of us. We're in the hole here, and you know it. Once they start looking to trim the fat, the rest of us start losing jobs."

"From everything she's told me, she intends to invest her own money into this place and expand your employee roster—something McFarland was never willing to do."

"I hope you're right."

Glancing back at Lily, he knew part of her enthusiasm was generated by her will to help the folks she'd met in The Grove. He didn't doubt Lily or her intentions to follow through with those plans.

Reginald broke away from the pack, took his coat and hat off a nail in the wall and strolled toward him.

"Reg," Juniper greeted. "Everything going well?"

"Smooth as can be." He lifted a pocket watch from his vest and clicked it open. "Only noon? Looks like nightfall out there."

"The rain has likely driven the crews in early. Cook will have the doors open for dinner."

"I could use a nice scotch."

"No booze allowed in camp," said Grimshaw.

Reginald gasped. "What kind of rot is that?"

Jim laughed.

"The kind that keeps men from sawing their own limbs off," said Juniper. "Is Lily about finished?"

"Not likely," Reg said, glancing back at her and their three accountants. "You'd better intervene before she exhausts every last one of them."

"Gonna make me risk a limb, huh?"

"Hardly," he said with a snort. He gave Juniper a long measuring glance that let him know he hadn't forgotten the scene he'd witnessed this morning. Juniper and Lily had awakened at first light, still tangled in each other's arms. After a few lengthy, intimate caressing stretches, they'd sat up to find a wide-eyed Reginald sitting across the smoldering fire. June figured he had some fast explaining to do, but Lily had simply greeted her cousin with a cheerful "Good morning" and had begun to pull out breakfast supplies as though spending the night snuggled up with her father's killer was nothing out of the ordinary. Juniper had followed her lead, and Reginald hadn't uttered a word about it. But Juniper had felt his gaze on him during the ride to camp. Once there, Lily hadn't given either of them time to sit around and speculate about anything.

"I'd say you're the only one suited for such a task," Reginald insisted.

"Think I'll go track down Davy," Jim said, shuffling down the steps. "Make sure he hasn't washed away in all this rain."

Juniper walked into the office. "Miss Carrington? Gentlemen?"

"Sheriff Barns," Lily said, glancing up as though he were just the person she wanted to see. "Do you think we could arrange a meeting with all the camp foremen? If we're going to compile information for improving efficiency, I would like to hear their input before we leave tomorrow."

"I'll mention it to Jim. I'm sure he can get them together after dinner."

Lily glanced back at the men sitting before her.

"All right then," said Allen, removing his glasses. "Should we adjourn until after dinner?"

"Very well," she agreed.

Allen, Johnson and Brown walked past him, each giving a greeting of "Sheriff Barns."

Juniper waited near the door as Lily pulled on her thick wool coat. She fastened each shiny black button then grabbed the umbrella she had propped against the desk. She walked toward him, not-quite-five-feet of pure feminine primness from head to toe to umbrella. She stopped beside him, her eyes suddenly bright with an excitement that bubbled over into a smile.

"Oh, June," she whispered, stepping close. She

glanced past him, making sure the coast was clear before stepping into his arms and giving him a quick squeeze. "The numbers look good," she said in a soft tone, as though conveying a secret.

"Not as bad as you anticipated?"

"It's going to take some funding to make up for McFarland's loss, but the potential is there." She drew a deep breath, regaining her schooled composure. "The mill's production capabilities will be worth the investment."

"That's good news," he said. "Is there a reason why you're keeping that a secret?"

"It's no secret, but it's hardly appropriate to give anyone false hope at this stage. There's still much to be done. I feel so much better having seen the actual proof. McFarland provided some paperwork while looking for investors, so I had some idea of the mill's capabilities, but not the details I needed to truly put my mind at ease."

"Why did you buy the camp instead of just investing?"

Lily's good cheer dampened at the thought of revealing the details behind her acquisition of McFarland Lumber. "We started out as investors," she said. "He put requests in with various companies. I looked over the information and expressed an interest. Upon meeting me, he refused to deal with Carrington Industries."

"Because…?"

"He refused to do business with a woman."

"Then why would he sell you the mill? I knew he was losing money and scrambling for more financial backing, but the change of ownership hit everyone here without any warning."

"He didn't intend to sell, nor did he bother to investigate his new investors. I own various companies and I used them to take control of the Pine Ridge Lumber Camp, knowing he wouldn't want to stay on with a woman controlling his company."

Juniper's eyebrows shot up and Lily felt the warming signs of color rising into her cheeks.

"So you can understand why he went out of his way to make this a difficult transition. He was not a happy man when I arrived to personally claim the title."

"I would have liked to have seen that."

"It was rather a fun morning," she admitted.

He laughed and took the umbrella from her hand. "I'm thinking you did this camp a favor," he said, holding out his arm to escort her downstairs.

Thunder clapped and rolled, rattling everything inside the hollow building as they walked through the millhouse.

"It would appear we arrived just in time this morning."

"The rain has made a mess of the roads. It's not going to be a pleasant walk back."

Regi and the others stood just inside the wide doors of the sawmill, all of them pressing down their hats and flipping up their coat collars.

"We haven't had a bad meal," Johnson was saying.

"You won't find better food in San Francisco," Allen agreed.

"A lumber camp is only as good as its grub," Juniper told them. "And we have the best in the Sierras. Cook is about the only reason this camp still has workers willing to put in a day's work. Any man who works is guaranteed excellent food and a place to sleep."

"I was told corned beef would be served tonight," said Allen.

All of their talk was starting to make her hungry. "Should we head to the dining hall?"

"Everyone but you," Juniper said evenly.

Lily gaped at him.

"No way am I taking you into the cookhouse with nearly a hundred men. You'll eat in your cabin. Reg can join you if he likes."

"If it's all the same to you, Lily, I'll go ahead and dine with the others."

"All right then," Juniper said, ushering her forward before she could respond. "We'll see you back at the cabin after you eat." His hand pressed against the small of her back, guiding her toward a steady veil of rain pouring off the rooftop.

"In a hurry?" she asked, smiling up at him as he popped out the umbrella.

He only grinned. "Hold this."

The moment her fingers curved around the wooden handle he lifted her into his arms, saying, "And I'll hold you."

"Juniper!"

"The mud will ruin your fancy coat." Rain spattered across her coat and skirt. The steady tapping echoed beneath the umbrella like artillery fire as he charged through the downpour.

Figuring there was no point in arguing with him, Lily leaned close and breathed in the refreshing scent of spruce, pine and *Juniper.* "I'll try not to complain," she said, discreetly kissing his jaw.

"Easy." His eyes darkened with blatant desire. "I can't get caught kissing the boss."

Lily contained herself as he hurried down the hillside and across the rain-soaked grounds. She was still quite warm and cozy when he bounded up the steps of her cabin. He tilted the umbrella back to shield them from any onlookers and plastered his mouth to hers. Lily slid her arms around his neck and kissed him for all she was worth.

By the time he'd released her mouth and set her feet on the small wooden porch, she was dizzy and short of breath.

"I've got to stop doing that," he said, shaking out the umbrella and closing it.

Lily could only smile. She rather enjoyed his surprise bursts of passion. "I wasn't complaining." She took him by the hand and pulled him into the cabin. The moment the door closed behind them she launched into his arms, and he was kissing her the way a starving man devours a feast. His lips shifted, touching her cheeks, her eyes, her nose, her chin.

Abruptly he stepped away from her. "I'll go grab us some food."

She'd rather have *him,* but managed to keep from blurting out the words as he pulled the door open.

"Bar the door behind me," he said, the steady sound of rainfall muffling his voice. "Don't open it for anyone else."

She did as he said, sliding the bar into place. Pulling off her jacket, she sat heavily onto the lower bunk of the first bunk bed. She expelled a hard breath, trying to ease the sudden rise of passion. The tingling swirls only increased as she recalled the way he'd looked at her as he'd stood in the doorway to the office, the pride in his grin... *She loved him.*

Lily was certain of it.

Juniper Barns. Just his name sent a hopeless surge of emotion expanding through her chest.

How can this have happened? How could she have fallen in love with the man who'd killed her father? Yet, after getting to know Juniper, she couldn't blame him for what had happened.

Her eyes burned at the thought.

She was leaving tomorrow. Would he come to see her in San Francisco? Did he want her? Just because he'd kissed her with bone-melting desire didn't mean—

The floor creaked behind her. She turned just as a force shoved her facedown onto the mattress.

Lily struggled and tried to scream but more than one set of hands held her pinned against the bedding, one holding down her head and shoulders as another secured her hands, the rope burning across her wrists.

"Good and tight," a man instructed. "She's a feisty little bitch."

She knew that voice. *Oh, God.*
Chandler.

Fingers clenched the back of her hair, lifting her head as a cloth went over her mouth, cutting off her cry for help.

"I don't know about this, Billy," said the other man. "We were supposed to grab one of those 'Frisco men."

A man's bruising grip wrenched her up. She stared at Billy Chandler and the man who'd been standing beside Mr. Grimshaw on the afternoon she'd arrived. *Traitor!*

"Lady Luck must finally be shining down on us," said Chandler, his crimson lips tipped in a sickly grin as he closed in on her.

Something wasn't right. Juniper knew it the moment he spotted what looked to be an open cabin door in the obscured distance.

Chills prickled up the back of Juniper's neck as he rushed forward, looking harder through the blur of rain.

Lily's cabin door was wide-open.

Tin plates hit the ground and he was in a full run.

"Lily!"

Her coat lay on the bed, a piece of paper beside it. Juniper's breath stalled as he read the sloppy pencil scratches.

Deliver the strongbox to the fork in the road at Piney Gultch Pass tomorrow at midnight or Carrington's man won't walk off the mountain alive.

He knew the place. A low spot of crossroads with a ridge on each side to offer adequate cover. But the money had already been dispersed. The men who'd escaped Chandler's place wouldn't have known that. They also hadn't expected to find Lily in this cabin.

He'd told her to bar the door! She hadn't been alone for more than fifteen minutes.

Crumpling the note in his fist, Juniper grabbed Lily's coat and ran outside to search for tracks. He circled the cabin. Rain pummeled the pitted ground, puddling water everywhere. He ran toward the woods at the rear of the cabins. A few rows in, he spotted the faint tracks of two horses heading up the mountain.

"Lily!"

Rainfall had already distorted the prints. They likely had a fifteen-minute lead. He'd never catch them on foot, certainly not with the rain washing out their tracks.

"Damn it!" He turned back. He needed a horse, a posse—he needed to know where Chandler was taking her.

He burst through the door of the cookhouse and slid to a stop. Water dripped from the brim of his hat. His chest pulling for breath, panic shaking him, his gaze raked over the men whose mouths gaped open; others froze in the midst of taking a bite.

Kyle stood up from his spot at a long table. "June?"

"Who here was on a crew with Chandler?"

Movement drew his gaze to the back of the room. Instead of a man coming forward, the timbermen sitting on either side of a slender man Juniper knew only as Rogers slid away from him, singling him out on the bench.

Juniper started toward him. Rogers swallowed hard and stood.

"Billy Chandler has taken Lily Carrington." He didn't slow his pace until his gun was shoved under the man's chin. "Tell me where he took her."

"I do-don't—"

"He wouldn't have gone up the mountain in this storm unless he had a safe spot. Every range of timber has a hidey place where men go to sit out storms or take a break. *Where is it?*"

"Ch-Chandler will kill me."

He clicked the hammer back on his gun. "Not if I kill you first."

"June," Kyle said softly from beside him.

He released Rogers long enough to shove the wadded ransom note against Kyle's chest. Juniper resumed his hold, his gaze pinned on Rogers as Kyle unfolded the crumpled paper.

"Ah, hell!"

He tightened his hold on Rogers's shirt, lifting the

man to the tips of his boots. "You're gonna lead Marshal Darby and me to every cave, shack and hollow tree you know about until we find Lily Carrington."

Rogers nodded vigorously. "Th-there's a couple places he's likely to go for sure."

"Günter!"

"Right here, Sheriff," his deputy answered.

He released Rogers as Günter made his way up the row of tables. "Assemble a posse, issue firearms and fan out. *Every man searches.* We're looking for two men on horseback, Billy Chandler and likely Ted Mathews. So long as Lily Carrington isn't in range, you can shoot on sight."

Everyone stared up at him in stunned silence.

"Move!"

Dishes clattered, benches scuffed the floor as the roomful of men rushed for the door.

He looked back at Rogers, who had paled to the color of a bed sheet. "You better not let me down."

"No, sir. If'n he's lookin' to keep dry for any length of time, he'd go to one of two places."

"Grab your hat and tell me on the way."

Kyle stood outside in the rain, already holding the reins of three horses.

"Rogers," he said as the man reached for a saddle. "Try to run from me and you'll die. I've never missed a target, moving or otherwise."

"No, sir. I sure don't want to see the lady hurt."

Lily's coat still draped over his arm, Juniper rolled

up the thick wool and jammed it into his saddlebag before mounting his horse.

Kyle rode in beside him as they started east. "We'll find her, June."

He knew he would. It was the inevitable time she'd spend in Chandler's company until he reached her that worried him. If Chandler hurt her, he'd be praying for hell before Juniper issued his ticket.

Chapter Sixteen

"**J**ust wait until I get you alone."

Soaked to the bone and shivering, Lily didn't doubt Chandler's intentions for getting her alone; he'd detailed them several times. They'd ridden through the rain for what felt like hours. She sat on Chandler's lap, a constant shower of chilling drops against her face. She counted her one blessing—she was far too numb to feel Chandler's bruising touch beneath her wet waistcoat.

She kept hoping to hear gunfire and Juniper riding up behind them. But all she heard was the steady hush of rainfall and Chandler's disgusting words. The drenched gag tied around her mouth prevented her venomous replies. Mathews rode a short distance ahead of him and she couldn't help but think he ought to be minding his back. Chandler had whispered his plans. He was waiting on his brother and intended to kill her and Mathews—once he no longer had use for them.

Up ahead, she spotted a white trail of smoke snaking

into the darkening gray sky. A shudder of fear broke through her cold tremors. Once they stopped, she wouldn't stand much of a chance against two brutish men.

They reined in outside a crude shack constructed of stripped bark. She spotted other horses out in the tall pine trees and recalled that some of the bandits had headed back up the hill.

Chandler hoisted her up over his shoulder as he dismounted. Her hands and feet bound, any struggle was useless. She pinched her eyes tight, terrified of what she'd find inside their makeshift cabin.

Please, God. Let Juniper come for me.

A door squeaked open and heat rushed out with the sound of male voices.

"You got 'em," a man said, sounding surprised.

"Sure did." He dropped her onto a dirt floor. Lily winced as pain shot through her aching muscles.

"It's a *woman.*"

"Not just a woman," said Chandler.

Lily struggled to her knees and looked up through the sopping strands of her hair. Four unfamiliar faces stared down at her. Behind them a fire crackled in what looked like an old boiler for some kind of machinery.

"The Carrington girl." The biggest of the group, a man with a wide brown mustache streaked with gray, stepped toward her. His startled expression gave her a flicker of hope.

"Let's see how negotiable Carrington is when he finds out we have his daughter," said Chandler.

"I heard she was his niece," said a lanky young man sitting on a crate near the stove.

"Won't matter how she's related to Carrington when Sheriff Barns is likely to kill us all," said Mathews.

"He should be wanting his pay, too," said Chandler.

"As much as he wants his woman?"

"Button it, Mathews," ordered Chandler.

"What's he jawing about, Chandler?" said another man.

"Barns was kissing her," Mathews announced, glaring accusingly at his accomplice. "We both saw 'em."

"Which don't mean anything," snapped Chandler. "What man worth his salt wouldn't be tryin' to get under her skirts? I never should have dropped her that first time! We'd all be on our way to Mexico by now instead of hiding out in this damn shack."

"Who the hell said they wanted to ride to Mexico?" said the older man with the mustache. "I got a family, for cryin' out loud! I haven't seen my wife in two months! I just want my pay."

"Barns is no fool." A stout man standing behind the others came forward. "You courtin' the sheriff?"

Lily vigorously nodded her head.

"Hell, she'd say she was courting the pope if she thought we'd let her go!"

"This don't feel right," said the man with the mustache. "I got no call to go hurting innocent women. We get caught, we'll hang for sure."

"We're not going to get caught," Chandler said.

The chilling quality of his voice made Lily's hair stand on end.

"What makes you think she's innocent? I saw her at my uncle's place. She shot my cousin point-blank between the eyes. She's willing to kill to keep what's ours."

"So we could pay everyone," she tried to shout through the cloth rubbing blisters into the sides of her mouth.

"Kidnapping women isn't what my son and I came here for," said the stout man.

"I didn't want to become no renegade outlaw," the kid on the crate put in. Lily realized he and the older man shared the same facial structure and black hair. "I don't want no part in money that comes from hurting the lady. We ought to take her back."

The others voiced their agreement.

"She's gettin' what's coming to her," said Chandler. "So are you."

Lily saw the flash of movement. She screamed as four shots split the air. Four bodies fell to the dirt floor. Her muffled screams didn't go far beyond the gag as the scent of gun smoke stung her nose.

Chandler's hand closed over her arm and pulled her up beside him. "Your quick-draw sweetheart's got nothin' over me," he said, smiling.

"You shot 'em."

Lily blinked away tears and looked up at Mathews. The man's tawny complexion paled as he stared in shock at his fallen co-workers.

"Of course I shot 'em! They were ready to turn us in because of some bitch in a skirt. You sayin' you have similar notions?"

Mathews shook his head. "No. Not me, Billy."

"All we need is the two of us. One to keep watch and one to collect the money."

Mathews eyed him pensively. With good reason. Lily knew Chandler had never intended to share the money with any of the lumberjacks.

"That setup workin' for you?" asked Chandler.

"Sure."

"This place is too obvious, anyhow. How far's that old millhouse?"

Lily glanced at Mathews, praying he'd stand up to Billy.

"Four miles, maybe."

"Good. Go grab up their food before it all smells of death."

Tears spilled hotly from Lily's eyes as Chandler dragged her toward the door.

Four miles. She glanced across the dreary distance. *Juniper, where are you?*

"There's your other four renegades," said Kyle.

Juniper stood in the doorway, his heart slugging slow and hard as his gaze moved over three men staring glassy-eyed at the ceiling. A fourth slumped against the wall. The entire floor was a black pool of blood-soaked dirt.

"Hell."

Someone had walked among the dead, their boot prints leading from the stove to the door.

"Those Chandlers are a cold breed," Kyle said in a low tone.

"Took her," a weak voice groaned.

The man against the wall leaned his head back, and Juniper recognized his wide curving mustache.

"O'Grady?" He rushed forward and crouched beside him. "How long ago?"

"Mill," the man said. "Blackwater. Just…minutes."

"I know the place," Rogers said from behind him.

Kyle moved in beside Juniper and tugged at the man's bloody shirt. "I got him," he said. *"Go."*

The old mill was nothing more than a cluster of broken-down shacks not far off the river. Rain dripped through cracks in the roof, creating puddles along the rough wooden floor. A cold wind rose up through the floorboards, adding to her chill.

"We'll go at dawn, then," Chandler said to Mathews, the two of them spooning cold beans out of a can at a dry spot near the center of the room as Lily shivered in the corner. The fact that they could eat after shooting down those men sickened her.

"You're sure they'll deliver all the money?"

"Hell, yes. My brother and I pulled a job like this up in Idaho last year. No doubt Barns sent a wire with our message to ol' Carrington—he'll insist Barns meet our demands. We ride on with the loot while they look for what's left of the girl."

Lily tried to fight off her fear, telling herself they were fools to believe Juniper was scrambling to contact some fictional masculine entity and gathering up money that had already been dispersed to employees. Juniper would come for her, there was no other solution.

"Least we got something to occupy our time for tonight," Chandler said, his eyes on Lily.

She just hoped Juniper came in time.

"I been itching for that woman ever since she sashayed into the millhouse last week," said Mathews, his confidence having perked up since he'd been promised a third of the money. "Those hips of hers move in a way that makes a man hard." He shifted the front of his trousers, and a shudder of repulsion went through Lily.

Chandler laughed and pushed to his feet. "You'll have to wait your turn."

Lily watched helplessly as he stalked toward her. "'Bout time we see what you got under all them skirts," he said, hauling her up and dumping her over his shoulder.

A door shut behind them and Lily's back landed on the rotted mattress of an old bed. Her wrists bound behind her, pain shot through her shoulders. Her breath stalled as she stared at a long knife held out before her.

"I got no patience for buttons and such," he said, the tip of his blade sliding down the high collar at her throat. "So you better hold real still if you want to spare that soft skin."

Lily winced as her bodice and chemise fell open, the whisper of metal sliding down her belly. He stopped at the bulk of fabric at her waist.

"This is gonna be good," Chandler said. He dug his hand into the waistbands of her bloomers and skirts and ripped his knife through them, severing every last petticoat. He cut the knot binding her ankles and she felt her legs being pushed apart.

She screamed against the gag and kicked at her attacker. His knife clattered to the floor. Her other boot pounded into his chest.

He swore, shoving her down, his fingers biting into her thigh just before his weight flattened her, knocking the breath from her lungs. "I see you're going to make this fun," he said, his hand moving between them, opening his pants.

Panic took hold—she struggled against him, desperate to dislodge his weight. Repeated rifle shots broke through the terror screaming through her mind.

"Lily!"

Though his voice sounded miles away, she answered his call, screaming his name through the roll of fabric.

"Son of a *bitch!*" Chandler growled each word through clenched teeth and scrambled off her.

Mathews barreled into the room. "Sheriff Barns is co—" His eyes widened at the sight of her exposed body.

"No kidding!" Chandler shouted, adjusting his pants.

Lily rolled onto her side and pushed to her feet, her legs unsteady as she lunged for the doorway.

"Oh, no, you don't!" Chandler knocked her to the floor. "Grab that rope," he shouted to Mathews.

Lily screamed as her feet were wrenched back and secured to her bound wrists.

"Did you see him?" Chandler asked, hoisting her onto his shoulder.

"Didn't spot no one. He's headed this way, though."

Clamped against his disgusting chest, Lily reared back and slammed her forehead into Chandler's face. He gave a shout, but his grip only tightened and shifted her to the side.

"Damn, you're a handful!"

"What are you gonna do with her?"

"Find a place to stash her." Chandler kicked out a rotted slat on the back wall, took one step and stopped. "Perfect."

Lily splashed into ice-cold water. *A trough,* she thought, relieved to discover she lay in just a few inches of green water.

"We'll just plug that hole."

She glanced toward her bent knees to see Chandler shove one of her petticoats into a rusted hole. The water in the narrow trough instantly began to rise. A steady trickling sound drew her gaze to a drainpipe feeding in a steady trail of rainwater.

"If I die," said Chandler, leaning over her, "you drown. So you better hope I make it back here to warm you up."

She wished she could tell him she'd rather drown. Juniper would defeat him.

She tried to turn, to get onto her knees so she could sit up. The attempt only drenched the rag tied around her mouth, making her choke as she sucked in a breath.

Oh, God. She could hardly move. It was no use. Water continued to creep up the side of her face.

Thunder boomed overhead, which she took as a clear sign that she was going to drown. The sound of pounding raindrops echoed all around her, along with the memory of Juniper's words.

I'd rather have gotten shot, Lily, than see you come to harm! I will not have your blood on my conscience. Do you hear me? I won't!

Her heart ached at the thought of him finding her this way. She should have told him this morning.... She should have told him she forgave him.

She's here.

His back against the empty millhouse, Juniper scanned the ghostly abandoned shacks spaced across the clearing. Steady rainfall impeding his vision and hearing, he moved quickly to the side of the next building.

He'd seen two horses tied in the trees and had left Rogers behind, not about to chance the kid getting himself killed.

He crept up to another open door. Nothing was inside but dirt and cobwebs. "Show yourself, Chandler! I'm not leaving without her!"

A flash of lightning silhouetted a man's shadow on the next wall.

Juniper raised his rifle, watching the shadow move closer. Once the man reached the corner of the house, Juniper stepped out and slammed the butt of his gun against his head.

Mathews hit the ground and didn't move.

Before he could take another step, a voice sounded from behind him.

"Word has it you're a fast gun."

Juniper turned slowly and realized Chandler had meant to surround him. He stood six feet away in the drizzling rain, his hands noticeably free of a gun. "I hear you're common filth," he said.

Billy Chandler grinned. "I hope this visit doesn't mean I'll be disappointed tomorrow."

"Depends. You hoping to be nailed into a pine box? If so, you won't be disappointed."

Chandler laughed, his good mood adding to the fire raging in Juniper's gut. What had he done with Lily?

"I'm not even holding a gun," Chandler said, raising his hands.

"You're armed. Not that it matters. U.S. marshals are asking that you be brought in dead or alive. Dead works for me."

Chandler gave a slight shrug. "So long as you want your woman that way, too. You shouldn't be so quick to kill. Without Mathews or me, the lady will die before you find her." He tucked his coat behind the grip of a holstered revolver. "Toss down your guns and I'll let her live."

Juniper tossed his rifle aside. "I'll take the lady *now*." He slid back the edges of his range coat.

"You that confident you can outdraw me?"

He remembered his vow to get Lily back. "I'm fast," he bragged. "A lot of men have thought they were faster than me. A lot of men have died proving they were wrong."

"Guess I'll be the first to be right."

"Not likely. There isn't going to be any exchange of money, Chandler, and on the off chance you manage to shoot me, you'll still be dead by nightfall. A U.S. marshal is on his way up. He already caught your brother Ned."

Chandler's expression fell. "Like hell."

"Why do you think he's here? Tell me where she's at right now and I might let *you* live."

Mathews groaned beside him.

Chandler's eyes widened, then narrowed.

Another flaw in his plan.

He reached for his gun.

Juniper drew, putting two bullets through Chandler's chest before the man's gun fired aimlessly into the mud.

Juniper holstered his guns as Chandler dropped to the ground. Beside him Mathews rolled and reached for his rifle. Juniper lunged. Drawing his blade, he slammed it through the man's gun hand, pinning it to the ground.

"Where is she?" he shouted through Mathews's screams.

"Last cabin!" he wailed.

"Rogers!" Juniper called toward the woods. "Get over here!"

A moment later the kid came running from the trees.

"Tie him up," Juniper said, pulling out his blade and pushing off him. He grabbed his gun and ran toward the other cabins.

"Lily!" he shouted, rushing through the front door of the last one. In the back room his heart stalled at the sight of torn white petticoats trailed across the floor, but no other sign of her.

"Lily!" He pushed a loose board aside and stepped through a gap in the back wall.

A shimmer of gold drew his gaze to the left. Her copper hair floated on the surface of a water-filled trough.

"No!"

He reached in, hauling her up, shouting her name as he tugged a roll of fabric from her mouth.

"Lily?" he whispered.

She coughed, water spilling from her lips, and relief broke through him, shaking him. He lifted her the rest of the way out, quickly cutting away her bindings. Her arms fell around him, then gripped him as she coughed against his chest, wheezing for breath.

"Thank God." He sighed, pushing her wet hair away from her face as she blinked up at him.

"J-June." She started to tremble.

"I've got you, darlin'." He pulled her trembling weight into his arms. "I've got you."

Chapter Seventeen

Juniper couldn't ease his hold. "You scared me, boss."

"M-m-me t-too. I was t-t-terrified I—"

"I know you were," he said, her cheek cold against his lips as he kissed her. He lifted her into his arms and the chill of her wet clothes stung him through his thick duster. Her lips were frightfully blue.

"—w-w-wanted to t-t-tell you…"

Juniper carried her around to the front of the cabin. "Honey, we've got to get you warmed up."

She drew a shuddered breath, and snuggled closer to his warmth. "…that I forgive you."

Those last few words rang out with crystal clarity, dragging Juniper to a hard stop just inside the shack. He stared down at her in the dim light. She forgave him?

"It w-w-was…all I could think. I don't blame you. He m-made a mistake."

Juniper couldn't begin to fathom what those words meant to him. It was too much to grasp.

Her shivers intensified.

"We need to get you warmed," he said, reaching the front door of the cabin.

"Rogers!"

"Sheriff?" he said, running toward them.

"There's a coat in my left saddlebag. Bring it here."

"She all right?"

"We need to get her to camp. Bring up the horses, all of them."

Juniper leaned against the inside wall and slumped down. Lily shivered uncontrollably. He held her tight, pressing his lips to her slick hair, sharing his heat until Rogers arrived with her wool coat. When the door squeaked open, he held his arm out.

"We'll be out in a moment," he said as the young man stepped back outside.

"Lily, we need to get this wet dress off."

Her teeth chattered as she eased away from him. She shifted her shoulders and the front of her dress fell open.

Shock and rage roared inside him as he brushed aside the torn garment and guided her rope-burned wrists into the sleeves of her coat.

Lily saw the horror and anger playing across his face as he buttoned her into the warm coat. Moisture hazed his eyes when he gazed up at her.

"Sweetheart…?"

"No," she said. "H-he tried, but you—" Her breath broke on a sob. "I was so scared."

"Shh," he soothed, pulling her close.

But she couldn't stop. Fear and relief battled for release in great sobs. She tugged him closer, needing to cling to him, needing his strength. When the tears finally subsided and she found her breath, he was holding her, his lips brushing gently across her cheeks, spreading warmth throughout her cold body.

"You're all right," he soothed.

She nodded, sniffing loudly as she continued to absorb his heat and strength.

"Time to go. Want me to carry you?"

"I can walk," she said.

He eased up, keeping her close beside him. Outside, four saddled horses waited, the man called Rogers sitting on one. Juniper led her to his horse.

"Where are—"

"Mathews is detained," he said. "He'll have to wait for a deputy to come up and get him later." He stepped up into the saddle then reached for her, lifting her onto his lap.

Lily instantly settled against him. His chest shifted abruptly against her cheek. She eased back and saw that he'd shrugged off his long coat. He draped the dark canvas around her shoulders, surrounding her with his heat as he pulled her snug against him.

"Let's get you home."

"Okay," she whispered. Feeling warm and secure in the arms of her sheriff, Lily closed her eyes and burrowed against him.

* * *

A blend of harsh voices intruded on her sleep, different from the gentle murmurs between Juniper and Kyle intermittently filtering through her dazed mind. She shifted against Juniper's warmth, subtly reassuring herself he still held her. The intrusive noise grew louder, forcing Lily to open her eyes.

They were surrounded by a sea of men. Startled by the sight of so many faces staring at her, she pressed her face to Juniper's shirt, her arms reaching for his neck.

He dismounted and cradled her tightly. "Miss Carrington is going to be all right. Everyone can get on back to their business."

"You don't gotta hide her from us," one called out.

"We're sure glad she wasn't hurt," shouted another.

"Ain't often we got a single woman in camp."

Juniper stopped. He turned, and Lily tightened her hold on him. "She's not single."

The steel in his voice tensed Lily's sore muscles.

"She's spoken for."

"By who?" someone shouted out.

"By *me*. Any man who so much as stares at my girl for more than a heartbeat will be dodging my bullets. Y'all got that?"

A murmur of grumbles went through the crowd. Lily didn't draw a full breath until Juniper had stepped inside a cabin and closed the door behind them.

"I'm *your* girl?" she asked.

His fierce scowl melted into a crooked grin. "If I

didn't stake a claim they'd be hounding at the door, waiting for the chance to woo you."

"The horror."

"Exactly." He brushed a soft kiss across her lips, then set her on a soft mattress. He lit a lamp on the small table beside the bed.

Lily glanced around a cabin a quarter the size of any other she'd seen in the camp. He gathered up a patchwork quilt spread across the bed and pulled it over her shoulders. She noticed the name May in small yellow letters on the ribbing.

Juniper's cabin.

"Sit tight, sweetheart. I'll be right back with something to warm you up."

Panic flared as he crossed the small room. "June?"

He paused at the door. "Günter's on the steps right outside. Would you rather I have him come in?"

She drew a ragged breath and shook her head. "No."

"I'll be right back," he said again. He stepped outside, and Lily pulled the blanket tight around her trembling body, shivering despite the warmth of her wool coat and quilt.

Nothing a few hours in Juniper's arms couldn't abate.

He was back within a few minutes, opening the door wide, saying, "There should be just enough room."

A man backed into the cabin, his arms gripping the end of a big brass bathtub.

"Right there on the floor," Juniper instructed. The long tub took up nearly all the space beside the bed as two men set it into place. They quickly retreated. Next came a procession of men hoisting buckets of steaming water. None of them so much as glanced in her direction as they filled the tub.

The moment the door closed behind the last man, Juniper started toward her, his expression dark with purpose. He reached for her foot and began unlacing her boot. Setting aside her boots and stockings, his hands moved methodically down the buttons on her coat. He gently pulled the garment away and lifted her into his arms, shifting her over the tub just a couple feet away.

Air hissed through her teeth as he lowered her into the steaming water. Cold to the bone, the warm water sent a prick of needling sensation across her skin. The raw abrasions around her wrists burned.

"Okay?" he asked.

She sucked in a jagged breath, and pain slowly gave way to soothing relief. "Yes." She curled forward, raising her knees, rubbing the sting from her skin.

"Lie back and wet your hair," he said from behind her, the strong scent of soap filling her senses. She glanced over her shoulder to find him kneeling at the curved end of the tub, his hands working a bar of soap into a white lather.

She glanced down at the steaming surface appearing dark in the soft lamplight. The thought of submerging her head into the water put the chill right back in her skin. She remembered the water rising in that trough, the shaft of fear that had spiked through her when she could no longer strain to keep her head above the murky water. Pain had throbbed through her chest as she had fought to hold her breath until she was sure she'd pass out or drown at any moment.

A shudder swept through her. "I'd rather not."

Juniper's hands froze on the soap. "I wasn't thinking," he said, his expression apologetic. He stood, grabbed a large tin cup from a shelf behind him then knelt back down. "Tilt your head back," he whispered.

Lily closed her eyes and did as he asked. She sighed as he doused her scalp with warm water. His strong fingers worked the soap deep into her grimy hair, sending ripples of pleasing sensations dancing down her neck to the rest of her body.

As he finished rinsing out her hair, a knock sounded at the door. "That should be Reg with your clean clothes. Here," he said, handing her the soap and a cloth. "He'll want to know how you're doing."

Before she could say a word, Juniper was out the door. Anxious to get out of the water despite the soothing warmth, Lily quickly scrubbed up. Finished, she draped the cloth over the side of the tub. The door squeaked open, preventing her from rising.

"June?"

"It's me," he said, though all she saw was a pile of petticoats and a light gray dress being tossed at the bed. He spoke in a low murmur to someone on the other side of the door.

"Send word if she needs anything else," she heard Regi say.

"Will do." Juniper stepped inside holding a silver tray. Her gaze was trained on her chocolate pot as he kicked the door shut behind him. His slow grin brought the burn of tears to her eyes.

"Figured this would be just the thing to get you good and warm." He slid the tray onto the table and filled the cup.

Lily began to stand.

"Stay where you are," Juniper insisted.

"But—"

"You're not done warming," he said. *Sit.*

Lily settled back into the warm bath as he handed her a cup of hot chocolate. Just the smell of the rich chocolate made her stomach churn. Wrapping her hands around the warm mug, she took a slow drink and shut her eyes as warm liquid moved through her. But it couldn't reach the chill deep in her bones.

"Better?"

"I will be," she said, looking up at him, "once you strip off those wet clothes and join me."

"That may not be the best idea."

"It's a fine idea. You need warming, too."

"Believe me," he said, his lips tilting with a smile, "I'm plenty warm."

"I'm not."

Juniper released a hard sigh. "Lily—"

"I need you to warm me."

He stared at her for a long moment, then turned away

and barred the door. He reached for his belt buckle, saying, "All right. So long as you know that's my sole intention, to warm you." He stripped off his damp clothes in a matter of seconds, and she noted parts of him were definitely heating up. She needed every bit of his heat.

"Scoot forward."

She did, smiling as he stepped into the long tub and eased down behind her, raising the water level to her shoulders. His arms slid around her middle as she leaned back, settling against his chest as his long legs stretched out on either side of her. Lily released a long, shuddering breath, and her body finally relaxed completely.

"Perfect." She sighed, thankful to have feeling back in her fingers and toes, not to mention every place where his skin brushed hers.

"How's your chocolate?" he asked after a moment. She held her cup up in offering.

"Sharing?"

"Of course."

He wrapped his hand around hers, took a drink and released her.

"Do you like it?" she asked, glancing over her shoulder at him.

"Nearly as sweet as you," he said, his arm sliding back around her middle.

"This is your cabin," she said, her gaze sliding over the tidy, functional space as she drank the rest of her cocoa.

"Yep."

"It's...*cozy*."

His low chuckle vibrated against her back. "It's a hovel. But having my own place beats bunking with twenty lumberjacks."

"Do you like being a lawman?"

"I guess." He lifted the empty cup from her hand, his long arm easily setting it aside. Lily could hardly see anything beyond the brass sides of the tub, and Juniper's knees raised on either side of her—which suited her just fine.

"Do you like being a business tycoon?"

She grinned at the title. "Sometimes. I like being a part of something I can watch continually grow. But I've never thought much beyond profit margins, never really understanding how people were affected by my decisions. Being here has been enlightening. I've been given a whole new perspective, not just for this company, but so many others." She caressed the long fingers laced across her stomach. "Despite all that's happened, I'm glad I came. I'm glad I met you."

Juniper kissed the top of her head, and she hoped that was some kind of agreement.

"I want to fix things," she said.

"I know you do."

She eased forward and turned to look up at him. "Do you think I can?"

Juniper was stunned she'd ask him such a question, yet she stared up at him as though his opinion had considerable weight. "I think you're amazing," he said in flat honesty. "A bunch of griping lumberjacks should be the last thing on your mind right now. You've barely thawed out. And now you're campaigning for them?"

The memory of how close he'd come to losing her brought the tension back into his muscles. "You could have been killed, Lily. God knows I can't get you off this mountain fast enough."

"I created this whole situation. You can't deny it."

"Sweetheart, this camp was having problems long before you took it over. Right now, my *only* concern is you."

She leaned up and kissed his lips. "I like the sound of that. Just me and you."

Her gentle smile brought back the words she'd spoken as she shivered in his arms: "I forgive you."

The words bumped around in his subconscious, yet he hadn't forgotten that just a week ago she'd had reason enough to want him dead.

Some things are worse than death, his heart cautioned. Wanting what he couldn't have; falling for a woman who deserved so much more than he had to offer.

Her hand found him beneath the water, jolting him from his thoughts. The gliding caress hardened him in a rush and had him swearing under his breath.

"Oops. Sorry." She flashed a grin that was anything

but apologetic as her hand continued to bump his thighs beneath the water. "I'm looking for the soap."

"I almost believe you."

Her green eyes widened, as though his doubt of her intentions shocked her. "I dropped it when you brought in the hot chocolate. See?" She held up the white bar. "Should I get the rinse cup or are you going under?"

Juniper couldn't fight his laughter, mostly because she delighted him like nothing ever had, and partly because there was no way in hell he'd withstand a scrubbing. "Darlin', I don't—"

"The cup," she said, rising up as though she intended to get out of the tub.

"Get back in here," he said, his hands closing over her waist, the sight of her slick skin making him groan against a lash of raw desire. "I can do my own scrubbing. Move back," he said, then leaned forward to dunk his head into the water between them.

Lily's hands slid into his wet hair the moment he sat back. Then she turned and shifted her knees over his thighs as she sat up, working her fingers across his scalp.

His breath burning holes through his lungs, Juniper stared at the pink water-beaded tips of her breasts just inches from his lips.

"You're torturing me," he whispered, his hand moving up the soft curves of her body.

"Am I?" she asked, her husky tone, the smile in her voice telling him she wanted his caress as deeply as he wanted to caress her. Unable to resist, he dipped his head and drew the firm pink tip into his mouth. Her fingers flexed in his hair. Her soft moan echoed his own.

"Lie back," she said in a ragged breath. "So you can rinse."

Releasing her, he leaned back into the water and furiously scrubbed the suds from his hair, resenting every second he wasn't holding her. When he rose up, Lily was over him, reaching for him, joining their bodies.

Juniper's groan vibrated through both of them. Her hips shifted, her body demanding, relentless, *so damn alive.*

At the first silken tug of her body closing around him, release ripped through him like a bolt of lightning searching across a dark sky. He grabbed her hips, halting the maddening movements, but he couldn't slow his own hot, searing pulses. With a shout that was her name, he spent himself inside her.

Catching his breath, he slumped back against the tub, annoyed by his startling lack of control. "Damn."

Lily followed him back, soothing him with gentle kisses. "I love watching you," she said in a breathless whisper, the tender core of her body caressing him, "and feeling your pleasure."

That quickly, a new charge of passion stirred. The fire in his blood exceeding the temperature of the water, Juniper lifted her off him and into his arms as he stood.

"June!"

"If I don't get you out of this tub, we're going to flood the cabin."

A while later they were cuddled up in bed and Lily was sighing with utter contentment.

"I never thought I'd find something I enjoyed more than my chocolate."

Juniper's low chuckle churned the wonderful swirls of sensation still shimmering inside her. "Should I take that as a compliment?"

"Of the greatest accord," she said, smiling, hugging him. "You, Juniper Barns, are decadence personified."

His lips grazed the shell of her ear. "I should feed you," he said.

She shifted against the warmth of his skin, her cheek nuzzling into the hollow beneath his shoulders. "Later. Right now I have everything I need."

Chapter Eighteen

He had to admit he didn't mind the coziness of his cabin. The tight space made it convenient to do just about everything in bed. They'd eaten breakfast, read through some files Günter had brought over for Lily and made love a couple of times in between. The one time they'd gotten dressed and sat at the table, Lily had done her best to give him a statement of all that had happened on the mountain, a task that was as hard on Juniper as it had been on Lily. She'd been tearful and shivering by the time they'd finished. He'd dropped his pencil and hadn't stopped kissing her until neither one of them could think beyond the passion rising between them.

Lily, currently snuggled against his side, was warm and sated. She'd been quiet for a long while, her head against his shoulder, her fingers brushing lightly over his chest as her toes rubbed against his calf.

Sweet mercy. A man could get used to this.

In another hour her carriage would be waiting to cart her down to The Grove. He hadn't told her yet that he wouldn't be going along. He had prisoners and dead scattered in all directions and enough reports to write to keep him busy for several weeks. His first priority was to get Lily home. Kyle would go along with the other hired escorts, staying with her until they reached San Francisco. June would have the peace of mind of knowing she was well protected.

"June?"

"Hmm?"

"What's to keep the men from locating their homes closer to the mill so they can see their families more often? Why can't we have a place where husbands can stay with their wives?"

He had a notion her mind had been steeped in business rather than daydreams. "Company land. Company policy."

"That's what I thought. The one complaint I keep hearing is that the men are so isolated from their families. Don't you think they'd be more content if they had the option to stay with their wives?"

"Having you in my bed makes me believe it would."

Lily smiled. This was the reaction she'd hoped for. She certainly enjoyed being in his bed.

"But there are valid safety issues to consider. You allow wives, you'll have children. Logging sites are hazardous, even for the workers."

"Couldn't we establish housing beyond the foresting, but close enough for the men to go home at night?"

"Jim has made that suggestion over the years. You'd have to designate some land and be willing to parcel it out."

"What do *you* think?"

He lifted onto his elbow, easing her head onto the pillow as he smiled down at her. "That you sure are pretty when you're talking business." His gaze trailed down her body. "Makes it hard not to get distracted."

She laughed and pulled the sheet up to her chin. "Pay attention."

"All right." He pulled her close and brushed his lips lightly over hers. "Tell me what's brewing in that mind of yours. I promise to pay attention."

When they finally emerged from the cabin, a clear, blue sky shone bright overhead as giant redwoods chased early afternoon shadows over the grounds. Walking through the camp beneath the weight of Juniper's protective arm, Lily buzzed with energy. Her mind was a flurry of ideas, and Juniper had listened to every one of them and offered suggestions. There was so much to do.

"Well, don't you look refreshed?" Regi stood on the stoop of their cabin.

"Miss Carrington," Juniper said with formal politeness as he stepped away from her.

"Sheriff Barns," she replied.

"I'm going to leave you to pack while I go check on a few things. She's in your care," he said to Regi.

"Oh, I do believe we're all well guarded," Regi said in a droll tone.

Lily didn't know what he meant until she watched Juniper walk toward two tall carriages and teams of horses waiting farther out. A group of large men stood near them, all wearing long dusters, each with a star pinned to his chest. Kyle stood among them and clapped Juniper on the shoulder.

"Who are they?" asked Lily.

"*That,*" said Regi, shuffling down the steps, "is our escort."

"*Six* lawmen?"

"Seven armed guards including the one called Marshal Darby. I don't know if they're all lawmen or if some were deputized just for the occasion. Your sheriff isn't taking any chances of you getting away again. Marshal Darby has been put in charge of our journey home."

"Juniper isn't going with us to The Grove?"

"According to Marshal Darby he still has prisoners on the mountain and fallen men to attend to today. Your sheriff's first priority is to see you sent off safely, of which I'm entirely grateful. I don't think I've seen a more frightening sight than your sheriff out of his mind with worry."

Lily couldn't pull her gaze away from Juniper. He wasn't going with them? Why hadn't he told her?

Regi's arm came around her. "Having fretted over you so much yesterday, I appreciate the extra precautions."

Did he even intend to tell her goodbye?

"I trust your bath and sleeping accommodations were agreeable?" Regi asked.

"Very much." Juniper had given her everything she'd asked for—and more.

"And your sheriff, was he agreeable, as well?"

"Nothing short of a gentleman."

"Uh-huh," Regi said.

She watched Juniper talk to the other men, his expression relaxed, as though he couldn't care less that he was about to send her off. Dear God, surely he knew how she felt about him.

"Well we might as well head to the coach. The last of our luggage was just loaded. After yesterday, I imagine you'll be wanting to rid yourself of this place once we return."

"Certainly not," she said, startled by Regi's assumption. "I'm not about to turn my back on them now. In fact, I'm certain we can greatly improve the conditions of our workers. I want to help them."

"Good God, Lil. Some of those men tried to kill you."

"And others died trying to help me." Just as Juniper had told her, the men who'd been shot in that ramshackle cabin had only wanted to provide for their families—they'd been misled, and died with intentions to set it right. "Carrington Industries is going to help this camp."

Regi held her gaze for a moment. "Are you sure your fondness for the sheriff isn't influencing this decision?"

"Of course not. I was interested in this company before I knew about Juniper. Being here has given me a new respect for my employees and what they do for our company."

"Developing a fondness for smelly beasts of labor, are we?"

She flushed at the memory of how callous she'd been toward employees she'd never met. "They're *men*, Reginald, with lives and families."

"You don't say? What a novel concept."

"I'm being serious."

"You're being human, love. And I have to say, it agrees with you. If you're going to improve efficiency around here, you may want to start with hiring a new mill manager."

"Replace Mr. Grimshaw? Why?"

"There's a good reason why he was of no help to our staff. He's completely illiterate."

Lily gaped at him. "How can that be? Are you sure?"

"Quite."

She glanced again at Juniper. He must know. What else hadn't he told her? She lifted her skirt and hurried toward the group of men.

"Excuse me," she said, looking past a cluster of broad shoulders. *"Sheriff Barns?"*

Surprised by Lily's sharp tone, Juniper looked away from the high perch of the driver and met her poignant stare. Her green eyes snapped with anger. "Are you all packed up?" he asked, glancing quickly at Reg, who didn't seem to share her distress.

"The luggage has been taken care of. Can I speak with you?"

Aw, hell. She'd obviously figured out he wouldn't be joining her in The Grove. Here it came...the accusations of unfulfilled expectations and unspoken promises. He knew he couldn't avoid this—but he sure as hell wished he could.

"Certainly." He held his arm out to her. She snatched his elbow with a grip that said she wasn't letting go until she'd said her piece. He started for the side of a cabin, away from onlookers.

"Five minutes," Kyle called after them. "We need to get moving."

Juniper ignored him and led Lily to the back of a cabin.

Her arms were crossed stiffly over the bodice of her gray dress as he turned to face her.

"Jim Grimshaw can't read?"

That hadn't been what he was expecting. "No," he said. "He can't."

"Then how can he be in control of this mill?"

"Because he knows this forest and this mill better than most men know the back of their own hand."

"There's more to running a mill than knowing the trees and equipment. All the correspondence—"

"Has been done through me or one of the other mill workers."

"So that's why he seemed so lost without the sheriff on the day we arrived. This won't do, not when—"

"Don't get the wrong impression. Jim runs this place. All I did was read his mail and take some notes."

"This camp lacks proper documentation. We can't improve our filing and—"

"That's got nothing to do with Jim. Honestly, Lily, Jim does a brilliant job. You won't find a man better suited for organizing your workers and workloads. What he needs is office help. We're understaffed. And Jim does the work of three foremen."

"So you're saying we need to hire an *office* manager, to take care of the necessary paperwork?"

"That would be my suggestion. Leave Jim to do what he does best—manage the crews and the work."

Her brow nettled, and Juniper grinned. He wanted to touch, to kiss. Hell, he wanted to lock her up in his cabin and never let her go. He wanted too much, more than he could ever give her.

"Couldn't he learn to read?" she asked.

Juniper shrugged. "Only if he can find the time. He already works around the clock for this camp. When would he have time for studies? Especially when his free time should go to his family, who don't see him but once a month or so."

"But with a new community—"

"Which at the moment is nothing more than an idea you have yet to fully research. Even if it's a go, the development will likely be a good year away."

"I know," she said defensively.

He knew she did. The lady didn't need anyone to tell her her business. He could just imagine the poor defeated saps who'd tried. God, he was crazy about her.

Her eyes widened, and he realized he wasn't exactly hiding his open amusement.

"What?" she demanded.

"Nothin'."

"You're laughing at me," she accused.

"I'm not making a sound," he argued, even as a chuckle began to rise from his chest.

Her expression fell. "Juniper?"

He tucked his fingers into his pant pockets to keep from pulling her into the kiss he sorely wanted. "Sorry. I just love watching you think."

Her stricken expression crumbled into something far more somber. *Hell.* He thought she might cry, and figured it might be easier to watch her leave with anger in her eyes rather than tears.

Nothing's going to make this easier. And he'd hate himself if she left in anger.

"If you have any problems or concerns after you get home, you can always send me a wire. I'll get it from either location."

Lily could only nod, her thoughts suddenly not having a thing to do with the company. He was pulling away from her—she sensed it in his tone, his rigid stance. He had filled every empty space in her heart, and he was going to just…send her away? With nothing?

"Why didn't you tell me you weren't going with us to The Grove?"

"I wish I could, but I'm needed here. I have men to bring in, families to contact. I'll be tied up with reports for a good long while."

She nodded her understanding. He had his job to do. But that didn't excuse his lack of courtesy by sending her off with no word of his feelings for her. She couldn't be the only one who'd fallen—he had to feel for her just as deeply. The way he'd made love to her, it was more than just physical desire.

"Will you come to see me in San Francisco?"

He lowered his gaze, and Lily's breath stalled, pain stealing into her chest.

"Juniper?"

He glanced up and she saw the truth in his eyes—he didn't intend to see her again. His breath expelled in a hard sigh.

"I suppose that's my answer."

"I've got nothing to offer you, Lily. After watching you in action, it's plain to see that you belong in San Francisco."

"I see. In other words, you've caught a glimpse of my business side and are running for safety."

"*No.*"

"What else am I to think?"

"That I have your best interests at heart."

"Not if you believe that includes a future without you in my life."

"You deserve better."

"I deserve to be with the man I love. But only if he loves me in return."

"Lily. I'm just...*you know what I am.*"

"Yes," she said, stepping closer. "A good man."

He shook his head. "The violence of my past follows me."

"I'm already a part of your past, Juniper. It's your future I care about. You wouldn't have to live in the city. I'd go anywhere, the hills, these mountains. I could—"

"*No.*"

"*I love you.*"

Sheer anguish filled his expression.

"You don't feel the same," she said, stunned by his reaction.

"Jeez, Lily. Not everything in life is so cut-and-dried!"

"This is. You're shutting me out, and I won't have it! Either you care for me or—"

"*I do!* You know I do. It's killing me to send you off, to not be the one to—"

"I'll be fine, as long as I know you're not shutting me out completely."

"I can't see any other way."

"Because you're looking back and not forward! Perhaps you need to put down your guns and stop living through your past, waiting for it to resurface! We could do anything, go anywhere."

He shook his head, fighting the alluring images of a life he'd sell his soul to have. But his soul had already been bartered, violence and bloodshed becoming a part of the life he couldn't escape. No good woman deserved to be bound to such a life, past or present. It was his past that had brought her here, exposing her to a violence that had nearly gotten her killed.

"I care for you," he said, aching to kiss her, his need to hold her tearing at his soul. Closing his heart to the pain, he took a step back. "And I…I wish you well."

Hurt registered across her pretty features as she comprehended his refusal.

"You two about done?" Kyle asked, stepping around the corner. "Daylight's burning."

"Give us a minute," Juniper said through clenched teeth.

"No need." Tears blurred her vision as she stared up at his hard gaze. He'd said all that needed saying. He wasn't willing to give them a chance. He didn't want her in his life.

She turned in a whirl of skirts and hurried toward the carriage, fighting back the burn of tears. Dear God, why hadn't she seen this coming? He'd warned her. His hesitation had been clear every time they'd been together. And she'd ignored all of it. She'd only been focused on how she felt when she was with him, the love blossoming in her heart—and *he* hadn't stopped counting down the days until he'd be rid of her.

How many times had he told her just that? *God knows I can't get you off this mountain fast enough.*

She hadn't fully comprehended the finality of those words. She hadn't let herself believe he wouldn't open his heart to her, as she had to him.

"Front carriage," Kyle said from behind her. He stepped in front of her to open the door and held his hand out to assist her up.

"Thank you," she said, refusing to meet his gaze.

"Is everything okay?" he asked, his hand closing over her arm before she could duck inside.

"Splendid." She was in love with Juniper, and he "wished her well."

She pulled away from Kyle's grasp and slammed onto the cushioned seat across from Regi. Her cousin's eyes widened at the sight of her.

"Oh, dear."

I tell him I love him, and he wishes me well?

Anger swelled inside her. He'd made her love him, had woven his way into her heart, making her long for more than her life in San Francisco could ever give her. She wanted love.

She would damn well hold him accountable!

"Sweetness?" Reginald said. "Are you all right?"

"Just fine."

"What of you and your sheriff?"

"I'd rather not talk about it." The coach rocked forward, and tears again threatened her eyes.

"Did you tell him?"

She drew a deep breath and glanced at Reginald. "Tell him what?"

"The obvious," he said, sympathy clear in his gaze.

Tears instantly hazed her vision and streaked hotly across her cheeks. "I did."

"My God, are you crying?"

Lily wiped at her cheeks, but tears continued to flow. "Yes, I'm crying!"

"Sweetness, what did he say?"

"He said he cared about me and he *wished me well*."

"Oh, Lily."

"I told him I loved him, Reginald, and he *wished me well*."

"You have known him just over a week, sweetness. This has to be sudden for a man. What was he expected to do?"

To love her back, to want to build a future with her.

"You asked him to stay on and oversee our transitions. He can't do that from your bedroom in San Francisco. What would you have him do, become your personal bodyguard and follow you around the office all day?"

"Of course not!" she snapped.

"Well then? Your days are filled with nothing but work and you're hardly one for relinquishing power. Where exactly would you fit him into your life?"

Realizing she didn't know the answer, she glanced out of the small window at the trees passing by.

Surely they could find a compromise between her life and his.

"Love has addled your usually rational mind," said Regi.

That was likely true. "I didn't tell him to just drop his duties," she protested, the hurt inside her refusing to relent. "I asked if he'd come see me."

"He will."

Lily wanted to trust the certainty in Regi's voice, but she couldn't. "He said otherwise."

"He's overwhelmed. We've left him with no small task. Pardon me for saying so, love, but you can be quite demanding."

She sucked in a sharp breath. She hadn't demanded Juniper love her. Had she?

"Give him some time. You made your offer. Be patient. Wait for him to come to you."

"And what if he doesn't?"

"We do what we've always done, love."

"Feed off each other's misery?"

He laughed and opened the newspaper sitting on the bench beside him. "See there, you're coming back to your normal self already."

No, she wasn't. Juniper Barns had changed her...for the better. He'd given her a gift—a gift that wouldn't be complete without him.

Chapter Nineteen

The offices downstairs hummed with activity. At nine o'clock in the morning, Lily was just leaving her private quarters on the third floor. She gripped the oak banister and stepped down onto the carpeted stair, lifting her ivory skirt. She would've been down earlier had she not tried on more than a dozen dresses. All of them fit too snugly across the bosom. She needed to go shopping soon, or at least call in a dressmaker.

As she descended to the base of the stairs, her gaze swept across the wide room filled with desks and filing cabinets, men milling about between them—the heart of Carrington Industries. She greeted a chorus of good-mornings as she made her way toward her office. A few months ago she'd have been in her office by 6:00 a.m. and worked until after supper. Yet this was the first time in six weeks she'd managed to make it downstairs before ten-thirty.

In spite of her absence, her company hadn't collapsed. Her staff had easily taken up the slack. Even

Regi had stepped up, taking over a number of her projects with surprising zeal and tact.

"Miss Carrington."

Lily slowed as one of her accountants hurried toward her. Light glinted off his glasses as he rushed past a side window.

"Mr. Allen?" *Nicholas* Allen she silently noted. "Glad to see you back at the office. I hope your children are feeling better."

His eyes widened behind his spectacles. She supposed her mention of family was still something new to some of her employees. After meeting with Mr. Dobbs's widow and his two grown children, she'd realized how very little she knew of her office staff, people she saw on a daily basis and had worked with for years. Her lack of interest had been inexcusable. "Emily told me all of your children had come down with the chicken pox."

"Yes, and I do apologize—"

"No apology needed. Four children with high fevers and blisters—your Agnes must have been a fright with worry."

"She was that. All four have faired well, aside from the itching. She's keeping them in mittens until they heal completely."

"Mittens in July? The poor dears."

"I can assure you it is their mother who suffers," he said with a wry grin. "I thought you'd like to see this." He held out a spreadsheet. "Pine Ridge is doing well."

She stared blankly at the page, fighting a sudden

rush of sadness. Since their return, Regi had handled all of the Pine Ridge business and negotiations. Just the mention of the lumber camp brought back the sting of Juniper's rejection. He'd made his feelings crystal clear over the past two and a half months. She'd not heard a word from him.

"That's wonderful news. Is Reginald in his office?"

"He was earlier this morning. We've been working on the housing presentation."

"I look forward to seeing it."

"I'll see you in the downstairs boardroom at one," he said, walking back to his desk.

Monthly reports, she thought. There'd been a positive vibe throughout the office, and a company overview would cheer her up.

Outside the two oversize offices at the front of the building, her secretary's desk sat empty. Regi's door stood slightly ajar. She decided to step in and congratulate him on his progress with Pine Ridge. A new, polished brass plate adorned the wall beside his office, boasting his new title of president. She never would have guessed how readily he'd take to his newfound responsibilities. But then, Regi had never let her down.

She knocked lightly before pushing the door open. "Regi?"

Sunlight poured into the room from the front windows overlooking the street below. She stepped inside the abandoned office lined with cherry wood paneling and sturdy bookshelves. File folders were spaced across his desk in neat piles, a few lying open, with pencils scattered between them.

Bold handwriting on an envelope at the corner of his desk caught her attention. She recognized the large, clear print. The envelope was addressed to Reginald; the sender—one Juniper Barns.

She knew they'd been corresponding, but seeing the handwritten proof felt like a slap in the face. Why hadn't he written to *her?* The man was more than capable of drafting a letter. She suspected he'd had something to do with the letters she'd received from the six men who'd stood trial for robbing the payroll. Each had thanked her for the letter she'd sent requesting the judge to consider their families and reduce their sentences. According to Reginald, the nine-month prison term they'd received for the robbery could have been up to five years or longer.

She'd appreciated their notes of thanks and apology, but what she wanted more than anything was to hear from Juniper. Had he simply wiped her from his thoughts the moment she'd left?

His sisters had already written to her twice. First to thank her for the chocolate and silver pot, and a second letter a month later, expressing ther enjoyment of her gift and their hopes to see her and Regi when the family came to San Francisco in September. By then she wouldn't be able to hide her condition.

She snatched up the envelope. Her thumb brushed over the dried ink. Addressed to her office and yet he couldn't be troubled to write even the shortest note to her? Did he truly have nothing at all to say to her?

Her finger slipped beneath the flap and ripped. What did he have to say to Regi that he wasn't telling her? She unfolded a handwritten letter, dated the week prior.

Dear Reginald,
Having fulfilled my obligations to Carrington Industries, I am hereby submitting my two-week notice of resignation, effective…

He was leaving.

Lily slumped into Regi's chair. *I've been patient. I've waited. He's not coming.*

"Sweetness?" Regi walked across his office looking crisp and dapper in his dark suit, a steaming cup of coffee in his hand, his expression creased with worry. "Are you feeling ill? Should I call for some sweet tea?"

"No," she said, forcing a smile. "I feel quite well, better than I've been in weeks." She couldn't force the man to love her. She could survive without Juniper. "Mr. Allen just showed me the increased profit reports for Pine Ridge. I came to congratulate you."

Regi stared at her a moment. He glanced at the open letter in her hand, then again met her gaze. "What's wrong, Lily?"

"You received a letter," she said, the ache in her chest expanding with each breath.

"One I see you have opened for me. The letter from Sheriff Barns?"

She glanced down at the page in her hand, and couldn't help but brush her fingers over Juniper's bold signature, the closest she'd been to him in nearly three months. "He's resigned."

"As we knew he would. That was the agreement. He'd stay on as sheriff until our new management was implemented. Next week we present the plans for the Pine Ridge Sierra Lumber Camp community, and his obligations to the company are finished."

His obligations to the company.

Her nausea was back.

"Lily, why don't you just tell him? He would be here in a flash."

"My condition is hardly a reason to—"

"Dearest, your *condition* is going to produce a child in just over six short months. Had I known the cause of your sickness before attending the trial, I'd have dragged him out of those hills by his ear."

Lily frowned at Juniper's letter of resignation, fighting another wave of useless tears. "I don't want him to be dragged anywhere. I am fully capable of taking care of myself and a child."

Regi moved beside her and leaned against the desk. "Lily, you have to tell him. He has a right to know."

"*No, he doesn't.* If he wanted to know of my well-being, he could have included a note with his resignation." She tossed the letter onto his desk. "At the trial he told you he was glad that I'd stayed in San Francisco and had allowed you to head up the project." That had hurt. Not only did he not miss her, he'd been pleased by her absence.

"I also told you he was lying through his teeth."

"You don't know that."

"I most certainly do. When I stepped from the carriage and you didn't follow me out, his expression was positively crestfallen. His first concern was for you. Had I even hinted that you were ill, I have no doubt he'd have ridden straight to this office. But I kept my word and my silence. He cares for you, Lily."

"Yes, he told me, right before he *wished me well* and sent me off to live my life without him. You were the one who said to be patient! I've been patient, Reginald!"

Regi wasn't the least bit put out by her show of anger. He'd rather see fire in her eyes than the sadness she'd been trying to conceal from him.

"Since when do you listen to me? For that matter, since when do you sit about and allow others to dictate how you should live your life?"

"I'm not!"

"Oh, no? Then why aren't you accompanying me next week? This housing community was your idea, Lily. Who is he to take away your joy of seeing your plans come to fruition? You should be there to see their reaction to this project."

Regi watched her eyes spark with interest and irritation. He wasn't about to let her walk away from Barns unwed and miserable.

"I am feeling better," she said.

"Then it's settled."

"But you have to promise me, Regi, not a word to him about me. You have to let me deal with Juniper."

"Agreed. So long as you talk to him."

"And you'll support me, no matter the outcome?"

"Of course." She would be blissfully wed or Juniper Barns would have hell to pay. "I'll make all the arrangements."

"Very well." She straightened out of his chair. "Don't be late for the one-o'clock meeting."

He smiled, glad to see some of the old Lily spark back in her eyes.

"Poor man has no idea what he's in for."

Chapter Twenty

"You sure about this?"

Günter stared at the tin star Juniper had tossed onto the desk.

"It's time." *Beyond time.* Since mailing off his resignation to Reg, he'd been counting down the days. In the past three months, he'd fulfilled all of his obligations to Carrington Lumber. With the mill running at full capacity, all the new positions filled, the office staff settled and court hearings completed—he was a free man. Free to take Lily's advice and the first steps toward finding his future.

Perhaps you need to put down your guns and stop living through your past, waiting for it to resurface!

She'd been right, of course. And he was done with waiting on the past. One more week, and she'd find herself being courted with a vengeance. He knew he'd hurt her, but never imagined she'd give control of Pine Ridge over to Reg to put further distance between them. She'd been so excited about her plans...and he'd clearly ruined them for her. But she was a part of this place—her name was practically legend among the men, Miss Carrington, their harrowing Joan of Arc. She'd consumed every spare moment of his thoughts for the past three months, making sleep downright unbearable. He'd get his sorry hide spiffed up, pick out the fanciest diamond ring his savings could handle and—

"Get your asses over to the millhouse, now!" Jim Grimshaw's voice carried through the open door, followed by muttered replies before the mill manager stormed into the jailhouse. "I'm rounding up stragglers for the meeting. Are you two coming over to help keep things under control?"

"You've got two deputies over there," Juniper said. "I'm just packing up my stuff."

"Can you take that new office assistant Carrington hired with you? The man is more work than help, following me around, shoving papers under my nose and asking me to read this and that."

Juniper shook his head. When the lady had an idea she dug in and saw it through. "I do believe your new office assistant is Lily's subtle way of hiring you a reading tutor."

"Subtle, my ass. I swear, if I hear the words 'sound it out, Grimshaw' one more time, I'm going to *knock* him out."

Juniper and Günter chuckled. He didn't doubt the promise buried in those words.

"Not that I don't appreciate all that the Carringtons have done for this camp. My Marybeth is counting the days until she can hang the new curtains she made for our future Pine Ridge house. Speaking of ladies, you might want to hurry on over to the millhouse. Your lady is causing quite the commotion."

"*My* lady?" Juniper asked.

"I suppose you want me to spell her name out, too?"

"Lily is *here?*"

Jim took a step back. "Don't shoot the messenger." At the sight of Juniper's plain trousers, Jim's eyes widened. "Where's your guns?"

"Packed. Are you sure it was Lily? Reg told me she was staying behind."

"Ain't a man who could confuse your fancy lady for any other woman. That millhouse filled up right quick when word spread she'd come for the meeting. If you ask me, she looked a little green about the gills. She didn't say nothin' but a soft—"

Juniper bolted out of the door.

"—hello when she emerged from the carriage," Jim finished.

Why wouldn't Reg have told him she was coming?

He bypassed the crowd gathered outside the millhouse and made his way around to a side door. It was standing-room only inside, men bunched into the large warehouse shoulder to shoulder. Directly across the wide storage room a group of Carrington men stood on a platform, Reginald's voice filling the room as he spoke at the podium. A swathe of light fabric shifted amid the dark suits.

Lily leaned forward, her profile stalling his breath. Russet curls tumbled toward her shoulders, her pale green dress emphasizing the green of her eyes. She stood a few paces behind Reginald with some men from her office. Her gaze searched the crowd of workers, her brow creased with the hint of a frown.

Had she waited a few more days, he'd have come for her. Keeping his gaze locked on her face, he edged his way toward the stairs beside the platform, his pulse accelerated, his palms growing clammy.

Hell, he thought, rubbing his hands against his pants. He'd never been nervous over a woman a day in his life.

He'd never known a woman like Lily.

At Reginald's announcement that the administration had passed the motion to build a nearby town for workers and their families, cheers rose up, threatening to lift the roof off the warehouse. Juniper watched Lily's mouth creep into a slight smile, and he felt a rush of pride. Just as she'd told him months ago—her promises weren't empty. She'd made good on every one.

As Reg continued to explain the housing development, Lily broke away from the others and shuffled down the steps. She moved as discreetly as a bustled woman could through a sea of men, making her way toward the opposite door. Juniper noted the four men in suits following her with a little more stealth, staying a short distance behind her. He was glad to see Reg had at least brought a decent escort. Outside, she joined a small procession of workers filing toward the long dirt path leading back to camp. A few men paused beside her, tipping their hats and offering a greeting.

"I see you're still sneaking off alone?" Juniper said as he came up behind her.

Lily's heart clenched at the sound of Juniper's voice. She'd been so afraid she'd missed him.

His arm brushed hers as he fell into step beside her. Not trusting her emotions, she kept her gaze on the path.

"Good afternoon, Sheriff," she managed to say in a steady tone.

"Actually, I gave up the sheriff title."

She risked a glance in his direction. His lips slid into a grin, and Lily slowed to a stop, transfixed by the warmth in his gaze. Dear God, she'd missed him so much. "And just what do you mean by resigning?" she demanded, months of repressed anger seeping into her tone.

"If you must know, I was on my way to San Francisco."

"You were?"

The quiver in her voice and sudden sheen in her eyes eased the fear that had been riding Juniper for three excruciatingly long months. "I was wondering...have you ever thought about getting hitched?"

A hush fell over the surrounding men who'd been following them back to camp. Lily stared up at him, her expression tense, and June was sure everyone could hear his heart pounding in his chest.

"Why?" she asked, breaking the thick silence. "Do you know someone crazy enough to ask for my hand?"

"I do like a challenge. And *I love you.*"

Her eyes narrowed, her jaw clenched—not exactly the response he'd hoped for.

"You hardly know how to show it. You sent me away with—"

"I sent you *home,* not away."

Lily crossed her arms, her beautiful face set in a stubborn scowl. "You sent me packing and *wished me well.*"

Low murmurs broke out behind him. The men closing in around them appeared none too pleased by her announcement. She wasn't going to make this easy on him. He'd do whatever it took to win back what he wished he could have accepted months ago—her forgiveness, her love.

"What I want for us, between us, I couldn't give you while wearing a badge. What you said about me that day, about me waiting on the past, you were right. I could never see my life beyond the violence I always knew would catch up with me. I've always expected to die in a gunfight. I've waited for it. Not anymore."

He watched her gaze drop to his hips, noting the guns that weren't there.

"Come what may, I'll greet it unarmed and take my chances on life."

He pulled off his hat and knelt down on one knee, initiating a roar of cheers from the men gathering around them. He reached for her hand hidden behind her crossed arms. Her expression gaped as her fingers slid limply into his.

"Miss Lily Palmer, you are the smartest, most beautiful and troublesome woman I have ever had the pleasure to know. I've been miserable these past few months. I'm crazy about you. Will you marry me?"

Staring into his clear blue eyes, Lily's heart swelled with love. She sniffed back tears. He'd even got her name right. She loved him so much. And he'd caused her three months of sheer agony. "Do you have a ring for me?"

His smile collapsed. "Well, I was—"

"It's not like you to be unprepared," she interrupted, not about to just leap into his arms after the months of torment he'd put her through. "One would think you'd put no thought into such an important proposition."

His brow pinched. "That's not true! I was about to—"

"Sheriff needs a ring!" someone shouted over Juniper's protest. A murmur moved through the crowd. A hand shot out over Juniper's shoulder, revealing a silver metal band at the center of a dirt-stained palm.

Juniper uttered his thanks and picked up what was surely a washer or spare part of some kind. His lips bowed upward into a heart-melting grin as he held the metal band out to her.

"You're lucky I love you," Lily said, unable to hide her smile.

"The luckiest man alive." He brought her hand to his lips, the gentle brush against her skin crumbling the last of her defenses. "How 'bout it, Lily? You want to be the first bride in Pine Ridge?"

"I'd love to."

Juniper slid the steel band onto her finger, then lifted her into his arms as he stood. Lily shrieked with surprise, then laughed, latching her arms around his neck as cheers roared around them.

"I've missed you," she whispered against his ear as he carried her into camp.

The caress of her lips turned his blood to fire. "We need to find a preacher. Fast."

"We have to wait for Regi. He'll be relieved to know I'm not having a child out of wedlock."

"A child?" Juniper stopped walking—he damn near stopped breathing as his gaze slid down the layer of green bunched around her middle. "Lily?"

Her brilliant smile sent his pulse soaring.

"Surprise."

"I need to sit down before I fall down." He pulled open the door of her coach, stepped inside and dropped onto the seat, depositing Lily on his lap.

His hand spread over her stomach. *"Really?"*

She nodded, her eyes bright with moisture. "In January."

His arms locked around her, hugging her close. Abruptly he pulled her back. "We have to get married today. *Right now.*"

Her laughter danced across his senses, soothing his

rush of tension. Nothing on this earth was as beautiful as her smile.

"Tomorrow," she said. "Regi will likely be answering questions for another couple of hours. It will be nightfall before we reach The Grove."

He kissed her lips, softly, reverently. Lily melted into his embrace. The slow yet thorough penetration of his velvety tongue dragged a groan from deep inside her as passion blossomed and burst.

"Then we'll be wed by moonlight," he whispered, "because I'm not about to lie down with you until you're my wife. And I'm damn sure not spending another night without you in my arms."

"Okay," she said, rather breathlessly.

"I love you."

"Thank goodness. I was prepared to refuse your resignation."

He laughed against her lips. "Does that mean you'll be wanting to hire me for a new position?"

She slid her fingers into his hair, sending his hat toppling to the seat. "Oh, you're in far deeper than simple hiring. I'm quite wealthy, you see, and my company is becoming a tad more than I can handle. What's mine is yours. I'm told I can be rather…demanding. Are you sure you're up to the challenge?"

"Oh, I'm your man. But don't think for a moment I'll be keeping my family cooped up in San Francisco year-round."

"Oh, really?"

"I'm not flat broke, you know? Do you remember that spot where I took you fishing?"

Excitement sparked as she recalled their walk through the river. "With great fondness."

"I've got a good-size parcel of land in that area. Figure a summer house would be real nice, and we could get our feet wet when we wanted to," he said with a wink.

Lily wrapped her arms around his neck, drawing him to her lips. "Our own mountain retreat? There's nothing I'd love more."

She'd come to these mountains seeking the life of Juniper Barns. And he'd just given it to her, heart and all.